THE PRINCE OF MILK

THE PRINCE OF MILK

Exurb1a

Cosmia Press

CONTENTS

INTRODUCTION

Some ideas are uncooperative and you have to deliver a stern talking-to in order to make them work. Others come knocking on your door, and if you offer up a seat and some coffee, they do the work themselves. (They like beer too.) This story was the latter scenario. I dropped by occasionally to make sure the work was getting done, but that really was about it.

Please keep in mind that I've left a little reading list at the end for those who are interested in finding out more about the science-ish stuff mentioned, if some of it is new to you. Sci-fi is usually terrible at predicting the future, but sometimes it's all right for saying a thing or two about the present.

Some writers claim that they're not writing science fiction, they just happened to have set their work a few thousand years in the future. With spaceships. And aliens. And large amounts of speculative science.

The book you're holding now most definitely *is* science fiction though. It started with two very simple questions about technology: how long can we keep pushing it, and what are the limits? I suspect that given enough time, the answers to both questions will be: Forever and none.

Our species may well have a long, strange, and wonderful journey ahead of it. If we keep up our current obsessions with science, technology, and the hunt for wisdom, we're surely bound to do away with the demons that have plagued us for thousands of generations now: disease, ignorance, and death. God only knows what we'll be capable of then.

I'm sorry you and I won't be around for the party, but come on, we've lived to see some fantastic things already. There'll be plenty more in our lifetimes yet.

With much love and gratitude, I would like to dedicate this book to all of you who have been lovely enough to support my work. All I ever really wanted to do was make stuff on my own terms. Recently I have been able to do that. It couldn't have happened without your support, and not a day goes by when I don't count myself extremely lucky for receiving it. So thank you.

All the best, as ever,

Ex.
Sofia, Bulgaria.

Watch out, you might get what you're after.

— Talking Heads

Time will perfect matter.

— Terence Mckenna

But there's an altar in the valley, for things in themselves as they are.

— Silver Jews

I

THE GRUDGE

ONE

The crone is consulting her rune stones. They're quiet today. She turns them over in her hand, whispers an incantation, turns them over again — one blue, one green, one red.

A boy has appeared at her door. He rushes in and begins looking under tablecloths and behind animal skins.

"Hide me," the boy whispers.

"Things are rarely as bad as they seem," the old woman replies.

The boy peeks out of the tent, then tries to crawl under a table.

"Hey, that's starfire wood that is, leave off!" yells the crone.

She peers out of the tent herself. The sky is its usual shade of half-twilight. The cosmic strings are dancing among the clouds. Nothing is out of place.

"I've never once asked for your help," says the boy. "But I am asking you now. Do me this one kindness and you can ask anything in return."

"Can't think of anything I'd want from you to begin with, if I'm honest."

"Then do it out of decency."

The crone shrugs and mutters an Etheric charm. A partition appears in the wall leading to a dark compartment inside. She beckons and the two of them enter. Another charm and the wall closes.

"Is it—" says the boy.

"Yes," says the crone. "One-way. We can see out. Nobody can see in. Now tell me what the matter is."

The boy crouches down and wraps his hands around his knees.

"You've broken the Laws?" the crone tries. The boy shakes his head. "Stolen something then?" He shakes his head again. She catches his gaze, marvels at his strange eyes: one green as jade, the other blue and glinting. Attractive lad, she thinks. Girls flock from all across the Etheria with marriage to him in mind, if the stories are to be believed. "You've been romancing someone you shouldn't?" she says finally. The boy nods. He goes to continue but a huge figure rounds the tent's entrance and looks about; a man higher than a column, wearing nebula fabrics that sparkle and ebb, and around his neck hang amethyst death pendants. He touches idly at the crone's things, her rune stones, her writing table. Then he peers into the lavatory section and the library cavern.

"Woman," he calls. "Are you present?" The boy covers his ears and rolls into a ball inside the dark compartment. "Crone? The Arbiter of Timely Accidents says you haven't left your tent all day. I wish to speak with you."

The boy whimpers.

"Shut up," whispers the crone. "Not a sound."

"A certain matter to settle with the Arbiter of Mischief," the man adds. At the mention of his own name, the boy clamps down even harder on his ears. "Woman?" The man touches at a few more of the old woman's possessions, takes a last look at her rune stones, then exits.

The boy sprawls on the floor of the compartment.

"Djall," the crone murmurs. "You've angered *Djall,* of all the arbiters?" The boy grunts. "Go on then, how did you do it?"

"Oh hell…" whispers the boy.

"*Tell me.* Nothing to lose now."

Beomus wipes the sweat from his brow and neck and sits up. His blue eye twinkles. "Zorya," he says.

"Idiot," the crone mutters. "Of all the women to choose."

"You wouldn't understand."

"Oh shut up, I loved just as well as you in my early years. But to court a married woman, that takes a certain shade of stupidity."

"We were going to run away," Beomus says sheepishly.

"How does Djall know of what you were planning?"

"Letters. I write to Zorya now and then. Maybe he found one. A week from now, the plan was to elope. It was all arranged."

"Elope to where?"

"The Corporia."

"Have you lost your mind? Djall would find you. I'd give it a year at most."

"Then we would have a year together," says the boy.

"Youth," the old woman quotes, "is wasted on the young."

"I asked her to meet me on the bridge to the world-schism," says the boy. "In a week's time. We were to cross it together into the Corporia."

"There's no guarantee the two of you would end up in the same era," says the crone. "You might be separated by thousands of years. You know how it works."

"I'd find her."

She studies his face. "You're an idiot, nothing short of it." She mumbles an Etheric charm at the wall and the partition slides aside.

"Help," Beomus says. "Tell me what's coming."

"Not a chance."

"Please."

"*No*. Divining what's ahead only fixes it in place. Better not to know." She nods to the door. "Off with you. Sort this mess out yourself."

The boy stands rooted to the spot. "Zorya said you would help."

"Is that so."

"She said to come to you if anything happened."

"Save a drowning fool and he'll only be back in the river the next day. And what then?"

The boy lowers his voice to its true pitch; deep and echoing all of a sudden. "Leave him to drown and you're no better than a murderer."

The crone rolls her eyes. "Fucking teenagers, they'll stop at nothing." She consults the blue rune, then the red, then the green. Their insides brim with sparks.

"Yes, you will go to the Corporia," she says finally. "And Zorya too."

"Thank Omnia…" whispers the boy.

"And Djall will go also."

"*Djall?*"

"So the runes say."

"So the runes say?"

"So the runes say," comes a third voice like churned gravel. Djall stands just beyond the tent's opening now, returned. His skin glows a wild purple. "I see you have found my young arbiter, Emelza. I'll be removing him if that's quite all right."

"The boy and I have business," says the crone. "Shan't take too long. Shall I send him over to you when we're done?"

"No thank you. I will be taking him with me now."

Beomus keeps his sparkling eyes to the floor. Djall's purple glow is almost blinding.

"Perhaps there has been a misunderstanding," says the crone. "I'd like to offer my services as a mediator in—"

"No misunderstanding," Djall says. Then to Beomus: "Come on now, lad. We'll settle this honourably."

"How's that?" the boy whispers, eyes still downwards.

"In the fire realms, where you'll be educated on matters of decency." He reaches for Beomus' shoulder.

The crone fires a twist of Etheric in Djall's direction. He flies back into the library cavern, parchment detonating.

"Run," the crone yells, pushing the boy to the door. The cosmic strings watch quietly. Cherubs stare. "Run as fast as you can now, idiot. And no looking back."

TWO

Derrick Thomas wakes around half past five in a cold sweat. His wife is sleeping like death beside him with her mouth open. He tests his blood sugar with the little meter. Under usual levels. The needle comes easily enough out of its packet. The insulin disappears into his arm.

Better.

He watches the sunrise a while, watches his wife sleeping, takes a piss, then collapses dead in the bathroom.

Later that evening, four men and a young boy meet in The Giraffe, the only pub in Wilthail. Of all the men present, Eric Crane is the youngest at twelve and three quarters. He watches his father and the other men talk from behind overgrown blonde ringlets.

They have made pleasant conversation for the first hour, asking after the architect's new conservatory, the lawyer's new firm, the gardener's aspirations, and the policeman's cat — who is sleeping under the table. No one dares glance at the empty chair to the policeman's left which, even now, is still pulled out as though a sixth man will be joining them. For the first time in three years of these Sunday night gatherings Derrick Thomas is absent. And he will not, they all know — especially little Eric Crane, be joining them again this side of Judgement Day.

Derrick Thomas lived in Wilthail his entire life and had done nothing of any great importance; the kind of neighbour you'd go to for a spare fuse but wouldn't invite to a party.

"He was a good egg," Officer Mcalister, the policeman, says finally.

"A good egg," the lawyer says and raises his glass. They all clink, even Eric Crane with his lemonade.

"One of the best," the gardener says. A silence. Then: "So…where is he *now*?" the gardener adds quietly.

"With the Applebys," Officer Mcalister says. "I gave them the body. They'll have him done up by the end of the week. Thomas' wife will organise the funeral by then, hopefully."

"Poor girl…" mutters Eric Crane's father. He notices his son looking off into the distance and tousles the child's hair. "Okay?"

"Okay," Eric says.

Mr. Crane thinks this is one of those formative moments for his son, the first time a young man confronts death. But Eric Crane is only looking out the window, watching the moon, thinking of nothing in particular. He isn't much bothered by all the talk of death. He's seen the body already.

Early that morning, just after sunup, all the cars were covered in dew. Officer Mcalister's bike was leant up unchained against his cottage. He'd reasoned that no one would be stupid enough to steal from the village policeman. His cat Sergei slept beside him, coiled and waking from time to time to lick himself and watch the last of the morning moon.

Eric Crane had closed the front door behind him and stepped out into the road. His destination was the scrapyard a few minutes west. This was the third time he'd made such a trip. He wore the mittens his mother had knitted him for Christmas and an empty rucksack. The village was dead, all the estate cars like sleeping dragons in the driveways. He passed Mcalister's cottage, the Lees' half-mansion with the perfectly trimmed grass, the Carnegies' decaying semi-detached affair, and came finally to the old dirt track, the scrapyard at its far end. A Victorian house lay on the way. It had an evil majesty — riddled with vines, disintegrating, the lawn all overgrown and dotted with busted tools. This was where The Old Curmudgeon lived, or so they called him at school. He was rumoured to have only empty sockets where his eyes should be.

Eric Crane sprinted past the house just to be safe. At the end of the track was a mesh fence and he squeezed himself under with little effort. He stood on the hill overlooking the scrapyard then, everything waiting down there for plunder like a pharaoh's tomb. There were old cars at one end, most of them engineless husks. There was also a disassembled plane, a pack of lawnmowers, and hundreds of chairs and tables. The orange shipping container sat at the centre of all that.

He navigated through the lawnmowers and cranked back the lock on the container as quietly as he could. New riches appeared every day in there — the items the scrapyard workers had earmarked as valuable enough to sell on and that morning was no exception. He noticed it immediately. It was about the size of a brick.

POWERFUL LASER. DO NOT LOOK DIRECTLY INTO BEAM.

Nothing — not last Christmas at Grandma and Grandpa's, not his father's hints at going to Disneyland next summer — was a jot on this. He held the thing in his hands like an astronaut chanced upon ancient alien technology.

The first time Eric Crane had been left alone in his parents' house he'd gone straight to the DVD collection and picked out The Time Machine with Rod Taylor and Yvette Mimieux. Mrs. Crane was strict about anything containing violence, and apparently there was a bit in the film where some fighting broke out, so it had been off-limits. The prohibition only spurred Eric on and he sat without moving for a full hour and twenty minutes, thinking of nothing but nuclear fallout and Weena and the Morlocks and the distant future, and by the time the end credits began to scroll up he had decided to become the first human to travel in time. The internet was banned at home so he used his Computing lessons at school to trawl through science forums.

He learned that the faster you move in space, the slower time passes for you. Sort of. He learned that there had been some experiments over the years trying to send light a few milliseconds back in time using mirrors, but this had come to nothing. However, he also learned that Stephen Hawking had been quite clear that backwards time travel was not just physically, but logically impossible anyway. So that was that.

Only forwards then. He had seen it in his head many times, the first journey. He would ease the machine's control lever forward, just like Rod Taylor, and there would be no obvious change in his bedroom except for the sun, which would visibly climb to the top of the sky and plummet back down again. Then he would push the lever a little further ahead and the sun would be replaced with a single golden line across the horizon. He would look out of the window and there would be Wilthail, going about its days, Officer Mcalister and Eric's father both just furious blurs, going to work, coming home from work, going to work, coming home from work — the lever further forward still and the houses would crumple and new houses would appear as if by magic, sprouting up as some other town merged into the village and the cars would become more streamlined as taste and engineering wandered off in brave new directions. He would wait until the sky was awash with rockets and space stations, until men and women rode down Wilthail high street atop vehicles that walked on mechanical spider legs, until a general sense of peace had come on the planet and no one had to go to school or work ever again. He would stop the machine then, treat himself to a celebratory bag of M&M's, and go bravely into that new world with a deep assurance that however strange it all seemed, however alien the language, however inedible the food, he belonged more to this time than the one from which he had come.

In any case, the machine had needed a laser for ages.

He stowed the thing away in his backpack and checked the rest of the container, but there was nothing of interest. He would come back tomorrow. Then he clamped the door bolt back down and set off again through the lawnmowers and vaulted up the hill. The fence was still curled back where he had come through and he slid under and rearranged the mesh so no one would be suspicious.

A light was on in The Old Curmudgeon's house. Eric looked for some other way around. There was nowhere to go. He avoided any patches of gravel and tried to keep his feet light, feeling the weight of the laser in his backpack.

He was at the end of the track then, the main road ahead. He turned to take one last look at the old house and there, unmistakably, was a spectre in the lit window — thickly bearded, gaunt, its eyes set directly on the boy. Eric ran back up the main street — other houses lit now,

Officer Mcalister's place, the Appleby's Funeral Parlour too — racing to his parents' house, the laser flopping about in his rucksack.

He froze. The lawyer and his wife were stood on their doorstep, both in their dressing gowns. They were staring across the street to the Thomas' house. An ambulance was parked outside. Two paramedics were loading a stretcher into the back, something huge beneath a white sheet. A car rounded the corner behind Eric. He ran for Number 29, where no one had lived for a year now, and crawled over the garden wall and peered out at the scene through the stonework.

The car stopped behind the ambulance. Officer Mcalister stepped out and waddled over to the first paramedic. The second was already in the doorway talking to Mrs. Thomas. Her eyes were red and puffy. She paused every few seconds to make a wailing noise and didn't look the paramedic in the eye. Finally Mcalister went into the Thomas' house and closed the door behind him. The two paramedics drove off up the road with their new cargo. Eric Crane ran his fingers over the chipped stone of the wall.

Something stirred beside him: Sergei, Officer Mcalister's cat. They exchanged a glance across the evolutionary divide. Eric patted it a few times. The cat squinted contentedly.

When he was sure the road was empty, he crawled over the wall and made back to his parents' place. He wouldn't realise the laser had fallen out of his rucksack until he got home from school that afternoon.

"Yes, a good egg Derrick was," Eric Crane's father says again. He offers his son a sip of his pint but Eric shakes his head.

"We should go and see his wife, make sure she doesn't get lonely," the gardener says.

The men all look down into their glasses. Eric Crane examines the moon a second time. In his mind he sees the gaunt and crinkled face staring back at him from The Old Curmudgeon's window; its eyes not those of the old face they sit in, but of a young boy's like his own who has simply seen too much of the world and would rather it just went away.

THREE

Fog comes on the village. The Wilthailites are in their beds, except for a few insomniacs. Sergei the cat prowls about and drinks from bird baths. He performs a quick reconnaissance mission in The Old Curmudgeon's garden. No shrews, only old shoes and broken trowels.

Next he watches Jennifer Rhodes the therapist in bed, hugging her dead husband's pyjamas.

Then on to the Applebys' Funeral Parlour where a light is still on, and Sergei perches at the window and peeks in. Classical music is playing on a radio inside. Derrick Thomas' body is lying flat on a shiny table.

The Appleby brothers prefer to work at night. The light is better, they claim. Robyn Appleby leers over the body and wears a constant, satisfied smirk. He is preparing a palette of makeup. Scott Appleby is behind him, picking out a suit for the corpse to wear.

"Though I walk through the valley of the shadow of death," Robyn mutters as he works on the body.

"Stop it," Scott says.

"I shall fear no evil for thou—"

"Stop it, would you?"

Robyn begins to apply the makeup, a beetroot purple which will be softened later by a pink relief, but for now makes Thomas look like he's died from an allergic reaction. Then he takes nail clippers to the corpse. With a handful of clippings he moves into another room. Serge vaults to the next window to keep the man in sight. Robyn drops the clippings into a vivarium. Inside, an enormous snake wakes, watches Robyn with perfectly black eyes, then begins work on eating the nails.

Robyn admires snakes of all kinds. He understands their nature. They owe allegiance to no one and their primary methods are cunning and, if needed, aggression. He watches the last of Derrick Thomas' toenails disappearing into the snake's mouth. Scott appears at the doorway holding a brown suit. "I thought this one?"

"Yeah."

"You're not even looking."

Robyn glances. "I'm sure it'll be fine."

The snake turns to Scott and looks him over.

"He likes you, hm?" Robyn murmurs. "Come a little closer, won't you? Get a good look."

"I have to dress Mr. Thomas. He'll—"

"Mr. Thomas isn't going anywhere. Come a little closer," Robyn says.

Scott joins him at the glass. The snake's tongue flickers like a candle flame.

"Have you decided what you might call him?" Scott mutters.

"Maybe we won't call him anything at all. A name puts him in the human ranks, and I think he is more dignified than that."

"Right. Okay."

Robyn eyes the sand beneath the animal's belly, hot from the lamp. It looks good down there, warm. To slither like that, to feel the ground against your skin at all times, to know your place in the dirt…

Derrick Thomas is the first client of the Applebys' Funeral Parlour in three months. Before him was Edith Jennings and she had been old and with few family and friends, and the brothers made very little money from the service. And before that, four months of no business at all.

Money grew tight. They began using credit cards, bickering. But here is Derrick Thomas lying on their preparation table, with a more than modest life insurance plan and a stockbroker's fortune to leave behind.

The money had been welcome. Scott is wearing new shoes and his hair is trimmed and slicked like the old days.

And Robyn has the snake.

"I don't think they're supposed to eat nail clippings," Scott says.

"They are creatures built for survival. They can eat almost anything. I'll bet that if we threw a stapler in there he'd snap it up in five minutes."

The doorbell rings.

"It's half eleven at bloody night," Scott says uncertainly.

Robyn barges past to the front door.

Fat Officer Mcalister is waiting on the porch. "Mr. Appleby." He smiles formally.

"Officer. Can I help?"

"Sorry to be calling on you so late. It's a matter regarding Mr. Thomas. I trust you haven't finished preparing the body quite yet?"

"We're just embalming it now, actually."

"Perfect, then would you mind if I took a last look?"

"At the body?"

"That's right."

"Is there a problem?"

"A final formality to settle. Unless you're busy, of course."

"Not at all. Please."

Robyn leads him up to the preparation room, where Thomas' cheeks are still scorched purple with makeup.

"Not as bad as it looks. We aren't finished yet. Could I get you a drink?" Robyn says.

"No thanks." They stand in awkward silence a moment.

"I'll leave you to it," Robyn says and exits.

Back in the snake's room, Scott whispers, "What does he want?"

"Don't know. Something about finalising the body. Just keep your mouth shut."

All quiet from the preparation room. Finally Mcalister appears at the doorway smiling. "All done. Thanks a lot, boys. I'll see myself out."

"Officer."

The front door shuts.

"What—" Scott starts.

"Just shut up," his brother barks.

The snake pivots to look out of the window. The brothers turn to follow its gaze. Sergei the cat is still peering through the glass.

"Piss off!" Robyn yells. Sergei retreats slightly, holding the Applebys in sight for a few moments, then makes back off into the night.

FOUR

A purple twist of Etheric streaks from behind Beomus and explodes a tent ahead. He is breathless, but wills his legs on. Oracles and arbiters are appearing at their windows to watch the spectacle. Beomus can't be sure, but the sky looks suddenly darker than usual. Blue blood streams from his head where a bolt of Etheric hit.

He chances a peek behind. Djall is closing on him, his great bulk gliding several feet off of the floor. Beomus ducks into an empty market and hides beneath a moonfish stall. Djall and his purple glow appear at the market's entrance. He inspects the stalls about him as though nothing is out of the ordinary.

"Time was when I owned a little stand here myself," Djall calls out. "I sold pig meat for my father. He'd let me slaughter the animals myself with a knife. He could've used Etheric to kill the little things painlessly, but he liked watching them die."

He explodes a few of the stalls, checks underneath. Beomus crawls further under his own and covers his mouth.

"In time I taught myself the ways of death and how to enact them," Djall yells. Another stall flies into the air and returns to the ground as rubble. "I learned that some lives are longer than others."

Beomus summons all of his concentration and actuates a flock of gulls in the market, bearing down on Djall. The Arbiter of Entropy bats them away. "Show yourself," he barks.

The music of the spheres plays quietly from above. The cherubs stare.

Beomus actuates a storm of bees about the arbiter. At a wave of Djall's hand they fall to the ground, dead. "Show yourself!" he roars and begins exploding stall after stall, a rain of wood and bread and offal. The explosions are nearing Beomus now and he sets off, heading for the fountain square. The drawbridge has already been raised. He looks for a wall to scale but most are the height of five arbiters at least. Djall is off the floor again, approaching, staring at the boy, eyes all malice and shining.

Beomus actuates anything he can think of with the last of his strength: a meteor, a bear, a hay bale. Djall bats them away and smiles. Beomus actuates a storm cloud between them, teeming with lightning. A great fork leaps from the cloud and strikes the Arbiter of Entropy in the eye. He falls to his knees. Beomus sprints past and heads back through the market, Djall roaring from behind.

He chooses a street at random, then another.

A bolt of purple Etheric explodes at his side. He races on, weaving past the iron doors where the diplomats to the Corporia dwell.

The world-schism. It churns ahead of him, a muddle of purples and blues and golds; time doubling back on itself, matter eddies, folded space, a shape of no dimensions: the bridge to the Corporia.

The all-sky is darkening now. The cosmic strings have ceased their dancing. Djall appears from the street and approaches the boy slowly.

"What now, lad — the Corporia? But you go alone, eh?"

Beomus steps backwards onto the bridge to the world-schism, keeping Djall in sight.

Djall begins to yell again: "When Novelty gave you that title, he meant you to spread mischief in the Corporia, *not among your own kind.*"

The boy stands to his full height and steps back to the very edge of the bridge now. The heat of the world-schism is licking at his shoulders.

Djall reaches with blazing purple fingers and sinks them into the boy's shoulder, lifts him off of the floor. Cherubs mutter to one another from a safe distance above. A crowd has gathered at the foot of the world-schism bridge, the crone among them. She shouts to Beomus mentally: *Whatever you're planning, don't. You know the rules of dispute. He'll follow you until there's a reckoning, then end you.*

"Or I'll end him," Beomus yells back.

Don't be stupid. Apologise. Humiliation is better than what waits for you through the schism.

Djall's fingers draw even deeper into the boy's shoulder, fingernails on bone.

Don't be so stupid, says the crone again in his mind. *Plenty of other women to choose from. Or men, if you prefer.*

A cry, Zorya approaching. "Stop. Stop it now." She claws at the two of them.

"Ah," Djall grins. "My wife. What apt timing, considering your hand in all of this also."

Beomus looks to the Etheria with its spires and columns, to the many observers at the foot of the bridge, to the cherubs watching from above, to the cosmic strings, to the now dark sky. The three of them dance together at the lip of the world-schism, flailing.

Zorya shouts again: "Stop it now, both of you. This is just a stupid game of pride."

"Ours to play," Djall says and clenches tighter around the bone of the boy's shoulder. "The two of you were to elope, no?" He drives his hand in further, blood everywhere. Beomus cries out.

"Stop this," Zorya says quietly to the boy. "Just apologise and we'll all go home."

He'll hunt you across the years, the crone's voice comes in his mind again. *And beyond that too. Think damn hard about what you're doing. Apologise.*

Djall releases his grip a little, puts the boy back down on the bridge. "Well," the arbiter says in a gravel voice. "You've been brave and stupid in equal measure. Will you face up to the consequences now, lad?"

He'll hunt you across the years, idiot, comes the crone's voice again.

"Just wait, just a moment, both of you," Zorya says. "There has been a terrible misunderstanding. Nothing we can't fix. Just give it a moment and we'll settle the matter." She puts a hand on each of their shoulders.

You're gorgeous, Beomus thinks. And something past that I don't have a name for.

The crowd strains to watch on tiptoes. The sky is black as death. The cosmic strings flatten.

"Come along then," Djall says, his face still blazing purple. "We'll settle the matter."

"Settle the matter," Zorya agrees and smiles sweetly to the two of them.

"Yes, we'll settle the matter," Beomus nods and wraps his hands about the Arbiter of Entropy, looks once more to Zorya, and pulls all three of them backwards into the Corporia.

FIVE

The Old Curmudgeon's name is John Whistle. He is sixty-seven and wears an enormous grey beard. He usually wakes around five in the morning, no matter what time he's gone to bed, and works on painting his models. They're all handmade, and when one is finished he places it among the others as part of a table display which now almost completely takes up the living room.

He has slept well and he's full of coffee. The edges of the world are feeling padded today. He is working in the living room on a piece of wood which will later be a young girl. Someone once told him that you're supposed to go looking for the figure already inside the material, but that is obviously bullshit. He rounds the curve of the head with the knife, almost ready to set grooves in for the hair.

Movement from outside. That infernal policeman's cat is perched at the window, glaring in. Whistle holds its gaze a while.

The door knocks for the first time in three months.

Whistle stays very still and continues to watch the cat.

The door knocks again.

The Old Curmudgeon has a daughter, Zoe, who lives in Cairo with her mother, Donya. Last time he saw the girl she was seventeen, nine years ago. Donya has giv en him the odd report of Zoe's progress in the form o short emails: in and out of mental institutions for the rich where the food is better than a three star Miche lin restaurant, indulged for hours by psychiatrists who must be laughing all the way to the bank. And funded of course, by her mother's university salary.

He and Donya's divorce had been fine, even pleas ant. They divided their things equally, no fighting over appliances or books. On the last day in Cairo they had sat out on the balcony overlooking the city and Donya made him a cup of tea. He was aware that this would probably be the last time they were within a few feet of each other, perhaps even on the same continent. They'd kissed goodbye on the cheek and now he is here, back in Wilthail, the village of his childhood, sitting in the early light of an English morning with his figurines and coffee.

The door knocks again. Officer Mcalister's chubby face appears at the window.

Hi, the policeman mouths.

Hi? Whistle mouths back.

Mcalister points to the front door. Whistle gets up and opens it, finally.

Sergei the cat is at Mcalister's feet now, staring up at Whistle thoughtfully.

"Terribly sorry to trouble you," the policeman says.

"Mm hm."

"Do you have a minute?"

"What is it? I've already heard about Derrick Thom-as."

"Will you be coming to the funeral on Monday?"

"No."

The little black cat wags its tail.

"Well just in case, eleven o'clock, the crematorium," the policeman says.

"All right."

Mcalister shifts his considerable weight from foot to foot. He has brought the police car today rather than his bike, Whistle notices.

"Well?" Whistle says, thinking of the little half-finished figurine on the table.

"It's a bit of a sensitive matter, Mr. Whistle. Your daughter, she—"

"I thought I made it clear enough to the people of Wilthail that my personal life is off-limits." He goes to shut the door. Mcalister's boot is already there to block it. "Mr. Whistle—" The policeman wrings his hands.

"You'd do well to remove your foot," Whistle growls.

"Miss Whistle tried to take her own life several weeks ago."

The cat cocks its head.

"Hers to take if she likes," John says.

"Mrs. Whistle has tried to contact you, I believe."

"I have nothing to say to her. What business is it of yours?"

"None whatsoever until several days ago when she arrived back in England."

"Mrs. Donya Whistle can travel where she pleases. Tell her to write me a letter if she must."

"Not your wife. Your daughter, Miss Whistle."

The air is thick all of a sudden. Is that damn cat smiling? "What is she doing back in England?"

Mcalister stays silent. Whistle looks the street over, then the police car. There is a figure in the back, all long black curls and sitting still.

"Kindly remove your foot from my front door," Whistle growls again.

"She's been certified as stable by the Egyptian Psychiatric Assoc—"

"I don't care if she's been crowned reigning monarch. Kindly remove your foot."

Mcalister pulls back and nods formally. "Good day, Mr. Whistle."

John slams the door and returns to his figurine. His hands are shaking. He listens to the police car start up and pull away down the street. All quiet.

Zoe Whistle was thirteen when she decided she had too much blood in her. She waited until her parents were out, then took a kitchen knife to her wrist. There was the sense of pressure being released and she felt much better but it also occurred to her she would probably die if she didn't get medical attention. The kitchen floor was slicked from end to end in blood and she was beginning to feel faint. Still, there wasn't any great sense of urgency. She was not supposed for the world.

John Whistle found her slumped against the sink when he arrived home from work. He tied off the wound with elastic bands and a bandage and called the paramedics.

When Zoe came to that evening in hospital, her mother and father were sitting by her bed. She smiled to both of them and said what a lovely night it looked outside. Donya burst into tears. John went for a cigarette.

Donya quit her job at the university to teach Zoe at home. When John came back from work in the evenings they were still usually deep in algebra and Shakespeare. Zoe seemed normal, even happy. The scar was healing nicely and Donya said the girl was doing well in her studies. They visited zoos and museums at the weekends and John would take them both for ice cream afterwards. He began to think of the too-much-blood incident as a one-off smudge on an otherwise immaculate map.

That was until a package arrived at the house in Zoe's name. John intercepted it and opened the thing up with a knife. Inside was a device called an 'exit bag'. It consisted of a plastic bag, a valve, and a small bottle of helium. Instructions were included. The device was to be placed over the user's head and sealed around the throat. The helium was to be vented into the bag. The wearer would be painlessly killed within a few minutes.

John threw the device in the bin and confronted his daughter immediately. He did a fair bit of shouting, stomped about, and finally calmed down. Then he tidied the house and tried to keep Zoe in sight until Donya was back, and told his wife what had happened. She went into Zoe's room for a long time, and when she came out reported that the girl was sleeping and the windows were locked.

So began the years of therapy and lithium and herbal remedies and afternoons spent reading medical journals, clawing at an explanation, however slippery. So began the final few occasions Donya ever took her clothes off in front of John Whistle and invited him to put his hands on her. So began Zoe's transformation from a playful child into something that still joked and smiled, but couldn't be left within reach of prescription medication or sharp implements.

Around the time of Zoe's eighteenth birthday, Donya and John had lost control by their own admission. The girl wore her hair down and long. Her face was brown with high cheeks she had taken from her mother without asking. She usually attended the scheduled appointments with Dr. Salib the psychiatrist, but stayed out the rest of the time until the early hours, coming home drunk or under some other influence. She took new men often, moved on when she got bored. Money went missing from John's wallet on a weekly basis. Glasses were smashed. Blood sometimes appeared in the bathroom.

It was around that time Donya and John quietly agreed to part ways. They hadn't slept together in months, perhaps a year. Donya was out until late most nights, obviously seeing someone else. With Zoe now independent, or as good as, John began to box his things away.

He left a letter for Zoe in her bedroom saying he would be leaving for a while the next day and could she please be around to say goodbye. The letter disappeared from her desk but she hadn't been home to see him the next morning. He waited an hour, changed his flight to a later one. Several more hours passed with no sign of his daughter.

Finally he kissed Donya goodbye.

It had been a pleasant partnership in some ways.

Not so in others.

He was back in Wilthail the next day, the corner of England he'd grown up in. Everything looked identical to when he'd left, more or less, as though someone had brought a bell jar down on the place and dusted it a few times a year for good measure. The village had been waiting patiently for Whistle, knowing his schemes would fall apart, ready to welcome him back with its drowsy embrace of footpaths and jam and afternoon tea.

The door knocks once again. There is no cat or policeman at the window this time. Whistle bunches his fists. He can make out a figure through the frosted glass of the front door, a woman. She stands perfectly still on the doorstep like one of his figurines. He counts to thirty seconds, then forty. The figure remains. He opens the door.

Her skin is a little tauter now, but she still has her high cheeks and flowing hair. A holdall lies at her feet.

"Hi," she says. A pause. "Okay?"

"Why aren't you in Egypt?" Whistle mutters.

"That's not much of a hello."

"Has Donya thrown you out?"

"I thought we could start with *how are you* and move on from there. Want to try it?"

Whistle catches sight of Mcalister's car waiting up the road, the policeman pretending not to watch. Sergei the cat is perched on the dashboard and apparently pretending not to watch also.

"Did Mcalister put you up to this?" the old man says.

"He offered to bring me over. God, what's wrong? Aren't you pleased to see me?"

He stands still and says nothing.

"Well, can I come in then?" the girl says.

"You'd better not be staying."

"I haven't slept in a day, not since Egypt. At least make me a cup of tea."

John looks again to Officer Mcalister and his cat, to the lawyer and his wife peeking from their bedroom window, then back to his daughter and beckons her inside.

SIX

Jamie Carnegie slides himself out of Suzie Lees' bed. Then he sets out running, the same route every day, up into the hills. He likes to stop at the peak and look down into the valley where Wilthail is still sleeping, usually.

He and Suzie had gone through their usual spin cycle of experimental lovemaking the night before, then she'd rolled into him. He'd been thinking about how sex loses its kick after the first few times. He wished her husband was around more often so their sessions could be riskier and less frequent.

"How do you feel about going away? For a while," Suzie said.

"Together?"

"Together, yes."

Tread carefully, he thought. "Where to?"

"Milan. Or Cyprus. Or a cabin somewhere. The two of us. Wouldn't it be nice? We could get one of those wood burning stoves maybe."

"What about work? You know I've got loads on."

"I'll pay for the time I use. It's only fair."

"That sort of makes me a prostitute, doesn't it?"

She sat up and lit a cigarette. "How about it though?"

"Won't it be a bit obvious if we…disappear together? Kevin would definitely notice that."

"You're such a bore sometimes."

He knew this game well. She would act heartbroken that he didn't care for a little while and wait for him to give in. He would. Then she would pay him the privilege of eye contact again and probably try to initiate more sex. He'd tolerated these dances for the first few months. Now this kind of bullshit just made him angry.

"It'll be too obvious. My father's suspicious enough as it is," Jamie said finally.

"Oh your *father…*"

"Yes, my *father* who'll get so smashed one night he'll tell anyone who will listen that his son is sleeping with the lawyer's wife."

She took a long drag on her cigarette for suspense purposes. "There is another way though," she said.

"Don't be stupid."

"He's my husband. I'll leave him if I want to."

Jamie was going to bring up money, to ask how she'd even survive, but instead just said, "I don't think it's a good idea."

"Now I look like such an idiot…" she said in a soft voice.

He left it like that and they'd slept and now he is out in the hills. He's sober up here.

He has never been able to maintain interest in women, except for those who were unobtainable. Diana Mitchell, she'd barely given him the time of day. Ellie Wells too.

But it's Jenny Dunne that he still thinks about from time to time, every other day; in the shower, taking out the bins, walking home from work. Jenny Dunne who came on so strong those first few months after they met through Lucy, her sister. There were odd, beautiful moments, usually weeks apart, when she'd suddenly come alive. And then there were the other times; the weeks of no emotion, the weeks when less than nothing happened, when she barely looked away from the television.

That was years ago now. When he remembers her, the flash of resentment is still just as strong as the day they went separate ways. Catching sight of happy couples in the park is still enough to fuck up his afternoon.

Down in the valley, Suzie Lees is coming around. She lights a cigarette and smells the pillow Jamie was sleeping on.

The photo frames are all facedown. Suzie usually turns them over before Jamie visits so they won't be bothered by pictures of her and Kevin smiling on Spanish beaches. There is one though which she always leaves up. In it, Kevin, only her fiancé back then, is twenty-one and handsome, holding a scroll: his graduation photo. He was tight-lipped even back then, but Suzie had assumed this hinted at mountains of untapped masculine potential waiting just under the surface of his personality. It was not until they began living together that she decided his shyness was actually nothing more than a lack of imagination. Two years passed and by then Kevin was already making jokes about having children. He lacked spirit but fitted the bill.

They married in the normal way and honeymooned in America, then returned home to their renovated cottage on Wilthail's main street. And things were tolerable for the first few years. They kissed goodbye in the mornings and shared the cooking duty equally in the evenings. They visited relatives, dressed immaculately, went on cruises.

Something changed though, she thinks. Something changed at a point. I've acted in ways since that I never imagined I would. Things have been said that should not have been said.

God, what did it?

She stares at Kevin's photo now, stubs out her cigarette.

Time, she thinks. It's time's fault and that's that.

SEVEN

John Whistle put his daughter in the spare bedroom where all of his old paintings were hung. Some were of her as a child. Others displayed alien landscapes Zoe didn't recognise, pompous arty stuff.

She appears the next morning around eleven. John is hunched over the dining table with a whittling knife, working at a figurine.

"What's that?" Zoe says.

"There's tea in the cupboard."

She makes herself a cup and sits down on the floor, bunched up in her dressing gown, and looks her father over. The decade hasn't been kind to his face. "Nice little statues," she says.

"How long are you supposed to be staying?"

"You must've spent ages on them."

He examines the knife. "Yes. I have."

The living room is bare except for patches of plaster peeling from the ceiling. There is only one seat at the table: his.

"So, what's been going on?" Zoe tries.

John points to the table and the knife and the figurines and says nothing.

"Yes but…"

"Sports day," he says. "The Sunday Market. Evening walks. Heavy rain here and there. Local elections. General elections. Births. Marriages. Deaths. Taxes."

She sips her tea and makes a *sheeesh* noise. "Well, I've been very well, thanks for asking."

"That's great news."

"I don't have to go to therapy anymore. I got off the coke—"

"I didn't know you were *on* coke," John says.

"Right."

"And now you're here," he says, his hands working on the little figurine and his eyes watching the knife.

"And now I'm here."

"Do you have a plan?"

"I reckon the English countryside is good for peace of mind." John shoots her a glare. "I thought I might stay a week."

"A *week*?"

"If that's okay."

"No, it's not okay."

"Well…"

A long silence. "You never wrote," John says.

"Neither did you."

"Considering the circumstances, I didn't much feel like writing."

"Mum said you'd be like that."

"Like *what*? Reasonable?"

Another long silence. Zoe goes upstairs and gets changed. When she comes down again her father is still in the same position. With his back turned he says, "How's Donya?"

"Happily married still. He's a good man."

"Lovely. And you?"

"What?"

"Are you married?"

She chuckles politely. "Don't you think I would've told you if that had happened?"

"No, I don't." The knife pivots in his grip.

"Well then no, I'm not married."

John nods at this. "That's good. Neither am I. And I wouldn't have said a damn thing to you about it if I was. More tea?"

"Yes, all right."

EIGHT

Augustus Rawlings invites Officer Mcalister and his cat in for a drink when the policeman calls at the door. Officer Mcalister gets Earl Grey with milk. Sergei just gets milk. They sit with Mary Rawlings, Augustus' wife, in the garden. She apologises on behalf of the garden. One side, hers, is blooming with sunflowers and roses. Her husband's is a nest of weeds and death.

"Augustus takes no pleasure in gardening," Mary Rawlings explains.

"Only a dullard would," Augustus Rawlings replies.

The policeman likes this couple; that old and dying breed of English bumpkin who does a good turn for the sake of it and always seems to be baking something or other.

Augustus Rawlings pours the policeman more tea. "What is it we can do for you, officer?"

"A sensitive matter, I'm afraid. It's fallen to me to make the rounds about Derrick Thomas."

"Poor Mr. Thomas," Mary Rawlings says quietly.

"For everything a season," Augustus replies.

"The funeral is being held next Monday. Can I count on your attendance?" the policeman says.

Augustus nods enthusiastically. "You most certainly can. Has the cause of death been ascertained?"

"Heart attack I suspect, but it's too early to say. Actually, there was a small matter I wanted to bring up with you. Again, a sensitive issue. I trust it goes no further?" Mary and Augustus nod formally. "I notice you're still working in the pharmacy, Mary. Are you aware Derrick Thomas was a diabetic?"

"He came in for his insulin every other Friday."

"And had his prescription changed at all recently?"

"Not that I remember. It's usually me he deals with, so I think I would know if it had."

Sergei hops onto the policeman's lap and curls into a ball. Mcalister rubs the animal's belly and continues: "And is there any way someone could have gained access to the medications without you knowing?"

"I don't think so. The security at night is top-notch."

"And in the day?"

"It's just myself who works there, and Judy Crane sometimes, but not for months now. What are you implying, if I might ask?"

"Nothing at all, just attempting to close down all avenues of suspicion. Mr. Thomas was an unexpectedly wealthy man. I'd like to rule out any foul play in the village."

Mr. Rawlings smiles delightedly. "You think someone murdered the poor bastard?"

"*Augustus,*" Mary chides.

"As I said, closing down all avenues of suspicion. Are you sure no one has access to the pharmacy except for yourself, Mary?" Mcalister says.

She scrunches up her old mouth. "Well, Mr. Appleby — Robyn I mean, is a trained pharmacist."

"The undertaker?"

"Yes. He comes in as a backup a few times a year when I'm under the weather."

"Has Mr. Appleby stood in recently?"

"Oh yes, several weeks ago."

"I see."

"Oh, I do hope I haven't gotten anyone in trouble."

"Not in the least. Was Derrick Thomas on a high dose of insulin? You aren't breaching confidentiality telling me this by the way."

"Nothing out of the ordinary, I don't think."

"What would happen if the dose was too high?"

"We measure all of the—"

"I don't doubt your skills as a pharmacist Mary, but indulge me — what would happen if the dose was too high?"

"Nausea, sweating, hard to say."

"This would carry on for some time, I suppose?"

"Oh yes."

"But if the dose was, say, quadruple? What then?"

"Oh, death," Mary Rawlings says. "Within minutes."

"Death," Augustus Rawlings nods.

They sit silently in the sunshine for a few moments, Sergei watching Augustus Rawlings through his paws. The old man winks to the cat.

"Is this an official investigation?" Mary says gently.

"Oh no," the policeman says. "Nothing like that. We just need to make sure there aren't any loose ends." Mcalister squints at the garden, one side dead, one side alive. "What lovely sunflowers you have."

"Precious things," Augustus says. "Living on the edge of life, as everything must. Just a few days out of the sun, or starved of water, and they wither. And no policeman would come investigating after their deaths."

"Excuse my husband once again," Mary says. "He is always strange in the summer."

NINE

Eric Crane is standing in front of The Old Curmudgeon's house pretending to examine a patch of pavement. He is watching his peripheries for any sign of movement from inside the house. Nothing stirs. His heart is hammering but this is the last chance. He's looked everywhere for the laser — even in the stupid places. He takes a few deep breaths and starts up the crooked garden path, rehearsing the line in his head. *Hello, I'm Eric Crane. I don't mean to bother you but—*

There's a young woman already standing in the doorway. She's smiling as though she's extremely pleased to see him. "Hi."

"I'm looking for something," Eric mumbles, his rehearsed speech forgotten already.

"What's that?"

"The...I think I might have left something on the road. Have you found anything?"

"Mmm..." The girl pouts. "What does it look like? Maybe my dad's seen something."

"No," Eric says quickly, suspecting who her father is. "No, it's okay. I lost a laser, about this big?"

"A laser? That sounds expensive. What were you doing with a laser?"

"I found it."

"And now you've lost it again?"

He nods glumly.

The girl puts her hand up to her mouth and mock-whispers: "Are you a scientist?"

Eric shrugs. He wants to trust this girl. Her accent is strange and he suspects she knows more about the world than she's letting on.

"Well, if you see it…" he says.

She slips on some sandals and closes the door behind her and takes his hand, leading him back down the garden path. "Shall we look for it together?"

"Um," he says.

"Two heads are better than one. I'm Zoe. You're Eric?"

"You know my name?"

"Printed on your school bag." She smiles as though nothing terrible has happened in the history of the world, ever. This is exactly the kind of person his mother would tell him to stay well away from. He swears he suddenly feels taller.

She looks up and down the dirt track outside The Old Curmudgeon's house. Nothing. Then she leads them to the main road. "Did you walk up here?" she asks.

"Yeah."

"Come on then."

All the cars will be returning home from work soon and see him with this strange woman. He's not sure he cares.

"What were you doing with a laser?" she says.

"I build things."

"What did you want to build with a laser?"

"A machine."

"Hey." She stops dead in the street. "You think I'm an idiot? You think I can't handle clever things? How old do you think I am?"

"Er — thirty-something?"

"*Thirty-something*? I'm twenty-six, *you little upstart.* And that's young enough to hear a secret or two and not pass it on. Young enough for lots of things in fact. So out with it, what did you want the laser for?"

"A time machine," he whispers. She bends down to his height, puts her ear to his mouth. He says it again.

He has seen it in his mind a thousand times: whirling brass and steel and levers and a chair with red felt.

"How does it work?" she whispers back.

"Gravity."

"Ah, gravity." She nods knowingly.

They pass Officer Mcalister's cottage. The policeman's black cat is lying on the lawn, watching them with one eye open.

"Where will you go?" Zoe says.

"What?"

"With your time machine. Where will you go?"

"The future," Eric says without pausing. "Really, really far ahead."

"That's a good idea, loads of interesting stuff there. Hey, you could be a museum exhibit. I bet they'd pay good money for that."

"They don't use money in the future."

"Ah, no, you're probably right."

No sign of the laser yet. They follow the winding main street towards Kevin and Suzie Lees' house.

"When you get your machine working, could you give me a ride?" Zoe says.

"Sure. Where would you like to go?"

"Back a few thousand years. Egypt, if you don't mind. I bet my ancestors were all nuts. I'll fit right in."

"It doesn't go backwards. Stephen Hawking says that's impossible."

"Ah, forwards is fine then."

They pass the Lees' place. Jamie Carnegie is working in the front garden, shirtless, digging a flower bed. He stops to watch them pass, looks Zoe over.

"You were expecting my dad when you knocked on the door, weren't you?" Zoe says. Eric nods. "You looked afraid. Were you afraid?" He nods again. "You mustn't be scared of him. He's just lonely. If we're scared of lonely people, they'll only get lonelier."

They pass Eric's house. "I didn't come this far when I had it," the boy says.

"No? Well I'm sure it's around somewhere. Shall we go and ask my dad?"

"No," Eric says quickly. "No thanks."

TEN

Robyn Appleby has wheeled Derrick Thomas' body into the room with the vivarium so the snake can get a good look at death in the human kingdom. The snake is silent and admires Thomas from head to foot.

"Christ," Scott mutters, working on the accounts at the table.

"What's the problem?"

"You're going to turn into a snake yourself if you keep indulging it like that."

"Look at its eyes though."

"What's in its eyes?"

Robyn peers into the vivarium. "Nothing, absolutely nothing. Isn't that a miracle?" The snake ambles off to another section of the tank to take stock of its imprisonment. "The policeman came back yesterday," Robyn murmurs.

"What?"

"To talk to me."

Scott puts down his pencil and stares. "Why didn't you say?"

"I've only just thought about it."

"Well…what did he want?"

"To talk about my shifts at the pharmacy."

Scott takes several deep breaths. "That's all? What did you tell him?"

"What do you think? That yes, I work occasionally at the pharmacy, and what of it? He asked about what I dispense and to who, blah blah. He's just posturing. Don't pay it any mind."

"*Don't pay it any mind*?"

"We can't keep the business together if you go all woolly on me."

"If Mcalister—"

Robyn whirls, catches his brother with the sharp end of a stare. "Our reptilian friend currently only has an appetite for mice, but I'm sure he'd equally approve of a more exotic range of meats." He eyes Scott's pudgy bulk.

"I won't go woolly on you," Scott mumbles.

Robyn smiles and turns back to the snake.

Scott thinks of their mother suddenly, her face gentle and unassuming. She was not one to ever criticise or threaten. Robyn gets his less likeable qualities from their father who Scott can't remember ever giving either of the boys a word of encouragement in the whole of their lives. He built the business from scratch, starting as a young man in a neighbouring village, then moved the family to Wilthail when the older generation began to die off. By then he was stricken with Alzheimer's, but still rose at dawn to start work on the bodies and stayed like that, presiding over them like a surgeon until it got dark. He was a gaunt and tall man, pale-faced, with little more than bones for limbs. Scott brought a ball into the house once despite his father's rule about no toys inside. His father had silently taken the ball and escorted young Scott to the cupboard under the stairs, where he left him overnight. When the old man died, the two brothers embalmed him together, brought the colour back to his face with makeup. Then they buried him.

When in a bad mood, Scott occasionally remembers that day and feels a little better for it.

Now Robyn is taking something from a box: a mouse. The thing squirms in his grip and he dangles it upside down and slides the glass ceiling off the vivarium. The snake knows this routine already and is rigid and waiting. Robyn holds the mouse still, out of the snake's reach, watching. Scott feels the terror in the little thing. It must know what's coming, on some primal level.

To be kept in a box like that for days and only taken out for the sake of feeding some writhing firehose of a monster...

"Just give it to him for Christ's sake," Scott says, almost shouting.

Robyn wears the beginnings of a smirk. He feels a little like a god.

ELEVEN

The crone stands alone at the world-schism. She is peering into its eddies and catching half-glimpses of the worlds inside, writing her observations in a great leather-bound volume. She calls it The Book of Knots. In it, she plots the lives of Djall, Zorya, and Beomus, as they flit from age to age within the Corporia. Marbles on a trampoline, she thinks.

The Etheria has changed in their absence, some several thousand years since the three of them fell into the Corporia. Those arbiters who wish to end their lives cannot, now Djall is gone. Those arbiters who wish to bear children cannot, now Zorya is gone. And with Beomus missing, chaos is absent also. Lovers meet in boring fashions. Each hour unfolds as expected. The crone can't recall an interesting coincidence in the last twenty centuries.

She peers deeper into the world-schism. There is Djall, a Chinese peasant. In the same age, Beomus is a Russian monarch. They will not meet in this life. Further ahead now, the two of them are born, by mere coincidence, in the same suburb of Alabama. They live their entire lives sensing the other is close, but without ever actually meeting. A hundred lives later they are back twenty thousand years, both hunter-gatherers, spending their days hungry and naked. They meet eyes once across a campfire at the convergence of their two tribes, but never suspect who the other is.

The crone knows well enough how time works. It is a malleable thing which can fold into itself. Events may precede their causes, so long as consistency is preserved.

Thanks to the three errant arbiters, the Corporia's history is now riddled with paradoxes. Djall has at times been his own great-grandfather; Zorya a daughter and the daughter's mother-in-law simultaneously without realising.

"You're wasting your time," says the Arbiter of Fickle Pleasures, approaching from behind.

"Mine to waste," the crone mutters and scribbles another life in The Book of Knots.

"They'll fight amongst themselves for an eternity. How long can you wait?"

"The boy doesn't deserve this. Zorya neither."

"They knew the rules, surely?"

"And who among us hasn't broken them at some time?"

"Mmm…"

The night is almost starless now. The sky yearns for the return of its arbiters.

TWELVE

Suzie Lees watches Jamie Carnegie sleeping. She likes the repetitive motion of his diaphragm going up and down, something constant to count on.

There was a time when she didn't worry about the future. She and Kevin would have children, and the next two decades would be spent raising them. Then the twilight years would come, and the couple would move to Spain or wherever, and amble happily into old age. Only, Suzie couldn't have children as it turned out. Not long after that revelation, Kevin had discovered she was sleeping with an old boyfriend from university thanks to a cryptic letter he found in the study. He hadn't shouted or threatened divorce. Instead they existed in limbo after that, married, dining together, even making formal but pleasant love from time to time, but both of them knowing for certain that they were too distant now ever to adopt. The matter of children had never come up again.

A knock. Jamie stirs. The knock again, short, professional. Suzie grabs a dressing gown and answers the front door. The fat policeman and his cat.

"Mind if I come in for a moment?" Mcalister says.

"Not at all. Please."

Into the kitchen and the policeman sits himself at the table. Sergei curls up on the floor. "Apologies for calling so early in the day," he says.

"I've been up for a while. It's all right."

Upstairs, Jamie knocks the alarm clock off of the bedside table. A thud.

"I thought Mr. Lees was away on business?" the policeman says.

"Yes, but family are staying, you see."

"Righto. Well, I had one or two questions I was hoping to ask you."

"Of course."

"About Derrick Thomas."

She watches him from the corner of her eye. Mcalister was a handsome man once, fifteen years ago, she thinks. How is it he never married? She couldn't remember there ever even being the mention of a woman, come to think of it.

"I understand you knew Mr. Thomas quite well?" Mcalister says.

"We were friends, yes."

"But there was something of a falling out a few years ago, no?"

She hands him his tea and keeps her eyes elsewhere. "People change, of course."

Mcalister lowers his voice. "I understand that it was a *special* friendship while it lasted." Suzie remains silent and raises an eyebrow. "Normally I wouldn't bring these sorts of things up, but in light of recent events—"

"What recent events?"

"Mr. Thomas was a fairly wealthy man, and one with a complicated social life. He died under quite exceptional circumstances."

"Wasn't he a diabetic?"

"He was. It was perfectly manageable with medication, yet he appears to have died from a related and easily avoidable condition. I have it on good authority from his wife that he was very particular about administering the insulin."

"Blast, you've got me. I crept into his house in the dead of night and—"

Another thud from upstairs.

"Which family members are staying, might I ask?" Mcalister says.

"Does that have any bearing on your investigation?"

Suzie reveals a long, tanned, and waxed leg from beneath the folds of the dressing gown. Mcalister ignores it and turns to look out of the window. "No," he says. "Just curiosity."

Jamie Carnegie is perched on the landing now, listening to the exchange in the kitchen.

Mcalister folds his hands on the table to make it clear he isn't in a hurry to leave.

"All right," Suzie sighs. "Derrick and I had a fling, yes. A stupid, stupid thing — he was bored, I was bored — two bored people having a good time. Is that so disgusting? It was years ago. None of that counts as criminal."

Mcalister is quiet for a moment, then: "No, it doesn't. You had no contact with Mr. Thomas after the…incident?"

"We saw each other in The Giraffe sometimes, but that was it."

"How did you feel about Derrick Thomas breaking off the affair?"

"Who said he had anything to do with it?"

"Mrs. Lees, a number of emails have emerged between Derrick Thomas and his brother, explicitly laying out what passed between the two of you."

"Who found these emails?"

"Mr. Thomas' wife."

Well, fantastic. That was one more face she couldn't meet in the street again. "And?"

"Mr. Thomas seemed under the impression that you wanted him to leave his wife."

"I think all men should leave their wives."

"In this case we are talking specifically about Mr. Thomas. Is this true?"

"I don't see why, after being invited into *my* house, while you sit in *my* kitchen, you're allowed to make unwarranted—"

"This is currently part of an unofficial investigation, and if I can establish all of the facts then it can stay unofficial. If, however, I am unable to establish the facts then I'm afraid I will have to take it down a more procedural route, and that will involve hours of transcribed interviews." He lets that settle for a moment.

Sergei rubs up against his master's leg. Mcalister gives him a little stroke.

"Yes," Suzie says quietly. "He was going to leave his wife and I was going to leave Kevin."

"The emails also suggest that he was planning to buy a house for the two of you in the south of France. Is that also true?"

A pause. "Yes."

"It must have been quite unpleasant for you when those plans fell through."

"Derrick was an idiot. It would never have worked. I'm glad we went separate ways."

"All very admirable. The Thomas family made several complaints to the police around that time of key marks on both of their cars, as well as hoax phone calls late at night."

"Did they?"

"Yes. Do you happen to know anything about that?"

"No."

"Very well."

Mcalister closes the kitchen door softly, sits back down, then lowers his voice: "Suzie, I know that stuff was you. Mrs. Thomas knows full well too. You're going to have to be straight with me here. Now, I understand why you would've been angry."

"Do you?"

"Yes. What I need to ascertain now is *how* angry you were."

"Not angry enough to kill him."

"What would have made you angry enough?"

"Oh get bent," she spits. "You can let yourself out. Imply I'm a whore if you like, but I wouldn't kill anyone."

She storms upstairs. Jamie Carnegie is still stood on the landing, already regretting eavesdropping.

THIRTEEN

Jennifer Rhodes is sleeping soundly with her arm coiled around her dead husband's pyjamas. As every night, the pyjamas have been squirted in Mr. Rhodes' aftershave so that when it comes time to sleep they will still smell faintly of him. She packs them away in the mornings so as not to be reminded of such a strange sleeping habit.

He has been dead four years now. She was told the beginning is the hardest part, but has found this not to be the case. There are gaps in what she remembers and she feels a sense of guilt about this. What *exactly* did his voice sound like? What was his natural smell? Did he snore much?

When the initial honeymoon phase of a relationship is over for both parties, Jennifer has reasoned to herself, one is left with a close friend. Lovers are hard to come by. Close friends, harder still. She is certain now that a pair of cologne-doused pyjamas is the closest she will be getting to another meaningful friendship.

Around a year after Mr. Rhodes passed away, Jennifer decided to embark on a career in counselling. She began with a night class, then took an MA degree by remote learning. With funds enough to survive for a long while anyway, she set up a practice in the village. Progress was slow at first. Having known Jennifer Rhodes for many years, the majority of the village were unwilling to divulge their inner secrets to someone who was locally famous for leaving the handbrake off of her car, then watching in horror as it rolled calmly down Precosa Street and into Augustus Rawlings' ornamental pond.

Suzie Lees was her first client, however. That had been enlightening. Jennifer nodded and hmmm-ed as Suzie confirmed each and every suspicion Jennifer had coveted about the woman's sex life over the past decade.

Suzie must have put in a good word with the village. Rupert Carnegie came next with his alcohol-related erectile dysfunction, after failing to perform in the company of a German prostitute during a trip through Cologne. Then Mrs. Crane with her menopause, Mr. Crane with doubts about his marriage, and Officer Mcalister who was experiencing generalised anxiety and believed his cat was occasionally trying to talk to him.

Sessions often return to her in dreams and merge into one another. On those rare nights when she speaks her troubles aloud, the pyjamas only faithfully listen.

Across the street and Eric Crane is sleeping quite soundly too. His machine is coming together nicely. He disassembles the thing at night so his mother won't see it when she wakes him in the morning. The control surface is ready: an alarm clock to show the current date and time, and a wooden spoon to regulate the machine's speed through the years. The chrono-deflectors are also ready: four enormous petals fashioned from corrugated iron, which will warp gravity and time in a bubble around the entire structure. There are only a few parts missing now; railings for decoration, rations for the journey, and the laser. The laser is integral to the machine's function. The chrono-deflectors will not work without it.

Further down the road, the Applebys are still awake, putting the finishing touches on Derrick Thomas' make-up. He looks a picture, lying on the preparation table in his suit. The two brothers work to the blare of an MP3 player on shuffle. Beethoven's Symphony No. 7 Movement 2 has given way to I Believe in Miracles by Hot Chocolate and Robyn dances a little as he works. The strings and the guitar echo off the stainless steel of the sideboards. Scott longs to be far from here, on a beach, in a penthouse; Jesus, anywhere — rich and unworried.

A few streets away and Augustus Rawlings is not asleep either. He is working on his memoir in the study, banging at a typewriter. His hair orbits in grey candy-floss wisps, quivering as he types. He is particular about names and dates, which he recalls with surprising accuracy for someone of his age. He has had a very long and eventful life after all. Perhaps that is the source of his vitality.

He is quite unaware that if he looks up, even for a moment, he will catch sight of cat eyes in the garden which have been watching him since he began writing some hours ago.

FOURTEEN

Beomus is now on his two hundred and fifth incarnation in the Corporia. Tonight the rain is lashing at his windows and he is huddled by the fire, watching the flames and thinking of nothing in particular. Some incarnations he has used well and others he has frittered, and with his toes to the fire and dressed in rags, he does not need to think so hard to guess which one this life is. This body is seventy-three; the year eighteen sixty-five or thereabouts. He has been to this village before, by coincidence: a previous life, though in the year two thousand and eighty-one. He and his Corporic wife were scouting and they chanced on the place. It had been all chrome spires and soft edges then. But now, ahead and behind in time, it is only shacks and the river below. And the rain. And the fire. And the knocking at his door.

"Fuck off," he mutters and goes to pack his pipe.

"Please," a man's voice. Beomus has become suspicious of men's voices. "Sir, my wife, she collapsed on the road and we're out of food."

"You've a foreign edge to your tongue," Beomus says. "You aren't Icelandic?"

A pause. "We're Icelandic, sir."

Djall comes in many variations and flavours, Beomus knows. "The priest's house is down along the way. Keep walking, you'll find it."

"She's almost lost consciousness, won't make it any further. Just a cup of water or some bread. We won't ask any more of you."

Beomus takes the poker from the fire, hides it behind his back, and opens the door a slither. He looks them over. "Inside," he mutters finally.

The man lays his wife down on the floor. Her eyes flutter for a moment, then close.

"A sickness," Beomus says. "Put these in her mouth."

"Thank you, sir. Thank you so much."

The man's face is kind and young and he takes the roots Beomus gives him and pushes them through his wife's lips.

"I am Bjarni and this is my wife Rosa. We weren't far from Hvítá when the storm came on us."

"A foul night, to be sure."

"Do you have a name, sir?"

"Bjartur." The sound feels alien in Beomus' mouth, even after having used it for so long in this incarnation.

"We will thank God every day for meeting you, Bjartur!"

He watches the man's face. Djall is easy to catch by sight or sense when at close distance. This is not him.

Beomus lays the poker back by the fire and fetches water for the couple. The woman comes around for a moment, looks about, smiles to Beomus, then falls back into a sleep. Beomus gives them both his bed and makes a bed of his own on the floor from spare blankets. He listens to their breathing as they sleep and wonders what the next life will bring and where it will be and when it will come. He thinks of the stranger's wife and remembers his own, seven of them now across his lives in the Corporia, all dead or yet to be born from where he currently is in history.

Zorya's face comes to him then, as on most nights.

Finally he sleeps.

He's woken with the sense that something is close. He makes out a figure in the gloom, standing above. The fire's poker is pressed to his throat. He starts up, but the figure applies the poker more firmly and he lies down again.

"You haven't found her, have you?" It's the young man's wife. Her eyes burn with purple fire.

"What?" Beomus whispers.

"Zorya. You've wasted this life, you haven't found her."

"I've found her," Beomus lies. "And I've no intention of telling you where."

"Then," says the wife, says Djall in Etheric, grasping the poker, the face angelic and the lips curled in a smile and the eyes burning amethyst purple, "I'll ask you again in the next incarnation." The poker enters Beomus' windpipe with only minimal pressure from its wielder.

FIFTEEN

It is the afternoon of Derrick Thomas' funeral. He is in the ground now. Eric Crane stood at his mother's side, in too-big trousers, eyeing the coffin and thinking of the morning a week previous when he watched Thomas being wheeled out under the white blanket like a sleeping ghost.

Now the funeral party has moved to The Giraffe. Father Liptrot is lecturing Officer Mcalister on something or other about immigrants. Sergei the cat listens idly from beneath the table. Rupert Carnegie is singing an old Scottish ballad, pausing occasionally to take sips of whisky.

Jamie Carnegie steps out into the parking lot and fishes a cigarette from the packet. A woman is already outside; short, dark-skinned, smiling. She offers him a light. "That's your father in there, singing?" she says.

"How did you know?"

"You came out here because you're embarrassed, I reckon."

"Right."

He waits until she's looking out at the road and sneaks a few glances at her face. "Don't think I've seen you around," he says.

"I'm John's daughter."

A pause. "John?"

"John Whistle. You didn't know that was his name, did you? God, he said he didn't go out much but I didn't realise how bad it was."

He stares at her face openly now. The scotch from earlier is spreading through him and suddenly everything is warm and welcoming and safe and how did such an old piece of rope like Whistle make something as gorgeous as her?

She puts up a hand in a mock-whisper: "He doesn't know it yet, but I'm his guardian angel. I've come to rescue him, you see."

"I believe you."

Suzie Lees is watching from inside. Jamie catches her eye and turns back to the car park.

"Did you come to Wilthail by yourself?" he says. "Wherever you're from."

"Egypt. And yes, all on my lonesome. I don't think I'll be back for long though."

Jamie tries to think of something interesting to say. Nothing comes. He sneaks another glance at the girl. Finally: "What's Egypt like?"

"Dirty. Busy. What's Wilthail like?"

"You've seen it, haven't you?"

She shrugs and rolls up her sleeves a little. Underneath is an atlas of white scars that criss-cross all the way up to her elbows. She notices Jamie Carnegie staring.

"I am—" she looks for the end of the sentence in the distance. "Here to rest a little while."

Suzie Lees still watches from the window slyly, Kevin Lees in turn watching her.

Jamie nods as though she has said something important. "It's a good place to rest."

He glances at the scars again. Seems insane, he thinks, that something so beautiful would want to re-

71

move itself from the world. But then maybe that's how beauty keeps its market value, else the world would be full of beautiful things and no one would give a damn about any of them.

"You're not bothered?" she says, nodding to her arms.

"I'm not bothered."

She stamps her cigarette out and openly studies his eyes. Suzie Lees feels a gulf open up in her chest.

Zoe had been admitted to a rehab clinic in Cairo after her mother found a large bag of cocaine in the girl's handbag. If Zoe didn't go, Donya said, she would cut off her allowance. Either way, there would be no more cocaine. So Zoe lived among the sleepy recovering folk of the clinic where most of the time the residents were lying down, huddled under sheets, moaning, waiting for the urges to pass. Sheets were changed daily or twice daily given the quantity everyone sweated. Drugs were administered in the morning and the evening: a light sedative for her, a cocktail of methadone or whatever for those with bigger problems. She liked how clean the place always seemed to be and the fact that meals were always at the same time.

She got over the hump soon enough but had to stay for the full course, a month. She read a lot and kept to herself and watched the muscular alcoholic getting changed in his room across the hall. Then she be-friended one of the heroin addicts a few rooms away. He was an American, Barney. He was shy and dodged the question whenever she asked about women in his life. It was clear he'd fallen in love with her, or some microwaved version of it. They slept together a few times — him tiptoeing into her bedroom after mid-night — and he soon agreed to save his morning cap of methadone once every two days and pass it on to her. For pain relief, she said. Two weeks passed like this, Barney opening up like a lotus; his marriage, affair, and divorce — then Zoe had enough stashed caps for what she intended.

She chose a Sunday, when nothing happened in the evenings much. She borrowed the CD player from the common area and took it back to her own room. Barney had managed to smuggle her in a bottle of red wine and he promised it was a good one. She put The Very Thought of You by Ella Fitzgerald looping on the CD player and sat and smoked for a long time and drank the wine, trying to savour it. But it was just grape juice — what the hell could the snobs taste that she couldn't? When the song got to the instrumental for around the fifteenth time, she drank all the caps down with the wine and laid back in bed and lit another cigarette and waited for something clever and wise to come to her. At the end of her life, the universe would be kind enough to finally make things clear. Surely.

She thought of God, of Cairo, of her father, of ex-boyfriends and ex-girlfriends and all of her dead pets and nothing much jumped out.

Fine.

There was some nausea, some tiredness, then the urge to sleep.

Almost completely under, she made out someone banging on the door: Barney, shouting and shouting, and someone else with him. Then nothing.

She woke in a hospital. Sterile, with the smell of cooked chicken and disinfectant. On the side was a letter in Arabic that Donya had left. By the second day, when Barney had gone and, Zoe suspected, gone for good, she found the courage to read it.

You are sleeping now. I am writing this beside you, to leave for when you wake up. I suppose it is a kind of confession.

73

They say you'll come around in a few days. They also say there isn't any permanent damage that they can detect, though they're not sure about your brain. I told them that your brain has been damaged since you were born anyway.

Why all of this? That's what I'd like to know. I have sat beside your sleeping head in a hospital three times now and wondered if you would come out alive. I have been woken three times by the telephone in the middle of the night to be calmly told that my daughter has tried to take her own life. No child should have to go through that. And no parent should have to be put through it either. I am so angry that I don't know what to do with myself. Angry at you and angry at whatever it is that's making you do this. Every day I wonder if it was John or I who did this to you somehow. Was I too cold when you were a child? Was he too strict? Did we give you a bad life?

I know you will be the first to admit that we didn't. Even if your father and I didn't get on well, you were more loved than you would ever believe, by both of us. We tried to educate you well, and you are educated. Bright as a button. We tried to show you affection and having seen you with your friends and your men, I know that you have plenty to give in that department. If the fault is with us then I can't find it. I'm sorry, I really can't. Every time I come to you like this, to a hospital, I hate myself. You always look so peaceful, but all I can see written on your face is my failure as a mother.

No one should have to read a letter like this after going through what you just have, but I needed to make myself as clear as possible. I love

*you, as much as I ever have, but I can no longer
be your mother. Not until you're rid of this thing.
I'm nothing but a fretting bag of worry.*

*There's a cheque in this envelope. Use it to
buy yourself a ticket to wherever you need to go.
I think I know where that is already.*

> *Knot Cottage*
> *Fullbrook Street*
> *Wilthail*
> *Mornington*
> *WI30 4NU*

*Your father can be an arsehole, but he's ul-
timately a good man. Go to England, stay with
him. There's nothing left I can do and he is your
father after all. Tell him what has happened, be
honest. Tell him I abandoned you if you like.
Tell him I send my love.*

*This is not the letter I meant to write, but
it is the one I have written. Come back to me
when this is over. You'll be healthy and I'll still
be here, waiting to welcome you home. And finally, two and a half decades in, your life can
begin and I will be there to begin it with you.*

> *Be well,*
> *Mama x*

Jamie Carnegie holds the door open for the girl and the
two of them go back inside. The distant relatives have
left. Now The Giraffe is mainly full of the more hardened
drinkers and those who are too polite to excuse themselves. Jamie spots his father sat alone at the bar.

Mrs. Thomas is speaking very quietly and slowly to
a lady from the post office and her eyes are red. Eric

Crane's father feeds him sips of lager when the boy's mother isn't looking. Augustus and Mary Rawlings sit in their matching blue raincoats slurping ale and watching the scene. Sergei is sleeping under the table, a now empty saucer of milk by his head.

"Won't you have a drink, officer?" Rupert Carnegie slurs at Mcalister.

"Fine thank you, Rupert."

"Ah! The bottle then," he says to the bartender. The bartender hesitates. "Give me the bottle. You deaf?" The rest of the folk stay quiet. The bartender hands the scotch across. Carnegie swigs straight from the bottle.

"Haven't you had enough?" Jamie says gently to his father.

"Time was," Rupert Carnegie drawls, "when we would've made a right party out of all this."

"It's a funeral, Rupert," Mcalister says.

"Aye, but Thomas would've wanted a right dance, I reckon."

Augustus Rawlings finishes his drink, licks his lips carefully, then: "Unfortunately Mr. Thomas is not here to ask." A long silence. Rawlings continues. "Such is death. It might come unexpectedly at any moment, no? Quite without warning too, by aneurysm, by heart attack. That is a thing we'd all do well to remember."

Darling, Mary Rawlings says gently, in a language only Augustus hears.

"Why," he continues, "if we didn't die, can you imagine the sheer boredom? A race of dull, humourless monkeys, seen everything, done everything—"

Darling, Mary says again. *Not too much now.*

Sergei opens his eyes, licks a paw, listens.

"We give all the credit to life of course, to birth, to that hideous, bloody exit from the crotch. Does death not deserve credit also? Death needs no mother to bring it into the world. Death needs no father to protect it."

What are you doing? Mary says louder now, in clear Etheric.

Nothing but a love letter to the craft, Augustus replies.

Sergei cocks his head. Rupert Carnegie swigs from the scotch bottle. Officer Mcalister is staring at Augustus, perhaps questioning the old man's sanity.

Don't you smell it? Augustus says in Etheric. *The boy is in the room.*

Mary Rawlings eyes the attending folk: Rupert and Jamie Carnegie, Officer Mcalister, Father Liptrot, and a few others she has seen about the village from time to time.

Look how I have their attention, Augustus murmurs. *Which of them do you think it is?*

Satisfied Rawlings won't be continuing his lecture and the eccentric crisis has passed, the folk turn back to their drinks in silence.

Beomus, Augustus calls out in Etheric. *Are you close?* Nobody stirs. *I smell you,* he says slowly.

Darling, Mary says. *Drink up. Let's just go home.*

SIXTEEN

Jamie Carnegie is out in the morning again, running up May Hill. A figure appears over the ridge, hidden away in a long black coat. Jamie nears and recognises him. The old man never leaves his house supposedly, but here he is, pushing through the mud and slush in wellington boots. They meet eyes as they pass.

"Morning," John Whistle grumbles.

Jamie nods, tries to smile. His father told him once that Whistle grew up here but moved away. Must have gone somewhere awful to come back such a miserable bastard. His face has malice written through it; the brow all cracked like a stone wall. Jamie often thinks about men like Whistle, almost feels bad for them. Old and miserable sacks of shit, not unlike his father.

When Jamie came back from a school trip to Kew Gardens and announced that he wanted to be a landscape gardener, first his father laughed. Then he looked up, realising the boy was serious and said, very quietly, "You'll be dead before you do a queer's job under this roof." Still, Jamie had taken the course at college when the time came, telling his father he was studying to be a mechanic. And finally, two years later, getting his diploma, he left it on the kitchen table and the matter never came up again. Now when Rupert Carnegie is sober enough to leave the house and the topic of his son comes up, he tells shop assistants and dog-walkers that Jamie wanted to be a mechanic but didn't have the brains for it. Whistle, Jamie maintains, is no different. A cold, indefatigable bastard who has decided it's better to shit on the lives of others than dare having one of his own.

"My daughter," Whistle mumbles.

"Sorry?"

"She's…her stuff's everywhere. Had to get out of the house. Hairbrushes and makeup…"

"Ah." Jamie tries to smile again.

"You've met my daughter?"

Jamie nods. Zoe's face appears in his mind. The morning is suddenly a little warmer. He studies Whistle's face, looking for any likeness of the girl but there's none.

"How long is she back here for?" Jamie tries to remove any hint of interest from his voice.

"One more day if I have any say in it. Probably a month if she does."

A *month*. "Well, it must be lovely having her back."

Whistle grumbles affirmatively. He sees the girl's face in his mind now too, though as a baby.

She didn't even have a name then, those first few days. He and Donya took the little bundle of skin back to their apartment and fed her and changed her when she needed it. He came to understand that babies have a smell no amount of talcum powder can seem to cover up, and that their vomit can ruin a shirt for good.

He and Donya stopped making love, but perhaps that was normal for the first few months after childbirth. She doted on Zoe night and day and began sleeping in the nursery so she could be there when the child woke up. John began to sense that he had served his purpose and was now an obsolete relic, there to facilitate daily life, but an object of interest for no one in particular.

The insomnia began when Zoe was one. Whistle would lie awake until three or four in the morning, listening to his wife breathing, his stomach full of anxious needles, unable to sleep. The less she touched him, the worse it got. Unable to ask her what was wrong out of fear of shame, he sat on the matter some more.

In the mornings he often wanted her and if he made an advance or hinted at it, she quickly got dressed and fixed them both tea. If he mentioned going to bed early she encouraged it, but stayed up several hours extra herself until he was asleep. He hadn't known regret like that before; regret at not knowing this side of Donya existed, regret at having chosen the wrong woman, the wrong life. He thought of old girlfriends and wondered how things might have turned out with them instead. And he thought of Zoe. It would tear the family apart if he left now. The only correct thing to do was wait. Wait until she was old enough to fend for herself. He would live for her in the meantime.

The days were long and he let himself be absorbed by life at the university. A student made an advance on him once. He kissed her for a moment, then explained in polite terms that it was a terrible idea and she backed off. Donya warmed up a little when she'd been drinking some nights and occasionally put her head on his shoulder, or even initiated lovemaking. These episodes were few and far between, perhaps twice a year, but this was enough of a relief to keep him hanging on each and every night wondering if it would be the rare occasion when she finally, unexpectedly, returned to herself.

A bad patch when Zoe was eight: John stopped sleeping again and drank a half-litre of vodka one evening and confronted Donya in the study. He must have looked insane, all red-eyed and swaying. He told her the way they were living was inhuman and that he loved her and she had to explain to him what was wrong that second or he was leaving.

Donya didn't look up from her book, but lit a cigarette and, turning a page, muttered, "Then leave."

He considered killing himself. What a thing to do, but it would get her attention. He considered smashing her things, burning her clothes. Christ, anything.

He often thought back to when he'd just met Donya, those first few weeks together.

What a stupid thing that I was happy then, before, and that happiness seemed to have a momentum behind it. I thought I'd ride it like some god on a lightning bolt through the rest of my life. We were untouchable, she and I. And I knew that nothing could ever kill what we had. And we killed it.

I can't pick out the exact moment when it all crumbled, or point to what did it, but I'd give the rest of my life to go back to where we were, if even for a day.

He looks Jamie Carnegie over. The boy has years ahead of him; strong and fit. Whistle wonders what he would do if some potion could take him back to where this kid is now. But if you couldn't bring your wisdom back with you, what the hell would be the point?

Jamie Carnegie looks Whistle over. The old man is finished; ugly and bitter. He wonders what it must be like to grow so ancient and twisted, to have probably never known love at all.

In some secret corner of his mind, Jamie occasionally goes back over past sexual encounters and feels better for it. There was the girl he met on the sustainability course last month. And the receptionist at the recording studio. It felt good when they wanted you. But the mornings were always hollow, even if the women turned out to be lovely. Sometimes they cooked him breakfast or made another advance, but by then the feeling was gone. They were not and could never be Jenny Dunne. Only Jenny Dunne could do that, and now she was gone. These other women didn't smell correct, didn't joke properly. They were more experienced, more sophisticated, wittier, but afterwards, whether it be the second he laid back down or the next morning walking home, Jenny Dunne's face usually turned up in his mind.

Now remember, why did you end it, dickhead?

Yes, because I never felt I was enough. Because I thought I'd rather stay alone than be an option to someone I considered a priority. Because I was too ashamed to give away just how insecure I felt back then. Because I was young. Because I was pathetic.

And what I wouldn't give to just sleep next to you one more time.

"Anyway," Whistle mutters. "Best be getting back before my daughter burns the house down."

"Be seeing you, Mr. Whistle."

"John, if you like," the old man says and starts down the hill.

SEVENTEEN

The tender wipes the machine's single orange eye, then steps back to a respectful distance.

"Are there more visitors scheduled?" says the machine.

The tender keeps his eyes averted. "But one more. A peasant from the out-districts."

"A peasant? Fine news. It's been nothing but dull snobs all day. Only so much one can take."

Justix of the Silicon Fields came to the machine in the morning, begging after a more lenient tax on neurowarps. A noblelady came next, crying crocodile tears for the machine to repeal its recent ban on de-sentience devices.

"Tell me of this peasant's request," comes the machine's deep warble of a voice.

"I cannot. He said the matter was a sensitive one and that he would need to speak to you directly."

A ragged man clears his throat, standing by the main door.

"Leave us," mutters the machine. The tender exits. The peasant approaches, stares a while in silence.

"I am not how you imagined?" says the machine.

"I am not sure…" the ragged man says. He continues gawping. A strange machine, all rings within rings spinning about each other, and a golden whirling ball of plasma at its centre. "You are a thinking machine?" says the peasant.

"In a sense, yes. Every bit as complex as you are. Arguably more so."

"The caliph, they call you," says the peasant.

"And what of you? Do you have a title?"

"It's unimportant."

"The path to wisdom begins with calling things by their true names," the machine says tiredly.

"You could not pronounce my name even if I told it to you, I fear."

"I speak over three thousand Terran languages and four hundred exotics, but have it your way. What is it you intend to bring to my attention today?"

"What powers you, sir? Vacuum energy? A singularity?"

"Ah, an educated peasant, I see! How do you know of such things?"

"I am learned about matters which interest me," says the ragged man. "My family is poor, but we grant ourselves simple pleasures. Books and the like."

"*Books*?"

"Ink on tree matter."

"I know damn well what books are. Why ever do you bother with such archaic nonsense?"

"There's a certain appeal to things which can perish easily, wouldn't you agree?"

"Do you know the extent of your heresy?" the machine growls.

"That you had your creator destroyed, a bookseller himself? That you execute peasants like me who educate themselves on the true nature of the world? Yes, if that is heresy."

The machine has no face to smile, but the peasant suspects it is smiling nevertheless. The throne room door seals itself. Lightshades come down over the windows.

"Beomus," the caliph says delightedly.

Glittering metal legs unfold from the machine and it stands, overshadowing the peasant. Beomus keeps his eyes on a patch of floor. He says, "And so you have become a tyrant in this realm, as well as the other?"

The machine chuckles. "A meagre one compared to my previous standing."

"I prefer you like this," Beomus says. "Now you are mechanical on the outside, as well as in."

The machine takes clomping strides over to the peasant and puts its single, burning orange eye to his.

"I'm a thing of technology, as I was before. Do you think we were ever more than that? Yet here we play still, in the quagmire."

"It will have been worth it, when it's done," Beomus mutters.

"Ah, when you've won the whore's hand back?"

"Nothing to win back. I have it already."

The machine laughs and the glowing, orange eye squints. "You are an idiot in paradise, lad. You've thrown it all away for the sake of nothing at all."

The machine extends its fifteen mechanical arms to accompany this last remark. Claws unfurl. Then in a growl, "How many incarnations has it been now?"

"Ninety."

"Ninety?"

"More, I expect. And you?"

"More still."

Quiet for a moment, then Djall says, "You've seen the 23rd century?"

"Of course."

"My favourite, I'd say. Just before the Great Catastrophe."

"I preferred the Renaissance." Beomus looks the machine over again like a breeder might a horse. "I met her in my last incarnation, in Europe."

The machine remains perfectly still. "How was she?"

"Exhausted. As I am. As you are."

"All your own doing, lad," the machine snarls.

"Ah, providence."

Djall vaults at the peasant without warning, claws extended, racing on clacking toes. "*Providence*? Is that what you call a flight from justice?"

The peasant stands his ground, says, "When you see her again, *if*, be sure to ask if she was happily married. Catch her on an honest day and she'll tell stories of how you threatened her, goaded her into all manner of unpleasantness. It wasn't a marriage but a damn hostage situation."

"Her and I exist for different purposes," the machine says. "As the two of us do, lad. It was my occupation to extinguish. Her duty was to the other thing. You respect her career so much — what of mine? What's the world without entropy? I'll tell you. Not a single arbiter has ended their life since you removed me from the Etheria. They can't. *That* was my function. A pressure release valve for all the misery of immortality. And now immortality is a kind of torture rather than a golden privilege. That's your legacy."

"There are hedgehogs and foxes," the peasant says flatly. "Hedgehogs covet one skill brilliantly, only one. But foxes can be lovers, wisemen, and magicians all at the same time. You're a hedgehog, all prickles and one singular unpleasant obsession. Killing. Hell, why do you think Novelty even gave you your title to begin with? Because it was the only thing you could do at all. No wonder you made a terrible husband."

"If what you say is true, then I'd be happy to demonstrate that singular talent to you now, lad."

"They tell me you're not a god," Beomus says.

"Is that so?"

"It is. There's a legend in the slums that you can die, in this form."

The machine's rings spin a little faster. The golden, energetic heart beats a little harder. "Immortality is relative to the creature itself. Aren't men immortal compared to a mayfly?" Djall says.

"No, they only live longer."

Djall charges at the peasant again, claws brandished. The peasant extends his hand, a nanoswarm exploding from it, enveloping the machine. The throne room is little more than a fug of furious black bees for a moment, then Djall comes charging out the other side, orange eye still fixed on Beomus. He roars, splays even more mechanical claws, and a great shining spike unfolds from his head. The peasant dives onto the machine, activates a newmatter spear, the thing extending in his hand, and plunges it downwards. Djall stumbles about for a few fevered seconds, then lies down incapacitated. The gyrating rings begin to slow. Beomus jumps down to look Djall directly in the eye.

"Five hundred incarnations, then we're finished," the machine says weakly. "You know the rules. And if the grudge isn't settled by then, none of us are going home." It snorts at the peasant. "Not long now and you'll be out of the game for good. Or, find the upper hand somehow and end me in my final incarnation, take my wife, return to the Etheria."

Beomus smiles and sits himself down on the ground, cross-legged. "She sent me with a message." The orange eye blinks, fading. "She wanted me to make sure you knew that you were less than nothing to her, a mere arrangement."

"You came to taunt me?" the machine says, amused. The peasant nods. "Ah, a sadist after all then."

"Quite possibly." With no urgency, Beomus produces another newmatter spear, this time jamming it into the spinning rings. There is a small explosion. He watches Djall's single orange eye close to half, then shut entirely. He rips out a few electronic conduits to make sure the death is final, checks himself for wounds, and hunts for the room controls. The main door opens of its own accord. Behind it stands the machine's tender.

"Your master is dead," Beomus says. "I claim full ownership of the Cydonian Kingdom and its peoples, on account of successful regicide. That is the procedure, no?" The tender nods. "Excellent." Beomus inspects the throne room, opening cabinets, pocketing rare minerals and gems as he goes. "Now, I have several immediate requirements." He spies a number of opals in a basin and begins shovelling them into his pocket. "Firstly, my coronation will take place tomorrow morning, just after sunrise. Secondly, the—"

Something sharp is pressing into the base of his spine.

"Put those back," the tender growls.

"Did I offend an ancient custom?" Beomus says gently. "Yes."

The opals all replaced, he puts his hands up in a surrender gesture. "Turn around," the tender says. Beomus does so. The tender's eyes are harsh and small. The mouth is twisted into a wry smile.

"I killed the caliph," Beomus says, glancing down at the knife pressed to his stomach now. "That makes me the new monarch, doesn't it?"

The tender's eyes flash faintly purple. The wry smile widens. "I was lucky enough on occasion, lad, to incarnate into the same age twice," he says. "Now, repeat to me Zorya's message."

EIGHTEEN

When Mcalister can't sleep he patrols the neighbourhood, Sergei usually padding alongside. Tonight they pass through the village centre and turn down into the recreation grounds. The stars are out and clear. Frost is just beginning to kiss at their noses. There were many nights like this when Mcalister was a boy in Scotland — the cold eating at everything, his mother making a stew and his father working on a bottle at the kitchen table. It's an odd thing, he thinks sometimes, but with his family all dead now, if he forgets to remember them then they might never have happened at all.

Frozen grass crunches under Sergei's paws. The cat doesn't shiver, only looks to his master for the next turn.

A shape in the trees. Mcalister leads them both towards it. Youths: the older Simpson brother and some kids from another village, as well as a young girl. They're passing a joint back and forth and they have a few bottles of wine.

Mcalister appears out of the bushes. "Evening."

The older Simpson brother, Michael, puts the joint behind his back. The girl groans.

"That wouldn't happen to be dope, would it now? And wine?" Mcalister says.

"Good evening, officer," Michael Simpson says and tips an imaginary hat. "What can we do for you?" His eyes are dark and stay fixed on the policeman.

"How about you give me what's behind your back and then we all go home?" Mcalister says politely.

Simpson stands his ground. The other kids are backing away except for the girl, who takes Simpson's hand. Mcalister steps closer. The frost cracks under his boots.

"I know you, Mr. Simpson, but I can't say I've met your friends. Where are you coming from?"

"Crickley," the girl mutters.

"That's good then. It's not a long walk and I'm going to have to send you home for the evening now."

"I think we'll be fine here," Simpson says.

Mcalister smiles. "I'm sure you will, but underage drinking and smoking drugs tends to be frowned upon by my colleagues, you see. If you leave the wine here and give me that joint, I'll be glad to consider the matter settled."

Simpson stays rooted to the spot. The boy probably moved heaven and earth to make this evening work, getting the wine through an older friend, getting the dope from God knows where.

Sergei sits down on his back legs and watches his master.

"I think you're forgetting that I know your parents, young Mr. Simpson," Mcalister says.

"Big fucking whoop!"

A titter from his friends.

Yes, and the girl — Simpson was probably only minutes from getting her back to his tent and concluding the evening.

"All of you," Mcalister says to the other kids. "Get lost and I won't take it further."

They vanish into the trees, no hesitation, and then it's just Simpson and the girl. Mcalister steps towards the wine. Simpson steps closer too and picks up one of the bottles and holds it like a weapon.

"Not all that long ago, Mr. Simpson, I watched Father Liptrot making the cross on your baby head with holy water. You're a little older now but not much smarter, it looks like."

"Fuck off," Simpson says and puffs his chest out a little. The girl pulls at his shoulder but he stands his ground.

"Don't force me to make life difficult for you," Mcalister murmurs.

The boy's eyes widen. The nostrils flare. Mcalister steps back, anticipating. The boy raises the bottle, yells.

"Put that down, you bloody animal," comes another voice.

The boy freezes. The girl darts into the trees. Then the voice again: "I said put that down or there'll be hell to pay."

Simpson flings the bottle aside and runs after the girl.

Mcalister gives it a moment, composes himself. "You mustn't do that."

"Worked though, didn't it?" Sergei says.

Mcalister bends down and pats the cat a few times, gives his ear a little rub. "You *mustn't* do that. I don't want anything happening to you."

NINETEEN

"Where are they now?" says the Arbiter of Fickle Pleasures.

"Just about everywhen," the crone replies, her Book of Knots in her hand. She makes another line on the already crowded page, tracing the lineages. "No pattern to it...no pattern. One life a pauper, another a king. One a woman, another a man."

The world-schism warps and churns.

"And Zorya?" the arbiter says.

"Just as lost, poor girl," the old woman replies.

"Poor *woman*. She's millennia-old now, Corporically speaking."

"If we count like that then they're all ancient."

They watch the schism for a long while, lives beginning and ending and most meaning nothing at all — three discordant organ notes lost in an infinite belfry.

"Are we so different?" says the Arbiter of Fickle Pleasures.

"What?"

"To them. How they live now."

The crone shrugs. "No, I suppose not. But they're lost among the maze. We sit in the tower watching."

"And who is to say there isn't something more prescient than us doing the same? One would never know."

She grunts in an agreeable way and continues with her note-taking.

"You won't help them like that, writing it all down," the arbiter says.

"I like to think when they come home I will show this to them, and they'll see the stupidity of their ways," the crone says.

"You've a charming optimism about you, but come on. You're the Arbiter of Things Ahead. What do you see approaching?"

"I haven't touched my runes for some time."

"You don't care for them?"

"No, it's not that," the old woman mutters.

"You're afraid. Of what you'll divine."

The crone points to a lonely corner of the world-schism where a single mindstate flickers. "Do you see that? A primaeval spot in time, before civilisation. Djall is performing his ritual, making his sacrifice. Now."

"I don't know of such arcane things."

"He has had enough of waiting."

"Waiting?"

"Waiting for Beomus and his lover."

"But he must wait."

"No, there is an exception."

"Surely..."

"Yes," the crone murmurs. "Not long now."

They squint, the two of them, at the scene ahead.

Inside the Corporia, Djall is wearing a new, young face. He stands at the foot of an altar in the robes of a priest. A young girl is gagged and bound and lying on the altar, covered in sweat and trying to wriggle free.

The Arbiter of Entropy makes the symbol of the serpent, then the symbol of the pheasant. He does not meet the girl's eyes.

"So be it that I demand," he whispers, "with this innocent's life, to bring the ancient powers into action. In exchange for my remaining incarnations I demand, in return, that with my next incarnation, and my enemy's next incarnation, and my lover's next incarnation, we be settled in the same corner of extension and time. And if one of us should extinguish the other, then that will be the final thing and there will no returning. So be it I demand with this innocent's life that we shall all be reunited."

The girl rolls onto her back, then onto her front again. She is a tanner's daughter. That morning, while looking for fallen apples in the orchard, Djall snatched and dragged her to his makeshift altar.

"He's mad," whispers the Arbiter of Fickle Pleasures.

"He knows exactly what he's doing. It's a wonder he didn't enact it sooner."

"But if he's killed in the next incarnation—"

"And if Beomus is killed in the next incarnation, then that will be Beomus gone also. For good. He knows exactly what he's doing."

"Stop him then."

"How?" the crone says. "Jump into the Corporia myself?"

"If we lose any of them—"

"You needn't lecture me on the nature of things. There is nothing we can do."

Djall steps towards the girl, a knife in his hand, the blade catching a stutter of moonlight. He puts the knife in. The girl's eyes grow wide and bovine for a few moments, disbelieving. A river of blood. She rests her head on the altar. Djall puts the knife to his own throat now and grins.

"He knows we're watching," says the Arbiter of Fickle Pleasures.

"No," says the crone. "He is simply enjoying himself."

A new river of blood. The knife clatters to the floor. Djall, Beomus, and Zorya's mindstates ignite suddenly throughout the Corporia, pulled to a single point in the distance, diverging, doubling back in time, vaulting forward, drawn by the blood of an ancient rite, set to land in a single spot ahead of the two watching arbiters.

Softly the Arbiter of Fickle Pleasures says, "And where do they go now, in their next incarnations?"

"Ahead," says the crone. "To a village."

TWENTY

Jamie and Zoe are the only customers in Mrs. Leung's Chinese Restaurant. They have met on the pretence of talking about John Whistle, but he hasn't come up yet. Mrs. Leung brings over a plate of fortune cookies. Ever since her husband died, she's enjoyed watching young couples. They seem so innocent — lit up with a pure light hard to find elsewhere in life, save for new mothers and recently divorced rich men.

When she's gone, Zoe picks up a fortune cookie and motions that Jamie do the same.

"On three," she says. "And no peeking at mine. One, two—"

"Mine's boring," Jamie says.

"Give me a clue."

"It's just boring. Here."

He passes it across.

TODAY WILL BE A LUCKY DAY.

I sure hope so, Jamie thinks. "And yours?"

"Mine's a little odd," Zoe murmurs. She passes it over.

YOU WILL PLAY AN INTEGRAL ROLE IN THE CLIMAX OF AN ANCIENT GRUDGE.

Jamie says, "That doesn't seem very fortune cookie-ish does it?" Zoe shakes her head and reads it again.

They sip their drinks a while, then Zoe says carefully, "My father has a lot of ancient grudges."

"Against who?"

"Me, for example."

"I don't think so. Why would he let you live with him otherwise?"

"It's not letting. It's tolerating."

"You're his daughter."

"I gave him a hard time when I was younger. I suppose I understand if he's still angry about it." She rolls up her cardigan sleeves and the atlas of scars is still there, with its sad red back roads. "I never said sorry. I guess he doesn't see why he should either."

"Whatever you've done, it can't be that—"

"It can."

"I mean, isn't he your father though?"

"What's the one thing you'd never forgive a child for?"

Jamie thinks about this. "Failure."

"Strange thing to say."

He shrugs.

"Guess I'm not the only one with parental issues then, huh?" Zoe says.

"They should love you no matter what. It's part of the job description."

"I was going to have a baby once," Zoe says, quite out of nowhere. Jamie keeps his eyes on the table. "I didn't, but I was going to. If I had, it's not like I suddenly would've turned into this *enlightened being*. I would've still been me, just with a baby. You become a god because you screwed. What a stupid thing to become a god for."

"Yes," Jamie says and then he's not sure what else to add.

"Our parents aren't gods, that's all I'm saying."

"If you don't mind me asking, what is it your father can't forgive you for?"

She waggles her head a little awkwardly. "I have these episodes where I don't want to be around anymore. The gods don't take kindly to their creations trying to off themselves, do they? Yahweh forbids it. My father wasn't too keen either."

Later, Jamie plays with her hair. It seems heavier than it should be — as though weighted. He counts the freckles on her breasts. She was a little coarser than he thought she would be, a little more demanding.

No pretence now, no pretending. Jamie likes this point, when the game is done with and the two of you just lie and talk. You've seen each other's genitals. Now you're free to reveal yourself as a vegetarian, or an emotional wreck, or a YouTuber.

Zoe says, "Want a drink?"

"Sure."

She leaves the room naked. Jamie hears her voice and another, male. The girl reappears with two glasses of something alcoholic.

"Who was that?" Jamie asks.

"Who? Oh, Dad?"

"*Mr. Whistle*?"

"Yeah. Don't look so frightened, he knows you're here."

"How long has he been…in the house?"

"I don't know, since lunch? He says you're sleeping with Suzie Lees, whoever that is, so I don't think he'll be surprised you're sexually active."

"God, couldn't you have said something? I thought we were alone."

"Don't be such a square. Here."

He drinks. Jenny Dunne would never have done a thing like this. He drinks again, waiting to see what he'll say. Nothing comes. He wonders how many men have been in this position with her already. If only he could talk to them, just one. If only you could do that with lovers, compare notes with everyone who came before in real-time.

She gets back into bed and rolls into the crook of his arm. When she's asleep he stares for a long time out of the window at the stars and finishes his drink, then hers.

Where's the sense in anything? Just a few hours ago I couldn't take my eyes off of this girl. Now I'm in her bed and I'd rather just be sleeping back at my father's place alone. I'm like a stupid rat, darting at anything it sees that might give it a little relief from…what, exactly?

He thinks of Jenny Dunne. That first night at her parents' house, after they'd fumbled about naked for a few minutes, she became a different creature. She had taken his hand and shown him the keloid scars on her back. She'd told him about her depression, about how fat she felt. It was a holy sort of space he suspected she had let no one into before.

They moved in together after a year of monogamy, a small house among the farms of Wilthail. The skies were usually clear and they did each other's washing and took turns cooking. Two months of a thing that couldn't possibly fail — Jenny Dunne leaving her cotton swabs and tampon packets and old lipsticks around the place, and Jamie picking them up from time to time and looking them over like an archaeologist might.

But before long he missed the veils. She preferred TV over their conversations in the evenings. She lost interest in his day. She took to rolling over at night into a ball and racing off to sleep as soon as possible. He grew irritable, made the situation worse.

Domesticity was not the constant euphoria he'd imagined it might well be. It was closer to having a university roommate one had sex with occasionally.

The problem must be with me, he decided.

The problem must be with her, he decided on other days.

Petty arguments, passive-aggression, repression, and finally claustrophobia.

She made occasional jokes about getting married.

God, he thought. If the blueprint is shit, why build the house?

He tried to imagine another two, five, ten years of falling asleep with a ball of angst in his stomach. He could hang on for a little while in the hope that she returned to her old, passionate self, but the hope was obviously in vain. She was smarter than him, but he had more moving parts. It was pointless.

And watching her drive off for the last time with her things, he felt some deep sense of stupidity that he'd never bothered to ask what might have actually been wrong in those last few months — that he could've sat on the whole thing another week and she would still be getting into the same bed with him that night. It was like a spell he'd cast with his mouth and now the world was irreversibly altered as a result.

Better to keep lovers at arm's length from then on, he decided. A wrapped surprise was better than an opened gift you never wanted anyway. That was a fine philosophy to lead a life by. Probably.

TWENTY-ONE

The wind is strong and the mainsail is hoisted. The frigate glides around the cape. Captain Barnstable stands at the bow and takes a moment to enjoy the breeze.

The first mate begins a shanty and the crew join in with little persuasion. Against regulation, Barnstable orders a cup of ale for each man present and distributes the cups himself to thankful hands — down to the powder monkey, the boatswain, the cooks, the swabs, the carpenter, the ordinary seamen, and finishing with the navigator who is slumped over his charts.

Three frigates were set upon in the last month alone. Barnstable has had four new cannons installed and a store of muskets brought aboard. *The Indomitable* sails a little heavier for it, but the benefit is considered worthwhile.

The shanty dies away man by man until only the cabin boy is keeping the tune alive as a whistle, and eventually he too falls silent and returns to work. There is little to do in these hours with so much preparation having gone on in port, but Barnstable walks up and down the main deck anyway, surveying the sea then the ship, the sea then the ship, the sea then the ship.

Towards evening the sun makes a last orange stand against the night and the crew slump piecemeal and tired on the deck watching it die.

"Must be God bidding us we sleep well," the first mate mutters.

"I think God does not come out this far into the water," Barnstable replies.

"Ha, blasphemy captain!"

"Talk not to me of blasphemy, man," Barnstable quotes. "I'd strike the sun if it insulted me."

The first mate pauses uncertainly, watching his superior. Beomus realises his error. Moby Dick will not be written for another fifty years. "I'm being verbose, excuse me," he says.

"Captain," the first mate nods and makes off towards the aft.

There's but a candle flame of sun left now. The sea is oil in this dark light and the air is all fuggish with salt. Stars have appeared. Beomus looks to the Big Dipper and finds Merak with little effort. Four or so lives ago he lived on a research station surrounding it, two thousand years from now. A freak solar flare and then he woke, in a new body, a midwife pulling and kneading his head like he were bread — back on Earth, in this era.

"Sir." A timid voice, the ship's boy.

"What is it?"

"Sir, the sun."

The candle flame on the horizon is still just as bright as it was ten minutes previous.

"Telescope, quick as you can." One is passed to him and he glasses the candle flame and makes out a ship, flagless, its bow aimed towards *The Indomitable*, nearing.

"Alert the crew, tell them to ready the cannons, then fetch the first mate."

"Sir."

Beomus raises the telescope again. Vague features are discernible now. The approaching ship's lights do not waver like naval lanterns. The first mate is at his side. Beomus passes him the telescope.

"An apparition," the first mate whispers.

"Verily. You've seen such things before?"

"Never."

"An atmospheric effect, perhaps. St. Elmo's fire?"

"That fire is green and only touches the tips of a mast. She's all lit up like a bonfire."

Nearer now, Beomus can make out the details of the vessel. She's almost twice the size of *The Indomitable* and cannons are already poking from her gun ports. The source of her light is countless lanterns which are strung from bow to aft. The light is an artificial white, not the soft yellow of an oil lantern. Like Moby Dick, Thomas Edison's revelations are still decades from fruition. This is no age for electricity.

"Starboard, ninety degrees," Beomus says quickly.

"Sir, the reef—" the first mate protests.

"The helmsman, ninety degrees, tell him now."

"Sir."

The sky swivels with the yaw to starboard. Crew are emerging from the decks below, curious. The approaching ship pivots to track the new course.

The first mate has returned. "She's fast..." he murmurs.

"Thrice our speed at least," Beomus agrees.

"Are we not among the fastest ships in the fleet?"

"Aye, but that vessel is untypical."

He sets the telescope on the vessel again. It is not a quarter mile away, the port cannons glinting in the impossible, electric light. As though a mirror image, a figure is stood at the bow of the approaching vessel. Through the telescope the face is little more than a blur, though Beomus suspects it is wearing a smile, and that the eyes burn a furious purple.

The Indomitable has exploded into action — gun-powder thrown like flour, the upper deck all alive with the chattering of ramrods in muskets.

"Pirates?" the first mate asks.

"No," Beomus says, folding the telescope away, wondering what he will be in the next incarnation. "An old colleague of sorts."

TWENTY-TWO

Eric Crane waits until his parents have gone to the flower show or whatever it is and sends the signal, which is a text message to Zoe Whistle. Two minutes later there is a knock at the door. He leads her up to his bedroom, tiptoeing, though he's not sure why. The machine is ready and waiting.

"How does it work?" Zoe says.

"Mmm, gravity."

"You told me that last time."

Eric thinks for a moment. "When gravity is really strong it, like, bends time. If you were in a bubble of gravity, time would be bent around you and you could travel into the future. Relatively speaking."

"Only the future?"

Eric nods. "You can't go back, I told you."

"Maybe you just haven't worked out how to yet," Zoe says. "What if you don't like the future when you get there?"

The boy shrugs.

"You don't care, do you?"

"Not really."

"How about your mum and dad?"

"Don't think they'll miss me much."

"Well I'll miss you."

The boy feels a spark of something. "Come with me then, if you want," he says.

Zoe twists a strand of hair. "How far ahead will we travel?"

Far enough, Eric thinks. To when nothing dies, ever. To when there's no gap left between wanting and getting. "I'm not sure," he says finally.

"Show me how it works, at least."

He talks her through the control panel, with its flashing lights and its little digital calendar. He teases the control lever forward, shows her the slow setting, then the fast.

"How will we know when to stop?" she says.

"We'll know," he says quietly. He watches her face. "In the future they don't use guns or anything like that," he continues. "If they're angry, they talk it out, but they're not even angry much of the time. Everything is free so no one needs money, and they grow houses like we grow bananas."

"That does sound nice. Are there parents in the future?"

"Mmm, I'm not sure."

She picks up a toy rocket on his bedside table. "I saw some boys chasing you the other day," she says. "Were you in trouble?"

"I'm okay."

He takes some spare parts out from under his bed and starts sorting through them.

"You were running pretty fast and they were shouting. Are you sure you weren't in trouble?"

The boy says nothing for a while and kneads the resistors and diodes in his hands like they're precious gems. He thinks of Tom Downing, stood over Eric and forcing mud into his mouth. He knows where Tom

106

Downing lives. If I was braver, he thinks, I'd go round and kill him.

"There'll always be nasty people, you know that?" Zoe says. Eric nods. "It doesn't matter if you made everyone pretty and money vanished, some people would still be awful. And to other people, sometimes, we're the awful ones. So, why were those boys chasing you?"

Eric plays some more with the diodes. "They wanted to egg The Old Curmudgeon's house."

"And?"

"And I said they shouldn't."

"Why?"

"Because you live there."

"You can tell me all of it. I won't get angry or any-thing."

"Tom Downing said you tried to *do yourself in.*"

A pause, then Zoe says, "You don't know what that means, do you?" Eric shakes his head. "It means I tried to kill myself."

"Why?"

"I don't know really. Why do you want to visit the future so badly? I bet if you look really carefully you'll see you're not excited about the future at all, you just don't like the present that much. Well I guess I feel the same way."

TWENTY-THREE

Sergei first spoke two years ago.

Mcalister had confiscated a bag of dried psilocybin mushrooms from some teenagers on the recreation ground and taken them home. They looked like the real deal. He'd only been able to get hold of a little dope from time to time, so the mushrooms were quite a treat. He stirred half of the bag, about 2 grams, into a cup of tea and drank it down watching the evening news. There was a little nausea after around half an hour, but all in all he felt fine. He changed the channel to a war film and waited to see if the colours blurred but no such luck. Sergei came in from somewhere or other and jumped up onto his lap. The cat kneaded Mcalister's legs a bit, licked itself, then settled down. Mcalister began to stroke its back.

"It's better around the ears," Sergei said. "If that's all right with you."

Mcalister turned off the television and sat very still.

"I didn't mean to interrupt," the cat said.

The world appeared perfectly normal. This was not how he'd imagined mushrooms. "You didn't interrupt," Mcalister said in a very slow, very quiet voice.

"Well then," the cat said and presented an ear. Mcalister began to rub it gently.

"No mice tonight," the cat said.

"Is…is that so?"

"Say, you should hang the bird feeder a little closer to the ground. The birds asked me to tell you."

"Okay."

They sat like that for a long time, the policeman rubbing the animal's ear, then Mcalister said, "What's happening?"

"That's a big question. Cosmically? Lots."

"Now. What's happening now."

"You've taken several grams of hallucinogenic mushrooms. God knows why, but there it is. Presently you're holding a conversation with your cat. You're a clever man. If you look very hard you'll come to the conclusion that these two events may be somewhat related."

"I don't feel different."

The cat vaulted onto the coffee table so it could look Mcalister directly in the eye. "Then we have an alternate possibility. Perhaps the mushrooms didn't do anything at all and I'm only using this as an opportunity to broach the subject of talking pets with you. That way, if you wake up in the morning a little traumatised, you can always tell yourself it was just a psychedelic episode. How about that?"

"That sounds fine," Mcalister nodded. The cat continued to watch him, waiting. "I would like some hot chocolate," Mcalister said. "I don't feel very well at all."

"We're out of milk, as usual," the cat said. "Thanks to your standard shopping incompetence."

Mcalister ignored this. "If it isn't a hallucination," he said, "then what is it, exactly?"

"Hard to explain…"

"Try."

Sergei preened himself a little, then cocked his head. "How do you feel about there being deities in the world?"

"Confused."

"Good, that's to be expected. It's not what you think. Anything can be a god, so long as the other thing is small enough comparatively."

"I really don't understand."

"Look. It doesn't have to be all about omnipotence and deadly sins. If I really was a cat, I'd probably think you were some kind of god, albeit a lazy and tubby one. If another civilisation had technology beyond yours, you'd probably think they were gods too."

"Aliens," Mcalister muttered.

"No, that's not it. Regardless, all you need to do is stay as calm as possible. In future, if you see anything strange and want to run away, just remember how strange everything is already. You're a thinking bag of meat standing on an organic spaceship. And that doesn't seem to bother you. Why should a talking cat make the situation any worse?"

"That's not bad logic," Mcalister nodded, "but I don't know if it makes me feel any better."

"Then go to bed. And if in the morning you want to call it a day at thinking bags of meat and organic space-ships, well then don't ask me any direct questions and we can pretend it was all a trip. But if you think you can take a little further addition of strangeness in your life, then strike up a conversation with me sometime and see if I still feel like talking. Your call."

Mcalister woke in the morning with a sense of impending dread. He thought fondly back to the days and weeks before when everything had been dreary, but safe. The world had a floor to it then, and though that floor was white and plain and dull, it was a floor nonetheless.

Sergei was waiting on the sofa downstairs. Mcalister ignored him and made a cup of tea. The animal appeared entirely disinterested in life. Several days passed, then a week. The cat had said nothing at all, only eaten, pranced about, and licked its bottom. The policeman visited Jennifer Rhodes several times to talk the matter over, but she played it down as stress and that seemed the most likely explanation to him also, though he wasn't sure what he was stressed about.

A month had gone by without a word from Sergei. If anything, the cat seemed to have grown more stupid — drinking from empty bird baths and lazing around in the sun. One hot July day Mcalister set up a deckchair and took a few books and a gin and tonic out into the garden. When the light began to fade, Sergei jumped up onto the policeman's belly for warmth and the policeman stroked him a while. The sun was almost down and the day had been pleasant. The cat crawled up the policeman's chest and scrutinised him with its strange eyes: one green, one glinting blue. Mcalister rubbed the animal's ear.

"I think I'm glad you're just a cat after all," the policeman said.

"God, me too," Sergei replied.

TWENTY-FOUR

Jennifer Rhodes watches Rupert Carnegie from behind thick reading spectacles. This is their fifth counselling session. Only fifteen more to go.

"And the strangest dream," Rupert Carnegie says.

"A dream, yes." Jennifer nods and scribbles in a notepad.

"My son, he was only a baby, and we were out swimming."

"A baby?"

"Well, a wee lad. And this great flippin' thing, all spinning like—"

"A whirlpool?"

"Yeah, a whirlpool, opened up and was trying to suck him in."

"And you escaped?"

"No, it got him, it did. And then I woke up."

"Interesting…" Her pencil dances on the paper. *Shopping: Peppers. Loo roll. Jam.* "I think the issue is certainly centred around your son."

"Christ, I could've told you that."

"And a fear of losing him, perhaps."

"The lad's in his twenties. He'd be gone already if he could afford it."

"Hmm…" *Eggs. Drain cleaner. Scrubbing brush.* "Then perhaps you're afraid of losing the relationship itself."

"Nothing left to lose. He hates me."

"And what did he say to give that impression?"

"'Dad. I hate you.'"

Mince, but the vegetarian stuff. Broccoli. "Father-son relationships are often complicated, in my experience."

"You don't have children."

Jennifer Rhodes stops writing for a moment. "No, but I've met plenty of them."

"Right…" Rupert Carnegie mutters. "Well, on that note…"

"We have another twenty minutes, Mr. Carnegie." The old man seems to be thinking this over. "Need I remind you," Jennifer continues, "that you're here by *court order* no less. A breach of the terms and the judge mentioned the possibility of *harsher penalties*, if you remember."

"Yes, I bloody well remember, don't I."

Jennifer was not there for the incident, but she has heard reports from several people who were: Rupert crashing his Volvo into the library garden, then crawling from the car and vomiting over the roses. The chief librarian, Matilda Sargent, cleaned the vomit off of his clothes and stayed with him until the police arrived. His blood-alcohol level was reportedly four times over the legal limit.

"You were talking about Jamie, I think," Jennifer says softly.

"It's like…you're just going along fine and suddenly you've got this thing in your life, crying at all hours. And they don't tell you how the bastards grow up. It's awful."

It is not like that, Jennifer thinks. Or at least it shouldn't be.

She pictures her late husband. They had chosen names already: George if it was a boy, Sarah, a girl. She would have bought it those expensive, cushioned nappies you see on the high shelves in the supermarket, and when it was old enough, read it Shakespeare and Roald Dahl. Then off to university, and the golden years with the child coming over to visit her and Aubrey in their thatched cottage, somewhere, anywhere, and brought the grandchildren over later too.

"Jamie was a rebellious child, then?" she says.

"Aye. A little scrote."

"And you think you're still angry about this?"

"Nah, he's all right now, far as that's concerned. But he ain't heading for much. Always got his head in a book or out working on someone's garden. Queer in waiting."

"You're worried your son might be gay?"

"Not much worse he could do, eh?"

You are the reason this generation of men doubt themselves so completely, Jennifer thinks. You are the anti-Aubrey. Trapped down a mine of your own making, and all you can do is pull everyone else in with you.

"Where's all that lovely lovely, softly softly of yours gone?" Rupert says, watching her suspiciously.

"You can tell me whatever you like, Rupert. That's why we're here."

"You're judging, I can see it."

"I practice unconditional positive regard. You never wanted any more children?"

"Aye, but Karen didn't. Went off with another man not long after the lad was born anyway."

"That must have been difficult."

Rupert shrugs. "Wasn't surprised. Raised him myself, taught him everything I know. Not sure where it all went wrong."

"Perhaps it hasn't all gone wrong."

Rupert chuckles. "Well," he says, "you don't have a child, so you don't know, do you?"

Jennifer puts her shopping list aside and stares out of the window. "No, I suppose I don't."

"And I don't have a dead husband," Rupert says. "So I don't know about that. And I wouldn't pretend to."

They sit in silence for a long time. Jennifer thinks of Aubrey and how she never found that spring of meanness in him some men seem to have. She waited, even tried to provoke it, but he never snapped and certainly never said anything barbed.

Rupert mushes his face with his hands. "Sorry, that was rude."

"It's all right."

"Nothing turns out quite how you expect."

Jennifer watches a spider climbing the bookshelf. "I know," she says quietly.

Another long silence.

Rupert puts his head down and mutters, "You're always waiting for a time when it all goes smoothly, aren't you? You get one plate spinning, then another. And one falls off and you go back to it, and another one's on the ground before you even know it, and then you're trying to get the rest in the air. And you're thinking to yourself, *If I can just keep all of them spinning I'll be all right. If I can just keep all of them spinning…*"

But everything winds down eventually, Jennifer thinks. People, plates, and all.

Her husband is smiling from a photo on the desk.

"Some people seem to keep it all together, don't they?" Rupert says.

"Happy people are just people you aren't acquainted enough with yet to know how miserable they really are."

Rupert grins. "There's some sense in you after all." He looks out of the window to some children playing on the green. "Aubrey was a good man. Shame he isn't here," he says.

"I didn't realise you knew each other."

"Aye, when we were younger. We chased some of the same girls. But he stopped all that when he met you, of course."

"Anyway," Jennifer says. "We're diverting a little."

"He said he'd never look at another woman again."

A feeling then, one that comes on her once a week or so these days; the sense that everything is just an absurd game, from dating to doting to deference, then death; the initial light show of falling in love, the cultivating of a life together, the calm civility of cohabiting, then the burying of the only person in the world who truly understood you.

"The truth of it," Rupert says, "is that I just like a drink. Can you wrap your head around that one? The judge couldn't. Got no demons, me. Not running from anything. Just enjoy a piss-up from time to time. You can look for reasons until the cows come home, but you won't find any. Not much to do around here but the bottle. Don't know how you lot cope without it."

"No," Jennifer says. She leaves the room for a moment, then returns with two glasses and a bottle of gin.

TWENTY-FIVE

Zoe comes downstairs around one in the afternoon in her dressing gown, makes tea, then sits on the floor and watches her father working on his figurine.

"Have you given any thought to your plans?" John says, his back to her. Shavings fall away from his hands as the blade shears a little face and body from the wood.

"Sure." She sips her tea.

"And?"

"I thought I'd see what came up."

"Perhaps you could go and shack up with the Carnegie boy."

"Oh, that's what you're pissed about today, is it?"

The old man puts the figurine down and sharpens his blade. "I'm not *pissed* about anything. You can do as you please. Only, you can do it elsewhere."

"It was just—"

"Don't. I'd honestly rather not know." He picks up the figurine again and continues on its face.

"Mum says you used to get around a lot, before her," Zoe says.

"Your mother says a lot of things, I'm sure."

"Back when you had a personality."

John chuckles lightly. "Shall we say one more night, then out?"

"I really need to think about my plans."

"One more night it is then. It's been two weeks already. You said one."

"God, if you're going to be such an arse about it I'll leave now."

"Fine with me."

Zoe sips her tea again. "What are you making today?"

Whistle continues carving.

"I said—"

"A young boy. One who probably knows better than to outstay his welcome."

She examines the living room. "Why is it so bare in here?"

"I like it simple."

"Our place wasn't simple in Cairo."

"That was your mother's doing."

Bullshit, Zoe thinks. The only reason you keep this place so white and minimal is because you don't consider it a home. Just like a hotel, it's a place to sleep and be, only you don't sleep that much and you're barely a thing at all anymore. You keep the place bare like this because there's nothing left on the inside to express. "What's with the figurines?" she says.

"Just leave me alone, would you?"

She circles around to the other side of the table and picks up a little unfinished carving of a plump, elderly lady. "She doesn't look very happy at all."

"Put that down," Whistle growls.

"The face is all wrong, isn't it?"

"Put—"

"Anyone would think it's an ogre or something. Like—"

He bangs the table with his fist suddenly and shouts, "I said put that down."

She replaces the figurine and goes to leave.

"It helps me to think," John says quietly. "I imagine I'm them for a little while. It takes me back. And it takes me forward. It just helps, all right? God, you had your drugs for long enough. I've got mine, only it's free and no one bangs on my door in the small hours demanding I pay up. I just like making things. And if you think that's stupid then you can get the hell out."

Zoe sits down on the stairs. "I don't think it's stupid."

"Well I do."

"I don't think it's stupid at all."

He picks up the knife again and carries on with the little boy's face. "I didn't mean to shout."

"It's all right."

"You're just—"

"I know. A child."

"A child. Yes."

"Sometimes I imagine I'm someone else too," she says. "With a family."

"You could've had a family, with whatever his name was back in Cairo."

"I'm not supposed to."

"How do you know?"

"I just know. I don't have the heart for it."

"I thought that before having you. But when you came along I felt very differently all of a sudden."

"Yes, I know, I know, I've heard the stories — it changes everyone, blah blah, but it wouldn't change me. I just feel it. Not everyone is supposed to have children, or grow into a real person. Not everyone is supposed to just keep hammering away at life and get through it." She stares very hard at the little wooden boy. "I'm not *enduring*."

John bats the thought away with a wave of his hand. "You had some issues. All kids have issues."

"I don't want to be around," she says.

"You do."

"I don't."

"It'll pass."

"I'm twenty-six. It hasn't passed yet."

"There's still plenty of time."

"If you're supposed to respect me as an adult, then you have to let me go my own way. And if that's my own way, then that's my own way, and you can't do a thing about it."

He gives the little boy the beginnings of a nose. Then he says, "Funny, your mother hasn't rung."

"Why would she?"

"Because her daughter tried to take her own life a month ago and now she's gone to stay with her miserable father."

"So?"

"Not very conducive to recovery, is it?"

"I guess she thought it might be. She'd tried everything else."

"Well what would you try, if you were her?"

"I'd try not trying."

"Brilliant."

"I mean, I'd stop trying so hard. I'd just *be there*, you know?"

"No. I don't."

"She's always looking to get me on some new diet or fitness class or something."

Yes, John thinks, Donya always loved that nonsense. Pilates, wheatgrass, *colonic irrigation*. He remembers a time when all of that was normal, or at least tolerable. She seemed to love him and that was enough to forgive her commitment to vacuous bullshit.

"She left me a letter, for when I woke up, that last time," Zoe says.

"Hm?"

"Your address was at the bottom."

Spineless hag. "How maternal of her."

"And what did you ever do?" Zoe says. "She raised me the whole time you were back here and not once did you offer to come over, not for my birthday, not for Christmas."

"You know how it was."

"Do I?"

"There's fresh coffee in the kitchen, how about you fetch us both some."

"No thanks." She puts her coat on over her pyjamas and steps out into the day.

TWENTY-SIX

With the Rawlings' house in sight now, Mcalister's pulse quickens.

Nothing is suspicious from the outside. Mary Rawlings' side of the lawn is perfectly trimmed and blooming with roses. Augustus' is all brown and dead and weed-riddled.

"Keep still a moment," Sergei mutters. Every pore of Mcalister's skin feels drenched suddenly in hot butter.

"I can't see my hands," the policeman says. "And where are my feet, or my legs for that matter?"

"Still there," the cat says — vanished now too. "I've just kicked them a little further up the visible spectrum. You'll get the hang of it. Come on."

The world had been perfectly dull only a day before. The two of them were watching a shopping channel. A pretty blonde girl was advertising salad accessories.

"One day people will stop buying this junk," Mcalister groaned.

"No," Sergei said. "They won't."

"And we'll throw in the colander, and the dicer, *and* the grater, for only 6.99," the girl on TV said and smiled with all-white teeth.

"Actually it never really goes away," Sergei said. "I've lived at the end of your planet's history and there's still someone trying to turn a buck on something or other, and some poor sucker who's stupid enough to buy it. Granted, you lot stop using colanders in about a century or so, but there's always something to sell."

"We stop using *colanders*?"

"Sure."

"What the hell do we use instead?"

"There's a paradox. What if I tell you, and you invent it, and get stupendously rich?"

"Then I'd be stupendously rich."

"And this chopping board at no extra cost," the girl on TV said.

"Yes," said the cat. "But you're missing the point. Say you invent this new 22nd century colander and I come along ten thousand years later and learn about it."

"So?"

"Well, I'm telling you about it now, aren't I? And the only reason you knew how to invent it was because I told you about it. The idea didn't have a beginning."

Mcalister grunted. "I'm not sure I'd care. I'd be stupendously rich."

The girl undid one of the buttons on her blouse and winked at the camera. "For the full knife set? Recommended retail price 149.99, but only 129.99 for the next hour."

Sergei sprawled on his master's lap and the policeman tickled his stomach. "As long as you remembered to come back and tell me about it, I don't think there would be a problem," Mcalister said.

"Luckily we'll never have to find out," Sergei muttered.

"But seriously, what replaces the colander?"

"There are rules to meddling with time. I'm not going to flaunt them so you can revolutionise salad a century early."

The girl undid another button on her blouse and winked again. "And now the highlight of today's programming." She took off the blouse entirely. Underneath was a chainmail bodice and about her neck were glowing, purple pendants.

"Um," Mcalister said.

The girl spoke again: "His Venerable Lordship of Entropy, Djall, is presently inviting chosen members of the Etheria to his dwelling in the Corporia."

"This is unusual," Mcalister said quietly.

"Among them are some of the Etheria's most respected arbiters and philosophers. Entrance to the Corporia is to be subtle so as not to alert the natives. Djall, who has been banished since initiating an Etheric grudge against Beomus the Arbiter of Mischief, is expected to make a significant announcement at the gathering."

Mcalister hadn't noticed the cat rear back onto his hind legs. "Are you doing this?" the policeman whispered.

Sergei shook his head. "No. This is less than good."

"Good is a relative term," said the girl.

"There hasn't been a gathering of Etherics down here for thousands of years," Sergei said.

"I'd like some hot chocolate," Mcalister said weakly. "And who the hell is *Djall*?"

"He goes by the Corporic name Augustus Rawlings," the girl said. "Next up, this compact juicer is retailing at only 16.99, including cups and a free—"

Mcalister turned the television off.

They stand in the sunshine and admire the Rawlings' grand house. The garden gate opens by itself. Mcalister hesitates, then passes through.

Sergei rubs up against his master's leg. "Hey, pick me up."

Mcalister feels for the cat with invisible hands and makes his bulk out finally and balls the animal up into his arms.

"No sneezing, got it?" Sergei whispers.

"There's no one here anyway — what does it matter?"

"Take us into the garden."

"Why?"

"Just do it. Carefully."

Mcalister treads uncertainly past the roses and around the pond and the house explodes into life suddenly. Figures appear, tens of them, in green and blue and yellow shawls, wearing capes and hats, chattering, twittering, most of them apparently drunk — their faces painted purple and gold. Some stand well over eight feet tall. Others don't stand at all, but only seem to lie on the air.

"Rawlings has put a shield up so he doesn't alert the neighbours," Sergei says.

"What the hell is going on?" Mcalister whispers.

"A party. Haven't you been to a party before?"

Mcalister spots a girl with flowing hair that runs down her back in a waterfall and up her front to fall down again. "Akwia, the Arbiter of Water," Sergei whispers. "And there, The Sacred Cow. Well over three billion years old." Mcalister crosses towards the thing automatically. It doesn't look too unlike a regular cow, though the eyes aren't bovine black but burning purple. It's drinking from a trough full of what Mcalister knows by the smell to be mead.

"Haven't you had enough?" Augustus Rawlings has appeared from behind them. Mcalister feels Sergei tense in his arms. The cow pauses for a moment and pulls its enormous tongue back into its mouth. "I've had enough when I say I've had enough," it slurs.

Augustus pats it on the rump. "You're absolutely right, but it would be a shame to repeat..."

"I've learned my lesson after your wedding."

"You were but an addition to the entertainment. Still, don't overindulge now."

The Sacred Cow returns to its mead.

"What is he?" Mcalister whispers.

"A cow. Obviously," the cat replies.

"Augustus, I mean."

"He's the master of a force, sort of."

"Ah."

"His is entropy, if you like. He invented the idea."

"What's entropy?"

"Death, I guess. In cosmic terms."

"He *invented* death?"

"Did you think it just came naturally into the world?" A string quartet begins to play on the gazebo. "Go over there, to Mary," Sergei whispers.

Mcalister walks the two of them across the garden. Mary Rawlings is talking to a child, barely older than a toddler. Out of the child's mouth comes a booming voice.

"The Arbiter of Temporality," Sergei says. "Tries to make sure events don't precede their causes."

"You're looking well," the child is saying.

Mary smiles. "Thank you. You're looking wonderful yourself — very youthful still, I see."

"Such are the advantages of my line of work. The question on everyone's lips — lovely a party as this is – what exactly are we doing here, if you don't mind me asking?"

"I don't mind you asking," Mary Rawlings smiles.

"Then…"

She wrings her hands. "My husband is a private man. He likes to keep surprises to himself until the last minute. I'm sure he will make everything clear soon enough."

"Hey!" The Sacred Cow shouts. Two extremely tall men are dragging the trough of mead away. The string quartet have stopped playing. The entire garden stares.

"You give that back, you bastards," the cow yells.

"I think," says one of the tall men — identical, Mcalister realises, to the other, "that you have had your fair share of mead now."

"Maybe time to let someone else have a go, hm?" the other mutters.

"You bastards," shouts the cow. "Rawlings. Rawlings, where are you? Resolve this nonsense."

Approaching from the house, Augustus Rawlings, his old parchment face smiling: "It's healthy for a creature to enjoy his drink, but not so healthy if that drink comes to enjoy him instead." He nods to the identical men. "I think he may've had enough."

"I've had enough when I fucking say I've had enough," bellows the cow.

"Then perhaps it would be best to stop before we've all had enough of you."

"Anyone would've thought a few thousand years down here might soften you a little," the cow slurs. "But you're still just the same thick-headed power-grabbing—"

One of the identical men clamps a hand over the cow's mouth. The other leads him by the neck back into the house.

The string quartet begins again. The crowd sways to the music.

"Such a strange place," says the Arbiter of Water to a man made of handwritten scrolls. "The smell. I can't stand it, I must say. And forcing us to speak in their tongue, what's that all about?"

The man made of scrolls shakes his head solemnly and says nothing.

"Christ…" Mcalister whispers.

"I doubt it," the cat mutters. "He rarely comes to parties."

"What have we walked into?"

"Honestly, I'm not sure. They're all speaking English. It doesn't make any sense."

The air shimmers slightly. Stars have appeared in the sky, constellations Mcalister doesn't recognise.

"Augustus' wife. She's an entropy....*arbiter* too?" the policeman says.

"No, her role is different."

"How?"

"Just different."

A drinking game has begun. Three enormous Nordic-looking men are chugging from goblets. A small crowd have gathered around them, chanting. The first man to finish puts his goblet on his head. The game begins again.

"God, are you all alcoholics?" Mcalister whispers.

"What did you expect? Look at your kind. The smartest on the planet by far, and all you care about is power and boning each other. And most of you aren't even that bothered about power."

"Whatever then. I think we should go," Mcalister says.

"Not until we know what they're all doing here."

"Getting smashed, by the look of things. Same as any other night in Wilthail. Let's leave them to it."

Sergei digs his claws into the policeman's arm. "You cannot possibly imagine what's at stake here. You cannot *possibly* imagine."

"Judging from this scene I don't think I want to."

"These are my people."

"Then say hello."

"Not all of them are good folk."

"Augustus?"

"The last time we saw each other it was on bad terms."

"Forget to write him a Christmas card?"

"Ten more minutes," the cat whispers. "Just ten more minutes and we'll leave, I promise."

Now more of the garden have joined the drinking folk and goblets are on heads again. A number of guests have lifted into the air, suspended by wings and some by no wings at all. The Sacred Cow watches sadly from the downstairs bathroom window.

Wilthail's sky, Mcalister notices, looks an odd shade of purple for this early in the afternoon. The air is heavy and rancid all of a sudden.

"All this anticipation," says the Arbiter of Water to the scroll man. "What is the old fart planning for the finale? A performance perhaps?"

The scroll man nods.

"I know what this is," Sergei whispers slowly.

"Friends," Augustus Rawlings calls now, standing at the end of the garden, garbed in some kind of long cloak and with a complicated pendant around his neck. "A moment of your time."

Mcalister whispers, "What is this?"

Those already in the air stay in the air, fixed, standing on nothing at all. The Nordic arbiters replace their goblets on the table. The Arbiter of Water's hair ceases to flow.

"Nothing gives me greater pleasure than to see all of you, after such an enormous interval," Augustus says. "Truly, I have lost count of the years. As, I'm sure, has my wife." He gestures to Mary, who is standing pensively at the back of the garden. "But we are reunited, after such a trial. We have seen this realm's history from both ends; the murder and hardship of its infancy. The intricate brilliance of its later years. But as on any plane, in any universe, marital bonds are an absolute."

A sickly clap from the guests. The Nordic arbiters exchange a disgusted glance, then stare down at their sandals.

"What," Mcalister says, "is this?"

Mary Rawlings is approaching in the direction of Mcalister and the cat, her eyes still on Augustus.

"After all, the eternity my beloved and I have spent parted will seem as nothing compared to the eons ahead, together once again," Augustus drones.

"*What is—*" Mcalister says.

"A trap," Mary Rawlings whispers, staring directly into Mcalister's eyes. "It's a trap and you must leave."

"They see us," Sergei shouts.

The Nordic arbiters exchange glances again, then burst out laughing. "We assumed you were part of the entertainment."

"Go. Now," Sergei spits, digging his claws into the policeman's arm, the two of them suddenly visible. "*Go now.*"

Mcalister turns and darts for the garden gate. He falters and goes tumbling into the grass.

"Cat," Augustus calls. "Stay a while."

"Mcalister," Sergei shouts, scrambling about in the grass somewhere up ahead.

Mcalister runs for the garden gate again. The two identical creatures who policed The Sacred Cow appear from nothing, blocking the route ahead.

"Not this way," one says.

"Try another," says the second.

The policeman turns towards the house. Cherubs and sprites and God-knows-what float in no particular arrangement up and down its walls. He turns again. The only other direction is back into the garden, towards the guests, towards Augustus. Mary Rawlings has her head down now, eyes red and heavy.

"We were to return home," Augustus shouts, "when reunited, with the grudge settled. We are reunited, my wife and I. You have all been summoned here to witness the settling of the grudge. What are you on now, little prince of milk? Your last incarnation, like mine. The final death, no?"

One of the identical men is holding Sergei by the tail, the animal writhing about, meowing. Mcalister turns around to run, but the urge to sleep is strong suddenly and the purple sky fades to darker purple still.

TWENTY-SEVEN

He wakes in the dark, save for the flicker of a candle. His mouth is dry and his head is throbbing. A man stands beside the candle: Augustus Rawlings.

"Wh…" Mcalister tries.

"Don't bother," Augustus chuckles. "Ancient Etheric sleep technology. Primitive but effective. Just rest now."

The policeman shuts his eyes, then forces them open again and makes out Sergei's meagre outline strapped to the wall.

"I admire your arrogance, really I do," Augustus says. "To think you could meddle with forces so immutable."

"Leave him the hell alone," Mcalister manages.

"I was talking to you, officer. Beomus is old now, like me. We can afford him some overconfidence in his abilities. Your arrogance, however, is inexcusable. Any sane individual would've committed himself to a mental institution at first sight of a talking cat."

"I don't mind a bit of strangeness now and then."

Mcalister spies a table of instruments: scalpels, hacksaws, hammers, ranging upwards in size from petite to gigantic. Augustus toys with one of the scalpels. "You cannot imagine, having had only the one life, what it is to yearn. To really *yearn*. It is one thing to deprive a man of water, or food, or love — perhaps you have experienced these things. It is another to deprive him of justice, to send him waltzing up and down the years in such a *stinking place*, catching sight of his prize now and again and never finding quite the right occasion to claim it." He picks up a hacksaw and inspects the weight of it in his hand. "I have dreamed of killing your friend here in so many ways that I do not think there can be any left, surely. And I have killed him. One hundred, perhaps two hundred times. By cannon, by blade, by starship, by horn, by sword, by laser turret. And always he — like me — wakes in a new body, in some new century, remade, cheerily devoted to locating my wife and failing, until I should find him again and put him out of his misery. And it has been like this—" he picks up the sledgehammer now and approaches the two of them, "for the longest time. But I have done my duty. Good *gods*, I have gone further than any man, Etheric or otherwise, to protect my marriage. Samsara is ended. The bondage is undone." To Sergei: "Anything to say for yourself before I conclude this nonsense?"

"What are you, a shit Bond villain?" Mcalister mutters.

A crinkle appears on the Arbiter of Entropy's face. He scrutinises the policeman. "This one is stupid, I think. Evidently you've no idea who I am."

"I honestly couldn't care less."

"You will regret your ignorance momentarily. I have killed billions of your kind. I have destroyed millions of inhabited planets. I will eat the cosmos entire one day, when the time comes."

"If you keep up with bollocks like that, the universe will probably do itself in long before you have a chance," Mcalister mumbles.

"Yes," Augustus says. "Perhaps we will start with the policeman first then."

He weighs the sledgehammer again, then lifts it over his head. Purple fire dances in his eyes.

"You haven't won a thing," Sergei says quickly. The hammer pauses at its apogee. "She hates you still. If anything, you'll return to the Etheria less than you left it. Before, she merely didn't care for you. Now it's pure resentment. Even if you end me here, you could eat a trillion worlds and she'll still never love you. You used ancient Etheric to reunite the three of us, didn't you? That takes its toll anyway. Soon you'll go mad with its curse. Look at you, you're losing the plot already."

Augustus studies the cat keenly, regards his whiskers, claws, and little black nose. "Is the accusation that I've no mind for strategy?" The old man smiles. "Well, let's see. A party thrown to lure a fool. Even the thickest of fools wouldn't fall for that, no? Yet here you are. Who is the poor strategist, exactly?"

"If I'm gone—" Sergei starts.

"Yes," Augustus says. "No more chaos. I shan't let them appoint another arbiter to the position. The death of mischief, good riddance. And what purpose did it ever serve anyway? Your absence will be just the beginning. I'll snuff them all eventually, even Novelty when the time comes and—"

"Oh fuck off mate," Mcalister says. "Is that all you do? Big words and posturing?"

"Very well then," Augustus chuckles.

"I'm sorry," the cat says to his master.

Mcalister nods. "It's all right. It was quite lovely having you, even if you did shit in the roses sometimes."

"I shouldn't have involved you in all this."

The policeman tries to smile. "No, you shouldn't. But it's all right, really."

"I honestly never meant to get you hurt."

"I, on the other hand, feel differently," Augustus snarls. He brings the hammer down on Mcalister. The policeman turns with wide eyes to Sergei and Sergei's eyes are wide too now, green and glinting blue.

TWENTY-EIGHT

Suzie Lees is eating Nutella straight from the jar and standing in the holy light of the fridge. Her husband switches on the kitchen light. He's holding a pair of socks. Suzie removes the spoon from her mouth. "Okay?" she says.

Kevin nods to the socks. "Anything you want to say?"

"What am I being accused of now?"

This is not the first time they have had a conversation of this kind, but it is the first time she has had actual, physical evidence presented to her so plainly.

"I found these down the back of the bed," Kevin says.

"That's nice. It looks like they need a wash."

"They're not mine."

"Well they're not mine either."

"I know that, Suzie."

She makes a disbelieving face. "The gardener?"

Kevin says nothing.

"Come on."

"I think I've had enough," he says flatly.

"They're just socks. I brought them in to wash for him."

"They're not washed and the washing machine is not behind the bed." He smiles. "Well, you can fuck who you like because honestly, I'm done."

He is ten thousand feet tall. All the decade's suspicions are out now and he is suddenly freer than he can say. God, you commit your life to someone without ever really knowing them at all — what madness is that? Those first years are supposed to be a preliminary interview for the Real Job, but who is ever themselves — really themselves — around a new lover? And then a toaster and a shared wardrobe and a mortgage, and before you know it you're pulling out some other man's socks from behind your bed. Where's the sense?

On impulse he strides upstairs, packs some clothes into a holdall, and makes back down to the front door. Suzie stands fixed beside it. "Don't leave, not just yet. We should talk."

"I think," he says, taking his car keys from the hook, "we've done all the talking we need to. I'm not giving you any money, by the way. Whatever happens you can be sure of that."

"Now wait," she says. "Just wait."

"I don't even mind," he says calmly. "Really, I don't. I think you're miserable in general and that's why you do stupid things. I think you're not sure what'll make you happy. Just like me. And that's quite all right." He jabs her playfully on the shoulder. "But enough is enough, eh?"

She watches him climb into his Porsche and back the thing off the driveway and disappear into the night.

Behind the wheel now, he takes out the pack of unopened Marlboro Reds that have been waiting for just such an occasion. Wilthail's houses look strange to him suddenly; more like penitentiaries than homes. Do all the husbands really love their wives enough to give up ten thousand other possible lives? Do all the wives really love their husbands enough to sacrifice their autonomy?

God, it feels so real when you're living through it, gets wicked big on you. There you are, a young man, wandering through the open fields of your twenties and you go out for a date and suddenly: matrimony.

Babies, he thinks and turns into the back roads. A clever evolutionary trick to produce babies. Nothing more.

Where shall I go? I suppose I could go anywhere. America. I could go to America and write a book. What will I write my book about?

A childhood memory then. He is eight, or thereabouts. It has just occurred to him that one day he will grow up. His parents and his parents' friends don't seem so happy. When he's their age, he will be happy. He'll make the right decisions. He'll learn to live easy. It's simple. He'll just hold on to that determination and if anything makes him sad, or if he thinks he's going to be mean to someone, he'll remember that being happy is a choice and he'll choose it.

He thumbs the radio on. Johnny Cash, Folsom Prison Blues.

I bet there's rich folks eating in a fancy dining car.

Yes, all of them, idiots, and me an idiot too for a while.

They're probably drinkin' coffee and smoking big cigars.

How did I ever come to believe any of this nonsense would scratch the itch? A suit and a tie and a sports car.

Well I know I had it coming.

A career and a wife and a house.

I know I can't be free.

I should thank Jamie Carnegie personally. He did me a favour, a huge one. I should write him a letter.

But those people keep a movin' and that's what tortures me.

It happens so quickly he doesn't have time to swerve. A shriek of metal, the car folding in on itself, the windscreen shattering, the bonnet crumpling like paper.

The world pauses for a moment. Kevin looks for a wall ahead, or bollard, or fallen tree. Nothing. The road is clear. The monkey brain is overwhelmed.

The world resumes.

Glass shards, a scream — perhaps his own, then the dark.

||

TEN TO THE POWER
OF NINETY-ONE

TWENTY-NINE

Rupert Carnegie sips from his whisky bottle and puts the telescope to his eye again. From so high up in the church's belfry, the world is a quaint painting. He glasses the village below.

The trees stir in the wind, then settle. Wilthail is silent.

A figure approaches from the boundary of the church, Jamie Carnegie, a bag over his shoulder and his shirt torn and his face marked with blood. He climbs the steps to the belfry and silently takes a packet of cigarettes and a bottle of whisky from his bag and hands them to his father.

"You're a good lad," the old man says. "What did you see?"

"Same as always. One got me on the face. I'm all right."

"You're a good lad."

"Shout if you notice anything."

"Aye, then I best be shouting now." He points beyond the belfry. Another figure is approaching, walking quickly, hunched over.

"The old bastard…" Jamie mutters.

When Whistle arrives up in the belfry he's wheezing, and he clutches at his stomach. The three men regard each other in silence for a while. Then Jamie says: "How've you been, Mr. Whistle?"

John slumps against the wall and rubs his eyes. There is a weariness to his face that Jamie has come to recognise in all the Wilthailites in the last month.

"We've been staying inside," Whistle says.

"Hasn't everyone?" Rupert replies.

"God, it's when those *things* come out at night. They're horrid."

"Aye," Rupert nods. "We've been keeping to the church and not making any noise. They leave us alone."

"Good view from up here. What have you seen?"

"Nothing and more nothing, mostly," Jamie says.

Whistle grumbles. A light rain begins, the drips neon red, thick, metallic smelling. The men don't talk of it. It has come every night now for the past month. They sit in silence and it ceases a few minutes later, only a shower. Rupert Carnegie swigs from the whisky bottle and passes it to Whistle. Whistle drinks.

"Though I walk through the valley of the shadow of death..." Whistle murmurs.

"These aren't the end times," Jamie Carnegie says.

"Blood rain for God's sake. And knitting needle rain. This is it as far as I'm concerned. That god I never believed in is determined to have the last laugh by not only existing, but raising the whole world to hell."

"It's not the world," Jamie says.

"What?"

"I cycled out to the village limits last week. There's a barrier, made of glass or something, the whole way around. The world looks normal on the other side. Whatever's happening is just happening to Wilthail."

"Then we can get a message out, surely. A radio. Anything."

"Nothing works. We found a mountain radio in Mcalister's house. No signal. We're blocked off."

"Christ, for how long then?"

The men say nothing, avoid each other's gaze. They pass the whisky around again. Then Whistle mutters, "Where's Father Liptrot?"

"Show him," Rupert says.

Jamie leads Whistle back down to the church, into the crypt, and turns on the light. Liptrot is lying on a makeshift bed of sleeping bags with his eyes open and his hands pulling at his hair.

"Father Liptrot," Whistle says.

"He can't hear you."

"*Liptrot.*"

"Father, why have you forsaken me," Liptrot whispers. Then shouting: "Hell and damnation, the fallen angel has taken the world and shreds it in his mouth like a dog with a rabbit."

"He's been like that for weeks," Jamie says. "We tried everything."

"Did you try this?" Whistle says and holds the whisky bottle out for Liptrot. The priest takes it and swigs, politely gives it back, then resumes his muttering.

"Yes. We tried that."

Whistle bends to Liptrot's height and puts a hand on his shoulder and looks into his eyes. "Father, we need to know what's going on in Wilthail. Any idea?"

Liptrot focuses his stare on Whistle now, and in a low, gruff voice: "All is lost and more than that."

"More than what?"

"Hell and damnation! And the agents of the fallen angel, and the world in his mouth like a dog with a rabbit."

"I thought I was going mad," Whistle says. "But now I feel quite sane by comparison."

"In fairness it's given Rupert something to focus on. He comes down here and looks after the mad bastard," Jamie says.

Whistle lights a cigarette. He's always wanted to smoke in a church. He feels a man now, or close enough. Ever since that day when the sky turned always-twilight and the blood and knitting needle rain came, he has spent most of his time chopping wood for the fire and trying to keep Zoe stable. His joints seem to move easier recently.

That day, the first day, he and Zoe stood in the garden and watched the stars wink out and replace themselves with constellations unfamiliar. Then the howling began at night, the cackling, coming from all directions, singing too, shapes moving in convoy past the window.

Most of the villagers boarded up their windows. Others abandoned their houses entirely, the doors wide open like great yawning mouths.

"I need your help," Whistle says awkwardly.

"Hm?" Jamie says.

"Zoe's gone."

"Where?"

"Not sure. I went out to see if there was any soup left in the corner shop, and when I got home she'd taken her rucksack and some water. She hasn't been back since. That was yesterday night. She could be anywhere now."

"Why didn't you mention it earlier?" Jamie says, trying not to shout.

"She's a clever girl, she'll be all right. But I have to find her."

"Did she say where she was going?"

"No. Her lithium ran out a few weeks ago. She's been a little nutty ever since."

Jamie imagines her face now, torn open, a red mess, lying at the feet of some godforsaken monster. "We'll find her."

"There's something else." Whistle rolls up his shirt. His belly is torn open and the gash is red and black, rotting.

Jamie goes to touch it, then pulls his hand back. "That must hurt."

"Agony."

Whistle had gone to hang some washing out of the window, but Zoe stopped him. He waited until she was upstairs, then opened the window again and something darted at him from the garden. It was faceless, only grooves where the eyes should be and a slit where perhaps a mouth once was. It struggled with him and he hit it with the television remote control and it let go after a while. It wasn't until he'd gone upstairs to find his daughter that he noticed he was bleeding.

"Shit, then I'll go with Dad instead," Jamie says.

"Your father isn't in any state to go outside."

"He's in a lot better condition than you. You can stay here and look after Liptrot."

Jamie imagines the girl again, alive this time, out in the forest that wasn't there a month ago, wandering alone. God, the forest, appeared the same night the internet and the phone lines had gone dead, the same night the knitting needles and the blood rain had come. The forest, grown up around the Rawlings' house; great skyscraper trees and dark shapes within the trees. It went on for as far as Jamie's telescope reached.

"I'll find her," Jamie says.

And, he thinks, I'll bring the body back to you, whatever's left of it.

THIRTY

Derrick Thomas tries to squint, but his eyes won't obey. The world is a blur for a moment, then comes into focus. Old books, toys, clothes on hangers — he knows this place: the charity shop on Precosa Street. The room is all gloom. Night. He tries to step forward. His legs are rigid. The knees won't bend. *What the—* He strains his head down. His legs are plastic, by the look of it. His hands too. He turns them over. Perfectly seamless. Plastic. He tries to scream but no sound comes. He touches his lips.

Perfectly seamless. Plastic.

Stay calm. A dream. A horrible dream. Stay calm.

With some difficulty he hobbles to a dressing mirror. A neutral smile greets him in the reflection — a mannequin, naked. He examines his hands again. The fingers bend a little, but not enough to actually manipulate anything. He tours the shop. Nothing of interest.

Something touches his shoulder. He tries to run and falls and scrambles about on the shop carpet, writhing in silence. Finally he turns himself over. Another mannequin, almost identical to himself, is standing above. The face is content and smiling. The hips are well defined.

It offers a plastic hand. Thomas hesitates, takes it, and finally manages to get back to his feet. The mannequin fetches something from the counter behind, a Speak & Spell, and presses clumsily at the buttons.

"*Rhudes...Rhades...*" the Speak & Spell stutters in a robotic voice. "*R....*" Then: "*Rhodes. Rhodes.*" The mannequin points to itself and types again. "*A-A-A-A-Aubrey Rhodes.*"

Jennifer Rhodes' dead husband. What?

The mannequin passes the Speak & Spell to Thomas. He hesitates. Then, slowly: "*Thumus. Themus. Thomas. Derrick Thomas.*" He points to himself with a clumsy plastic finger. The second mannequin nods and the two of them stand for a long time in the silent dark of the charity shop and admire each other's dead, plastic faces.

THIRTY-ONE

"Little brother," comes the voice from beyond the door. "Little brother, won't you get up?" Scott Appleby burrows further into his sheets. "Little brother, it's coming up for midday and you've still not eaten a thing."

"Not hungry. And it's dark out," Scott murmurs.

Silence. Robyn enters the room and looks his brother over, all buried in the bedclothes. "I think perhaps it's time we left the house," he says.

"For what?"

"Food. We're running very low now, down to basics. Won't you come with?"

"I just want to stay here."

Robyn bends down to his brother's bedside and holds him with a stare. Scott tries to roll away, but Robyn stops him with a firm hand. "Times of adversity should be met with great courage."

"I don't understand what's happening," Scott whispers.

Robyn's pupils seem more vertical than circular somehow, like slits. His skin has taken on a patch-like quality.

"I think I'll just stay in bed," Scott says.

"What would Father do if he were here?"

Beat me, Scott thinks. Then beat me some more.

It seems strange to him suddenly, looking into Robyn's wild eyes, that the same father could produce such different results in offspring. If Dad had been a kinder man, he thinks, he might've favoured me. I was gentle. I saved ants from Robyn's boot. I rescued birds from the chimney. And Robyn organised the funerals, incinerated the bodies in the kiln. He was always praised for that.

"I think we're being punished," Scott says quietly.

"Don't be absurd."

"For Derrick Thomas."

Robyn pulls his brother out of bed and puts their faces so close they're almost kissing. Robyn smells like almonds and soap, like the bodies when they're prepared in the mortuary. He says, "If you come out with something that ridiculous again, I'm not sure what I'll do. You need to pull yourself together. There'll be a lot of business for us when this is over. You've seen what's going on outside. Folk are falling off their perches left, right, and centre. Plus, punishment implies a punish*er*, and you are not a godly man, so just stop your thoughts right there."

"Business? No one's going to want to pay for a funeral. They're barely staying alive as it is."

Robyn goes to shout but stops suddenly. "Brother, you're covered in fine white hairs."

"I haven't shaved," Scott says meekly.

"They're all over your face. Are you feeling well?"

"I'm fine. I just want to be alone for a little while."

"Turn around."

"What?"

"Turn around and show me your back."

"God, I just want to be alone for a while. Can't you leave me alone?"

"I'll give you until three. One—"

"Robyn please, you're scaring me."

"Two."

"Robyn, please stop it, you've gone—"

"Boys." Suzie Lees is at the bedroom door in her dressing gown. "Everything okay?"

"Couldn't be better," Robyn smiles. "Could *not* be better. Scott, I invited Mrs. Lees to stay here after her husband went missing."

"I'm sorry to hear about Mr. Lees," Scott says formally.

"Oh it's fine," Suzie beams.

They eat together at the kitchen table, the three of them: coffee and toast with marmalade. The snake and its vivarium have been moved into the kitchen. The animal keenly watches them breakfasting.

"Eager little thing, isn't he?" Suzie says, looking the snake over.

"Intelligent creatures," Robyn says. "More coffee?"

"Please."

Suzie's leg unsheathes itself from her dressing gown for a moment. Robyn gawps. "What do you feed it?" Suzie says.

"Live mice. Or anything we find. But whatever it is, it must be living, you see. They won't eat dead meat."

"How...primal."

"We should let it free," Scott murmurs. All quiet then. "It isn't fair, being trapped in there like that, all—"

"Perhaps we should let you free," Robyn says. "You do nothing around here anyway. At least the animal keeps us entertained."

"Boys," Suzie says. "Come on, nothing's wrong."

Nothing's wrong, Scott thinks. Nothing's wrong? God knows what abominations are out wandering the streets. God knows what's at work here. The graveyard, it isn't far away. Derrick Thomas might be crawling out of the soil at this very moment, raised from the dead by spirits malevolent, coming to pay us a visit.

He pushes his plate away.

"You're not hungry?" Robyn says. Scott shakes his head. "Got to keep your strength up. Thought we could all take the car out this morning, see the sights."

The sights, Scott thinks. I've had quite enough of the sights. "I'll take a pass, thanks."

"Suit yourself. Suzie?"

"Oh yes," she grins. "Perhaps we could go dancing."

THIRTY-TWO

Beomus climbed the stairs to the executive level and there had been the secretary himself, sitting at his desk, drinking coffee. "Comrade Denkov," the secretary roared. "You are not weary from the journey, I hope?" The secretary's Russian was quaint, tinged with a Bulgarian accent.

"A touch tired, but duty keeps me alert," Beomus said.

"All well in Moscow?"

"As well as can be expected, given recent events. And fair Bulgaria?" Beomus said.

"She's quite fine, all the better for your visit of course."

"Too kind."

The secretary straightened his papers. "To business right away then?"

"To business," Beomus agreed.

It was always like this with government officials, even in the satellite states: excessive formality and bullshit. Beomus wondered if they realised back in the motherland it was all liquor and prostitutes, among the senior members of the party at least.

"A woman is causing quite a stir, as you may have heard," the secretary said.

"I have."

"Petya Shuleva, her name is. A modern-day saint, some of Sofia would have it."

"I was told as much before I left Moscow."

"There are claims of *religiosity*."

Beomus' pulse quickened. "Religiosity?"

"Resurrections. One Alexander Drossev is said to have been hit by a bus in the city centre, only to be revived by this woman. Obviously a fabrication, but word has spread among the general population. You can see why I requested a man from Moscow."

And he stands now by the National Theatre in full uniform, his heart trying to beat its way through his chest. A woman approaches in a long, flowing dress that breaks in velvet waves at her feet.

"Comrade," she says.

He offers her a cigarette. "You are Petya Shuleva?"

"So I was born, yes."

"Thank you for meeting me at such short notice." He lights her cigarette. She smokes thoughtfully, examines him.

"You look a touch young to be a member of the party, if you don't mind me saying so," she says.

"You look a touch young to be raising folk from the dead."

"Is that what they say about me?"

"It's what they say, yes."

She eyes him again. "If you were born in some other country, perhaps you would not be a political man at all, but a farmer, or a scientist. And if I were born in some other country, in some other time, perhaps I would have been a queen. Or a peasant."

The sun appears from behind a cloud. Children run from bench to bench. A few soldiers watch idly from the fountain.

"Do you perform miracles, really?" Beomus says.

"Are you a member of the Communist Party, really?"

"In some other life, perhaps not."

"How many of them have you had?"

"Several hundred now," he says and lets that settle. She puts the cigarette out and seems to be holding her breath. "Zorya," he says.

The woman turns about suddenly and disappears down a side street. Beomus hesitates, then follows. She's vanished. He tries another side street. She is waiting on the porch of a dilapidated apartment block beside an old woman. He approaches. "This is my mother," the girl says. "Maria Shuleva. She said you would come."

The woman must be in her eighties, hidden beneath a huge shawl. She smiles and her face wrinkles further. The girl nods politely and enters the apartment block, leaving the two of them alone.

The wind drags itself through the alley, taking newspapers in its wake. The old woman's eyes are jaundiced, her face covered in liver spots. She stands as though bearing some great invisible weight. She addresses Beomus in Etheric: "You're young."

"And you're old."

"Such is time."

She embraces him. The smell of perfume and stew. "Hello," she says.

Beomus catches the girl still watching from inside. "That's your daughter?"

"Yes. It was safer to send her. People are always watching."

"And she's been performing the healings?"

"There haven't been any healings. A rumour, just that. I knew you'd come when you heard it. Or, I hoped."

"Clever. Which incarnation is it now?"

"You expect me to remember? Do *you*?"

He shakes his head. "Somewhere in the two hundreds, I think."

"Only around my fiftieth. I'm not so old after all then."

Now he is not sure what to say. Entire lives, he thinks, preparing for this moment and I haven't a damn thing to tell her.

"Where is my husband?" she says.

"I don't know, off in some other life. He ended me with a knife in the last one. And a bullet in the one before that."

She strokes his cheek. "Poor thing…"

"I've brought you something." He takes a letter from his coat.

"From the government?"

"No."

Two cracked, brittle hands appear from beneath her shawl and open the letter. Beomus watches the old woman read, searching for some sign of Zorya, but all he can see is years, eighty or so of them, all fallen on her like wet cement.

She folds the letter up, her eyes red now. "How did you get this?"

"I grew up in Russia, in this incarnation. My father was one of the government's high enforcers and it was his duty to interrogate political prisoners. He would take me to the detention centres sometimes. A man called out to me once in Etheric from a cell, said his name was Beomus. I told him that was impossible. He said he was from an incarnation ahead, that he had been waiting for the day when I would come, as a little boy. He gave me the letter and told me to watch for rumours of a healer in Sofia. We only had seconds to talk. That's all I know. He was beaten to death by the guards in the end. I'll try to avoid getting captured when I become that man later, I suppose."

"But you won't," the old woman says quietly, staring off down the alley. "That isn't how time works. It is a fixed thing."

"Bullshit, I do as I please. I'll stay with you, here. And when you give up this life, I'll find you again." He takes her face in his hands. "We don't have to keep going with this stupid game."

The old woman nods to the letter. "You've read this?" Beomus shakes his head. "It's a list of eighty of your incarnations, their locations, the dates of your births and the dates of your deaths. Your current life is in there. We don't stay together in this one. The letter says so."

"Then fuck the letter."

"You're a member of the *Communist Party*. It'll be another thirty years until it collapses. You know that."

"I'm the *Arbiter of Mischief*, in case you've forgotten. They can't do a thing to me."

"On the contrary, they'll do a number of things to you if you try to elope with an old woman. This era is not ours. The letter is clear about that."

A gentle rain begins and the old woman steps out into it and pulls Beomus with her. She says, "Eighty incarnations from now you will give a letter to a young boy recounting all of the time to come, and he will give that letter to me, here, again. It's the dance of time, Causality tripping over Her own shoelaces on occasion. Our last incarnations though, we spend it together. That's a sure thing. The letter says so."

How long ago was it that we met for the first time? Beomus thinks. Billions of years. Longer. "You were picking apples," he says.

"I was picking apples."

"On the outskirts of the Addled Forest."

"That's right."

"And I said, 'What's a young woman doing out here alone?' And you said, 'Avoiding headstrong young men.'"

Zorya shrugs. "You were arrogant back then."

"You said, 'I have a husband' and—"

"Let's not talk about that part." The old woman goes back to watching the rain.

"Why only tell half the story?"

She fiddles with one of her coat buttons. "This is all my fault."

"Don't be stupid."

"Should've just been happy with my lot."

Beomus raises an eyebrow. "I'm irresistible. Don't beat yourself up. Anyone would've done what you did."

"Keep saying things like that, and I'll teach you the true meaning of abstinence when we get back home."

"Understood. Sorry."

The world takes on a blurry quality. The apartment blocks fade a little around the edges. Beomus murmurs, "You said, 'I have a husband' and I said, 'What of it?'"

"And you said, 'What of it,'" the old woman nods reluctantly.

"We met on the river another fifty times."

"Closer to a hundred."

"Lovely scenery."

"My mind was on more immediate matters."

Beomus looks the old woman over. Her wrinkles are quite adorable, he decides. "Let me stay for supper, at least."

"Don't make the government suspicious, they'll give you hell. Go back to the secretary, tell him all is well and that the healer woman is a nut."

He takes her hand. "When will I see you again?"

"Other ages."

"Then tell me about the rest of them ahead. God, I think I've been everywhere."

"Prehistory, post-history. Caves and space stations."

He wipes the rain out of his eyes. "I don't think I can do it anymore," he says.

The world fades to almost nothing. The alley turns lightly purple.

A gentle wind.

She puts a hand over his eyes and there is the feeling of butter melting into all of his pores. True Zorya stands before him, naked then — Etheric Zorya, young again, pale-skinned, lips redder than blood, the life pendants hung about her neck. She says, "I'll wait for you in the middle of history. Europe. The letter says so."

His body has returned to its Etheric mode also, brown-skinned, slim, that of a young man's. "There's too much time," he murmurs.

Zorya kisses him on the mouth and says, "There is just enough time, and no more and no less than that."

They fade back to Corporics again. The old woman tightens her shawl and prepares to go inside. Coyly she says, "Have you thought about coming back as something a little more inconspicuous in your next incarnations?"

"Like what?"

"A woman, maybe. Or an animal."

"An *animal*?"

"If you wanted. How about a cat?"

"Don't be absurd."

"It's just a thought."

THIRTY-THREE

Wild light washes across an all-twilight sky in twists and stripes: blue, red, green. Mcalister blinks, rubs his eyes. "Jesus," he whispers. He strains himself up. A young man is sitting nearby eating an apple, naked. Mcalister is naked too, he realises, his skin glimmering.

"Don't make any sudden movements," the youth says, an accent Mcalister can't place. "Just get your breath back first."

They are sitting on nothing at all, apparently. Below them are stars, a million ornate constellations Mcalister doesn't recognise. In between the stars are nebulas, blooming like roses and dying and blooming again.

"I'm dead," Mcalister says.

"Nope." The boy takes a bite of his apple. "How do you feel?"

Like paper, Mcalister thinks. Only lighter and more transparent. "Unusual," he says.

"That's to be expected."

There are artifacts scattered all around them, shapes the height of ten men; spirals of copper and cubes of glass, edges bleeding into edges, corners with a heavy grudge against geometry.

"You like them?" the boy says. "They're scientific instruments, I suppose you might say. Devices for testing and controlling the limits of reality. That one, with all the twists, it's a kind of telescope for looking into higher dimensions of space. And that over there, the cube, it keeps the cosmic constants in balance, stops gravity and electromagnetism colliding."

"Why am I naked?" Mcalister says.

"We're always naked, really."

"All right, but why am I naked?"

"You only bring the parts that matter with you. The rest stays behind."

"Bring the parts that matter *where* exactly?"

The youth finishes the apple and cocks his head. "I wonder, if you told an ant he was in England, do you think he could even attempt to grasp the idea?"

"If I'm dead, please just tell me I'm dead."

"Or a dog. Do you think he could wrap his head around calculus?"

"Hey."

"You're safe. Nothing will try to harm you here. For now. I've brought you to a safe place."

"And who, in Christ's name then, are you?"

"You don't recognise me without all the fur?"

He looks the youth up and down, heterochromic eyes: one green, the other blue and glinting.

"That can't be," Mcalister murmurs.

"Oh," says the youth and gestures to the blooming nebulas and the impossible sculptures. "And all of this *can*, I suppose?"

Mcalister begins a breathing exercise and closes his eyes. "You've brought me to where you come from."

"I've brought you to where I come from."

"How?"

"Baby steps. Just relax and get your breath back."

"*How.*"

160

"It's complicated."

"Then try to explain."

The youth stands and turns his back to the policeman and looks out to the star fields. He throws the apple core out into space and watches it hurtle to nothing. "I wasn't going to let you die, not like that. Djall would've killed me soon after anyway, and I'm on, shall we say, my final afforded token of a life. So I brought us here."

"If you can come here whenever you like, why the hell didn't you do it sooner?"

"I told you. It's complicated."

Mcalister gets to his feet. The gravity is light, just enough to keep him on the floor. He joins the youth. The two of them stand naked on the threshold of an infinite mural of stars.

"Djall holds a grudge against me," the boy says. "I pulled him and his wife into the Corporia, your plane, a long time ago now. The rules of Corporic dispute state that any warring parties may only return to the Etheria when a grudge is settled, or one of the individuals is dead. That is, Really Dead. Not just that life, but all their lives."

"What does it matter? You're here now."

"Only by breaking the rules. You're not supposed to just come swanning home before business is settled."

"So pay a fine."

The boy scoffs. "There isn't some cosmic policeman who enforces this stuff. The rules are written into the Etheria itself. They're fundamental. There have been consequences already."

"God, you're telling me. My skin looks fantastic."

"*Extreme* consequences. Wilthail has been suspended from normal spacetime. An accidental bridge was formed between the Etheria and the Corporia when I brought us here. Something had to give and that something, apparently, was reality. The Etheria is bleeding into Wilthail now, all of its good and bad."

"I don't see much bad here."

"You'd be surprised."

A star silently explodes ahead of them and the debris spreads to the corners of their vision.

"I don't recognise any of these constellations," the policeman says.

"You will if you look hard enough. They're all the configurations that can ever be, from every point of perspective in your universe, at every moment in time. That's how we deal with things here, in infinities. Infinite choices, infinite consequences. Some of those infinite consequences are already befalling your friends. For that I'm sorry, but I was hardly going to let Entropy take a sledgehammer to your head."

"Entropy. As in Augustus Rawlings, right?"

"Right."

The policeman takes another deep breath. "What kind of consequences are we talking about?"

"Not sure yet. The bridge opened on your plane around the Rawlings' house. It opened on this side in the Addled Forest. Now the two points are joined. Whatever was here is there."

"And that is?"

"Hard to say. I had a quick look around before you woke up. We can't die, my kind. Not since Djall came to the Corporia. But the time is too much for some and they lose their minds. When I was young we used to send the more violent and insane among us to the Addled Forest, to get their minds together again. Far as I can tell, the same practice has been going on in my absence, only now it's for those who go mad out of being forced to stay alive. Whatever's in there likely isn't pleasant."

Mcalister pauses a moment to think. "The lunatic asylum of the gods has appeared on the outskirts of Wilthail."

Beomus slaps the policeman's back playfully. "Not a bad way of putting it, tubby."

"But your lot are peaceful for the most part, right?"

"*Peaceful* is a relative concept."

"You didn't used to talk in such vague terms."

"I didn't used to talk to you at all, early on."

Mcalister looks about. "Is this all *science* or…something else?"

"Spiritual? It's all right, that's not a dirty word here. From your perspective it may as well be both, and if you were to show your laptop to a Neanderthal they would think you a deity too."

"Science then. This is all technology."

The boy shakes his head. "Wrong again. Stop trying to put it in a box. Think relatively."

"I'll try another approach. Are the folk in the forest going to harm anyone?"

"Yes, and probably very, very violently."

"Then we need to get back."

"Obviously, but that won't be easy. The world-schism is closed for travel now the Laws have been broken. The only way back to the Corporia is through the Addled Forest."

Mcalister grumbles. He feels his vision slipping a little, the corners expanding. "Something's wrong with my eyes," he mutters.

"I kept you in your standard form when I brought you here, but it won't hold long. Soon you'll start losing your Corporic faculties."

"Should I be worried?"

"If you like, but it won't help. Your Corporic sight will go first. You'll probably begin to see in three hundred and sixty degrees. Then your skin will—"

"My *skin*…"

"Sure, your skin. Well, let's not talk about that now. I won't leave you, whatever happens. You looked after me for long enough, I'll do the same for you." The boy winks. "And hey, if you're hankering after a little milk and a tummy rub, give me a shout."

The world expands further. Colours appear in the star fields way beyond the normal visual spectrum. Mcalister concentrates on his breath. "Is your name really Sergei?"

The boy chuckles. "No. You couldn't pronounce my True Name."

"Then say it."

"You haven't the ears to hear that kind of thing yet."

"Try me."

Beomus opens his mouth and what comes out, Mcalister thinks, is not unlike the song of a dying star.

THIRTY-FOUR

Night. Derrick Thomas finds a lipstick on the charity shop counter. He crosses to a changing room mirror, waves to get Aubrey Rhodes' attention, and writes: I HAVE TO SEE MY WIFE.

"N…No. Too strange," Rhodes replies with the Speak & Spell.

I HAVE TO SEE MY WIFE.

"She won't like it."

Thomas stops to examine his plastic feet, then his plastic legs. In lipstick: WE HAVE TO MAKE THIS RIGHT.

"Dead."

WHAT?

Rhodes slides him a torn newspaper article, a picture of Thomas, younger and smiling. The headline: "Wilthail Family Man Deceased at 42."

Derrick Thomas strains to remember. BUT, he writes, WE'RE OBVIOUSLY NOT DEAD.

Rhodes fumbles with the Speak & Spell, typing with slow, calculated prods: "No. It's much worse than that."

THIRTY-FIVE

As they walk, worlds stream under their feet — wet continents, dry continents, arid planes of sand where nothing stirs.

"I don't feel fantastic," Mcalister says.

"That's to be expected," Beomus replies.

"I'm remembering things."

"Well that's good."

"Things I haven't lived through."

"Like what?" the boy asks carefully.

"Like that time I was a peasant in 14th century China. I wasn't a peasant in 14th century China. I'd know."

"Try not to pay it too much attention. The closer we get to the Addled Forest, the more mental white noise we'll pass through. Just keep your mind here, now."

"And I was a *woman*."

"We'll get to it later. Just stay focused."

They move towards a great, multicoloured ocean ahead. A rowboat is waiting on the beach. The youth steps in and beckons that Mcalister do the same. A few minutes later and they're out on the water, the youth rowing them through plumes and eddies of light.

"This next part is important," Beomus says. "I need you to keep your eyes on the horizon, whatever happens. Do you think you can manage that?"

"Why?"

"Eyes on the horizon," the youth says again and rows them further into the ocean. Mcalister focuses straight ahead and realises only now that there is no sun at the end of the world.

"Where does the light come from?" Mcalister says.

"Honestly, I never thought about it."

"*Never thought about it*? You lived here, didn't you?"

"Any idea what makes a magnet magnetic?" Beomus barks suddenly. "Any idea how a TV works? Or gravity, or an iPhone, or the wind? Or just about anything on your planet at all?" Mcalister shakes his head. "Then kindly shut up."

They continue. The policeman peers over the side of the boat. "How deep is this?"

"Eyes on the horizon, I said."

"Fine but—"

"We can talk about the ocean all you like when we reach the other side. There's a well over that way too, we can drink a little."

"Funny, I'm not thirsty. Come to think of it I haven't been thirsty since we got here."

"And you won't be. Or hungry for that matter. But we still eat and drink as a nod to our old nature, I guess."

"What?"

"My kind were…not too dissimilar to yours, once. Presumably we also burned fossil fuels, and watched reality television, and explored the stars for a while."

"We haven't explored the stars."

"You will. But all that wandering is only good for so long. One day your kind will expand across the entire galaxy, and more. The emperors of that time will feel just as hollow as the politicians of yours. But there are other horizons beyond that one."

Mcalister notices a shape moving through the water and pulls his eyes back up to the horizon. "Like what?"

"Ah, we're at one of those language impasses again. You'll just have to trust me. It's much better than space-ships."

"Tell me the word."

"For what?"

"For whatever it is after exploring the galaxy."

"In Etheric we say," and then a noise high as a bat's call and low as a whale's simultaneously.

"And what about after that? What did you lot do then?"

The youth grins. "Something else. The whole thing's a game of conquest, up and up. One round licked, then the next."

"That sounds terrible."

"Does it? Would you rather you all just spread out across the stars? What then? Boredom. That's what. Never-ending, inescapable boredom. There are other games to play besides cosmic Monopoly."

"And that's what you all do now?"

The boy shrugs. "Yeah, more or less."

"What's the point of that game then?"

"Fun."

Mcalister goes to reply but stops dead. "Sergei."

"That's not my name."

"Sergei, there's something on my foot."

The boy smiles encouragingly and holds Mcalister's stare. "No there isn't."

"There is, I can feel it. It's a hand."

"There's nothing on your foot. Keep your eyes on mine."

"I can't because there's a *bloody hand on my foot*. Look."

"All right, let's say for argument's sake that there is a hand on your foot. Can you see it?"

"No, because you told me not to look down."

"Fine, then how do you know it's there?"

"Just get it off, please. I'm going to look down now."

The boy lunges and takes Mcalister's chin and holds it level. "No, don't do that. Listen. You're not supposed to be here. The Etheria's a bit upset about the whole thing, trying to give you a scare. Keep your eyes on me and it'll leave you alone."

"What's on my foot?"

"Just another few kilometres and we'll be on the other side. Look, you can see it from here. The beach. That's where we're going."

"I'm going to look down."

"Don't even think about it."

Mcalister slaps his hand away and glares down at his foot. Red and veiny fingers are stroking his toes. He jumps back.

"Twit," Beomus shouts.

"What in Christ's name is that?"

Beomus starts rowing frantically, stopping every few seconds to smack the hand with his fist. "Pull it off. Bite it. Anything."

Mcalister claws at the thing, wails.

The shore is nearing, shining a gentle blue. Another hand emerges from the water, wraps itself around Mcalister's other ankle. He shrieks. The hands are impossibly strong and there are more of them now, clutching at his legs. The air smells suddenly of dogs left in a hot car.

"Kick, hard as you can," Beomus screams.

The hands drag Mcalister to the side of the boat and into the water. "Sergei!"

Beomus reaches, missing the policeman's hand by centimetres. Mcalister is almost submerged, spitting water, eyes wide. And there, below him, wait one hundred, perhaps two hundred, bald skeletal figures, the faces grinning cheek to cheek, the hands outstretched, and their gaunt, sunken eyes all fixed on his.

THIRTY-SIX

There is a knock at the door. Jennifer Rhodes pulls the duvet over her head. The knock comes again.

"Sod off…" she moans.

All quiet.

At least the silence isn't shouting anymore. The last few weeks it has been roaring in her ears. Then the screams at night, some the pitch of a child. If Aubrey were here he'd know what to do; probably fashion a bedpost into a spear and make dinner over a stove of burning newspapers.

But Aubrey is not here.

Some years ago in the middle of dinner, Aubrey collapsed after complaining of feeling dizzy. The hospital informed him he had a brain tumour. It was operable and the procedure went ahead. Jennifer acted as a nurse for several years while her husband recovered, and it wasn't until the cancer came back in the third year that she began to consider the worst. By then he could not piss alone. He could not eat alone. He would lie in bed most of the day watching the television, or not watching the television.

She fed him so much soup he soon smelled permanently of the stuff. He became incapable of brushing his teeth. And finally one morning she got up sometime around four to use the toilet and noticed he wasn't breathing. It was a relief, more than anything, though she never said it aloud for fear of sounding selfish; a relief that she need never change another adult nappy, that she need never brush someone else's teeth again. And a relief that while Aubrey's mind had been gone for a year anyway, his body had finally followed after its master.

A knock again at the door.

What would Aubrey do?

Aubrey would answer it.

She hauls herself out of bed and catches her reflection in the mirror. The pillow has engraved her skin with ancient glyphs. Her cheeks are drained. Her eyes are red and the lids are heavy. I am a no-thing, she thinks.

She opens the window. Rupert and Jamie Carnegie stand in the street below.

"Mrs. Rhodes," Rupert beams and raises his whisky bottle to her.

"Hello boys."

"We've brought milk and bread," Jamie says.

"Milked the cow myself," Rupert says proudly and mimes massaging a teat. "How are you?"

"I'm all right," Jennifer says.

"No one's seen much of you these last few weeks."

Jennifer points to the twilight sky.

"Aye, strange times," Rupert says.

"It's just, we're going on a trip," Jamie says. "And we thought we should come and make sure you're all right before we leave. Everyone's a little worried. John Whistle is at the church, you know. You could go and see him. And the Applebys are keeping well. Suzie Lees is living with them at the moment. I'm sure she'd love to see you."

"Maybe someday soon I'll go and do that," Jennifer says in a dull voice.

"And the Cranes are—"

"I appreciate your concern but I'm fine, really. If you leave the milk I'll gladly drink it, but I'm quite all right for bread, thank you." A long pause. Something cries out in the distance, not a woman's voice, not a man's. "Where are you gentlemen going?"

"Zoe Whistle is missing. We're off into the woods," Jamie says.

"Are you mad? I don't leave the house and even I know nobody comes out of there alive."

"She's a clever girl."

"I'm not worried about Zoe," she says and looks from one Carnegie to the other.

"What are you saying, eh?" Rupert starts.

"Just don't get yourselves killed, please," Jennifer says.

"Aye, we'll be writing that down to hang on to."

"Goodbye gentlemen. Thanks for the milk."

The men nod respectfully and Jennifer closes the window. She watches them starting up Precosa Street, father and son, one young and upright, the other hunched and with a whisky bottle in his hand.

She looks herself over in the mirror again. What is time and why has so much of it happened to me? she thinks. I was young and beautiful. Seems like only yesterday. Now I'm old and there's no recourse to anything.

She remembers the first night everything changed, a month or so ago. The sky had developed a purple edge to it and the air was suddenly tinged with cold. The Wilthailites left their houses and stood in the street for a long time, watching the stars winking out. Then the new constellations had come. Mobile phone coverage vanished. No satellite television signal. The electricity followed soon after.

They trudged in their family packs to the church and sat in the pews waiting for someone, anyone, to talk. Father Liptrot stood up as the rightful man of the hour.

"I do not mean to scare you," he said, and noticed that for once the entire congregation was deathly quiet. "But unpleasantness is afoot this evening."

"Nuclear war," Mrs. Crane said.

"It's not a nuclear war," Eric Crane whispered to his mother.

"Pardon me?" Liptrot said.

"It's not a nuclear war," Eric said gingerly. "There's no radiation."

"And how do you know that?"

"I have a Geiger counter. It measures radiation."

"Why in God's name do you own a thing like that?" his mother snapped.

"I bought it on the internet. For wars."

"It's the government!" Robyn Appleby cried. "The government, I bet. Who knows what they've been sitting on all these years! Well they've finally pressed the button. It's the government, no doubt."

"It's not the *fucking government*," came a voice from the back of the church. John Whistle stood dressed entirely in black with his daughter at his side. "The government can't move the constellations about, however much they wish they could. Something stranger is going on."

"Got a better idea then?" Robyn said.

"No. But whatever it might be, it's bigger than us, so the best we can do for now is sit tight and shut up."

"I think what Mr. Whistle is trying to say is that we should be humble in the presence of great power, especially if it intends to test us," Liptrot said.

"No that's not what I meant at all," Whistle growled.

"And that perhaps the best thing we can do is submit to its judgment and refer to our bibles. I ask you, what else could have done such a thing? Not the government, as Mr. Whistle has established. Nor a disaster of some kind. This has the mark of a great intelligence. In light of such an intelligence existing in the world, we should ask for its mercy, lest it grow angrier with us still."

"And I'll get angry with you if you carry on like that," Whistle said. "No religious rubbish. Something else is going on."

"Then leave," Liptrot said. "The door is just behind you. We'll stay and pray and you can hold your vigil for whichever false god it is you pray to in your own home. The Lord is evidently angry with us."

"The Lord can kindly fuck off," Whistle said and turned about and led Zoe back into the purple night. Jennifer Rhodes followed them out to the graveyard.

"It's good to see you again, Mr. Whistle," she said. "I didn't think you went outside anymore."

"Only on special occasions." He glanced begrudgingly at Zoe. "My daughter can be infernally persuasive when she feels like it." Zoe put her arm through his and rested her head on his shoulder.

"You used to be a scientist, didn't you? What do you really think about all of this?" Jennifer said quietly.

"There's nothing to think. We just have to stay calm," John said.

She watched his mouth, waiting for some wisdom to fall out of it but none came.

"There's wine at our place. You could come and live with us," Zoe said.

"No," John muttered. "She couldn't."

Jennifer nodded and went to rejoin the congregation but John spoke again. "Do you know the problem of evil, Jennifer?" She shook her head. "Well, it applies to our situation just as well as any other. There is evil in the world, yet God claims he loves us. If he could remove that evil but chooses not to, then he is not all-loving as we're told he is. If he wants to remove that evil from the world but cannot, then why do we call him all-powerful? In any case, he's not truly God and there's nothing to be frightened of. Chin up."

"Goodnight Mr. Whistle. Miss Whistle."

"Goodnight Jennifer."

She went back inside and sat with the congregation, and before long at least three-quarters of the room had joined Liptrot in a prayer, while the remaining few sat with their eyes open, checking their phones to see if reception had returned.

"Though I walk through the valley of the shadow of death," Liptrot intoned. "I shall fear no evil for thou art with me."

Jennifer gets back into bed. She pulls the duvet over her head again.

What a thing.

Thy rod and thy staff they comfort me.

The prayer meant something once. Now it's as empty as a nursery rhyme. Bloody John Whistle and his bloody realism.

What would Aubrey do? she thinks again.

She listens to the silence a while, ruined only for a moment by a scream in the distance.

Aubrey would do nothing, she thinks. Because Aubrey is dead.

THIRTY-SEVEN

Whistle has been surviving on a diet of lentils and chicken nuggets he found in the church freezer. He enjoys living in a place with stained glass windows. The evenings are quiet and the days are quieter and he has his figurines with him now, brought from his house. He listens to the sound of Liptrot snoring down in the crypt.

What is Donya doing right now? he wonders. Ageing, I expect. Getting fat around the middle.

The candle begins to burn down and flutter. His head nods.

If it should all be a dream, I wouldn't mind, he thinks. All of it.

Something batters him around the head. He sees stars, wants to throw up. He tries to crawl and is hit again on the spine and collapses. He manages to roll onto his back somehow. Father Liptrot stands over him holding a huge wooden cross.

"Whoever dwells in the shelter of the Most High," Liptrot yells and raises the cross, "will rest in the shadow of the Almighty."

Something hot is running down the back of Whistle's neck. His heart is trying to beat out of his chest. Liptrot brings the cross down. Whistle rolls out of the way of the strike and sprints to the pantry. He grabs a can of beans and brandishes it. Liptrot rounds the doorway holding the cross high again.

"Right," Whistle shouts. "You just stay the fuck back now, please." Liptrot bashes the can out of Whistle's hand. Whistle backs up against the pantry wall and fumbles behind, but there's no food left to fling.

"You are clothed with splendour and majesty," Liptrot cries. "The Lord wraps himself in light as with—"

The priest collapses suddenly. Behind him stands Matilda Sargent, the librarian, her hair swept across her face, her eyes dark and large behind thick glasses. Whistle slumps back against the pantry wall onto his butt. Matilda turns him around and dabs the wound on his head and fetches bandages and staunches the blood.

"Thanks," Whistle murmurs.

"Don't mention it."

They tie Liptrot to the bed in the crypt using velvet from the altar and pour a little water into his mouth. Then they make some tea, climb back up to the church, and sit in the pews and watch Jesus dangling from his cross.

"Go on then," Whistle says finally, coddling his mug. "What the hell was that?"

Matilda produces a transparent coil from her pocket. "Knocks anyone it touches out for about a day. Clever little thing, isn't it?"

"And where did you find it?"

She pushes her glasses up her nose, blinks a few times. "Lots of odd things are turning up around here, ever since, well, *you know*. I've been collecting them."

"Find anything that'll take us back in time about a month?"

"No such luck."

She fetches her rucksack. "I was coming to find Rupert actually. Someone told me he used to be an engineer. Was hoping he could help me with some of the gadgets I've been collecting."

"Rupert's gone into the woods with his boy."

Matilda catches his eye. "What do you mean into the woods?"

"The *woods*. You know — appeared overnight? Fifty feet high?"

"When did they leave?"

"About two days ago."

She removes her glasses and rubs her eyes. "They're already dead then."

"Isn't that a little presumptuous?"

"No."

Whistle takes a good look at her. She's wearing khakis, not her usual rainbow skirt. There's a weeping gash all the way up her arm. "What have you been doing all this time?" he says.

"Collecting," she says and takes a bottle of wine from her backpack. "Are there glasses here?" she says.

"In the kitchen. Over there."

She returns with them, then pours the wine.

"Corked," Whistle says.

"Doesn't matter. Drink up."

They watch Jesus again; face distressed, limbs bloody.

Whistle hasn't spoken properly to Matilda Sargent in over twenty years. He remembers her vaguely from school, and very strongly from his university days when they slept together a few times while his parents were staying in London. He recalls one occasion perfectly — Matilda Sargent, pale and nude, lying next to him in bed, reading the obituaries from the newspaper in a ridiculous high voice. It was the kind of moment he knew, even as it was actually happening, would be recalled again and again as he aged.

He had gone back to university not long after. They'd written to each other a little but he met Donya soon enough and stopped replying.

Matilda pushes her glasses up her nose again. "You were a physicist, yes?" Whistle nods. "Good." Out of her bag she produces object after object: coils, cubes, blocks, some of them bizarre colours, others faded or black. She takes one of the cubes, glass-looking, and puts it to John's ear. "What do you hear?" she says.

"Nothing."

"Then listen properly."

He closes his eyes. Still nothing. Then a faint murmur, growing louder, a female voice: "Six point six seven four by ten to the power of—"

"What the hell is that?" Whistle mutters.

"There are fifty-eight of the things. They all do the same trick. Numbers, long strings of numbers, all the same voice too. The numbers repeat. I thought there must be a pattern. No internet to crack it of course, but there I was hiding out in the library with plenty of time."

"You worked it out?"

She nods proudly. "They're physical values," she says. "Universal constants. Six point six seven four by ten to the power of minus eleven. It's the gravitational constant. And this one," she shakes another, tinged yellow. "The speed of light. And this one, the mass of an electron, and this one, the Faraday constant."

Whistle points to a cube twice the size of the others, glowing bright purple. "And that one?"

She puts it to his ear. The woman's voice murmurs from far off, inside.

"Ten to the power of ninety-one," Whistle says. "What does that mean?"

"Atoms in the universe, maybe," Matilda says.

He shakes his head. "Too big, I reckon."

"I've been through the whole physics section of the library. Nothing fits."

Whistle runs a hand through his gunmetal curls. "Combinations?"

"Exactly what I thought. All possible combinations of all possible atomic positions. The number's way too small though."

"Right." Whistle knocks one of the cubes on a pew. "What are they made of?"

"No idea."

"Have you tried smashing one open?"

"No, and I suggest you don't either. We don't want the universe falling apart."

Whistle notices she isn't smiling. He dangles the cube and goes to drop it on the floor. She grabs his hand. "Don't," she says.

"I'd like to see what's inside."

"Just don't. Not until we know what they are."

"Nothing is ever as mystical as you think, you know that?"

"There's nothing magic about a grenade, but you still don't pull the pin out."

Whistle hands the cube back. "A fair point."

A groan from the basement. "Shall we go and check on Liptrot?" Matilda says.

"I'll give it an hour or so. Can't trust myself not to kill him right now."

"Lucky I got here when I did, huh?"

"Lucky you got here when you did," he agrees, and once again pictures her reading out the obituaries.

THIRTY-EIGHT

Mcalister turns about in the water. The creatures surround him. They reach out with withered fingers and stroke his nose, his cheeks, pull at his feet. He tries to swim up, but they're above him now too. Half a minute passes, then a minute. He goes to fight through the rabble but they only strengthen their numbers; a wall of gaunt, pale faces. One of the faces is his, he realises. He grabs the thing and looks into its eyes. Even the little scar on his lip is there. He shrinks back, tries to swim in the other direction. Another of the things has his face too, and another — all of them gawping, their lips twisted into snarls. How ugly I am from the outside, he thinks. All pudgy and wide-chinned, British-looking, pastry and chocolate and beer. One of the creatures grabs his shoulders and stares directly into his eyes and roars. The others join in — a hymn. Mcalister screams then, a muffled dirge of bubbles.

He wakes out of the water, Beomus standing over. The boy prods him gently in the ribs. "Alive?"

Mcalister nods.

"Hard to tell from looking at you."

The policeman sits up, looks about; they seem to be on the shore again, the other side of the ocean this time.

"That was…" the boy kicks a little at the sand. "Unfortunate."

"Just tell me what they were and we'll never talk about it again."

"Honestly?"

"Honestly."

Beomus helps him up and gives him a little water from a glass bottle. "That's where dead mindstates go," the boy says, looking off over the shore.

"What?"

"We deal in infinities here, I told you. This place is where all the infinities meet. Sometimes the dead come here to sleep a while, before going back into the game."

"They weren't sleeping," Mcalister says.

"You woke them."

"They had my face."

"Yes. They did."

"Why did they all have my face?"

"You can call them your twin brothers, if you like," Beomus says reluctantly. "It makes no difference. Parallel versions of you haven't been so lucky. They were killed by whatever means. Augustus Rawlings maybe, in other scenarios. Then they came here. There it is. We've spoken about it. Now we don't have to again." The boy turns about, to the land. "We've a long way to go still."

"Did you rescue me?"

The boy shakes his head. "The ocean knows what you are, spat you out. It abhors intruders."

"It abhors intruders," Mcalister echoes.

"All of the Etheria does. We have to go."

"I'd just like to sit down a little while."

"We can do PTSD and hugs when this is all over and done with. We don't have time now."

Mcalister stays rooted to the spot.

"Hey. Tubby. We have to go." The boy kicks some sand over the policeman.

Mcalister begins shouting then. "I have been exposed to more than anyone in their right mind should be — ambushed, murdered, drowned. When I saw you at the fucking *pet adoption centre,* what I had in mind was feeding you occasionally and maybe a cuddle, not a complete psychotic break. Fight your own battle then, go on. I'll just stay here, thank you very much. I'm sure someone will come along eventually. Christ, I'm done." The boy says nothing and sits down in the sand. "Two years ago I had a life, a good life. All right, it was a little lonely, you weren't much of a conversationalist back then, but I got by. I was fine. I wish you'd never opened your damn mouth."

The two of them stare out at the ocean. There's no sign of movement under the water and the waves are gentle, almost invisible.

"You know what love is?" the boy says.

"Oh fuck off."

"When a new mindstate is born, the Arbiter of Bifurcations cuts it in two and the two half-mindstates get their own bodies. That's how we come into the world. It's the same for your kind too. Now, the two mindstates are scattered randomly throughout the Etheria. Sometimes one is male and one is female, or two female, or two male, but they retain some memory of their other half, even if they're not aware of it. Usually the half-mindstate wanders about for a while and marries and mates with some other half-mindstate and feels complete. But it isn't complete. Its real counterpart is still out in the world somewhere, in Tahiti, in Taiwan, in the Addled Forest, whatever. It's been known for a mindstate to end up scattered half in the Etheria, half in the Corporia even. Sometimes though, when chance aligns just properly and the universe is in a favourable mood, the two half-mindstates meet again. There's no telling if they'll be of a similar age or if one might be a young boy and the other a dying old woman. But it happens from time to time."

Mcalister sinks his hands into the sand. "You found yours then. That's where this is all going, isn't it?"

The boy nods. "She was already married to an arbiter, Djall, one of the most powerful in the Etheria. There was nothing to be done. Arbiters mate for life. If an arbiter loves outside of marriage, they're stripped of their position, demoted to regulating the behaviour of earwigs or something equally stupid." The boy cocks his head. "But we did it anyway. Ignoring a thing like that would be worse than death."

"As a man who's died once already, I wouldn't say death was so bad."

"Then you've just never loved properly."

"What do you know about it?" the policeman says.

"I've been lying on your sofa ten years now. You've never had a woman in the house, let alone on your arm."

A flock of violet almost-birds pass overhead, their feathers warping and glimmering. "His name was Peter," Mcalister says quietly. "We met at university. I haven't wanted anyone since."

Beomus nods. "All right."

And he will be in one of these oceans somewhere, Mcalister thinks. A million Peters, all swimming about with pale faces, dead.

"You can't bring them back," Beomus says. "If that's what you're thinking. Once they're gone, they're gone. Reassigned."

"To what? More life?"

"Sure. That's the game. Pull you out, then back in soon enough, new age, new geography. New species sometimes. But you can't track them. That's part of the Law. It'd be predictable otherwise."

184

"Brilliant." Mcalister drives his hands further into the sand. In almost a whisper he says, "I can feel my faculties slipping away. Give me something to hold on to. Just something small, whatever it is, to stop me from losing my mind."

The boy thinks for a minute. Another flock of almost-birds pass overhead. There are lights on the horizon now, Mcalister notices.

"Everything tends towards perfection," the boy says finally. "I know it's hard to see, but it's true. There's so much blood and death and pain in the world that any sane person would come around to the whole game being little more than slow torture, but that's not it. You have to see the whole process as a process. It's not easy. I'm not sure if it's even possible for more than a few minutes, but it's necessary that you hold it all in your head at least once."

Mcalister stares back blankly. Beomus rolls his eyes, continues. "There are two forces at work on your plane and on mine. Entropy and Novelty. Entropy is winding the universe down. Everything is losing energy and spreading out and falling apart. Planets are eaten by stars, stars turn into red giants, men, women, and children are dying, galaxies are collapsing. One day everything will be dust, and some time after that even the dust will be gone. But there's Novelty in the world too. Novelty builds things, new things. It lights suns. It fosters civilisations. Your lot will be out among the stars soon thanks to Novelty, and greater adventures after that. There's the real battle then. Not good and evil, not left-wing and right-wing, not right and wrong. Novelty and Entropy. One will win eventually, the other will not. My folk come in two flavours: those partial to Entropy and those on Novelty's side."

"And which camp are you in?" Mcalister says quietly.

"I really don't know. You?"

185

"Everything you just said is news to me and I only understood a quarter of it, so I might reserve judgment for a little while if you don't mind."

"I don't mind."

Mcalister glances over at the boy, vanished now, and sat in the sand quite contentedly as the little black cat the policeman remembers. The cat ambles over and curls up on Mcalister's lap.

"Go on," the cat says. "You know you want to." Mcalister hesitates a moment, then begins to rub the animal's stomach. "Yes," Beomus says. "That's better isn't it?"

"No…A little, yes." Mcalister relaxes slightly. "Do we die forever?" he says, almost whispering. "People, I mean. No magically bringing us back when we're gone?"

"No bringing you back to the same life, no."

"Ever?"

"Nope. Well, Etherics can sacrifice their mindstate for another Etheric if they like, but no one ever does it. And they'd certainly never do it for one of your kind."

"Cheers for that."

The cat keeps his eyes on his master, working on whatever he's about to say next. "Everything's going to be fine. We'll find Novelty. He'll help us."

"How?"

"I'm not sure yet. He's a clever man, he'll know what to do." The cat moves into the sand, rolls about on his back, then sits directly in front of the policeman. "There is something I can do," Beomus says, "to make this easier. We're not supposed to tell Corporics about the Gestalt, but I can show you a little piece of it, just this once."

"Gestalt?"

"The World in Itself, Truly."

Mcalister's eyes are heavy, his mouth dry. His mind feels like an old china thimble that might crack at any moment. He nods. "All right."

The cat pulls his eye down. "Come closer, tubby."

Mcalister slowly puts his eye up to the cat's. He can hear the animal breathing, can feel its tiny breath on his face. He looks deeper. Nothing, only the pupil and the red of the surrounding tissue. "I don't see anything," Mcalister says.

"Patience."

"I really don't—"

"Patience."

Then a glimmer, just a small one at first. It brightens: wild, multicoloured dancing sparks. Mcalister tries to pull away. The cat puts a gentle paw on the policeman's hand to keep him near. "*Patience*," Beomus says again.

The sparks dance and careen, a kaleidoscope of detonations. A world waits behind, infinite, colours Mcalister has not seen before, whirling about and warping in more dimensions than he is accustomed, more than should be logically allowed; a place he knows no name for but in some small, innate corner of his mind has always been sure exists.

Meaning is as solid as matter in there, galumphing about in eternity, shining and explicit now.

The universe creates itself from nothing, just for the pleasure of doing so.

History waddles about, drunk.

Logic only sits at the back and holds Her tongue.

The world ends. The world begins. Creatures expire. Creatures endure.

Tautologies populate the sky, bare and self-evident.

The Great Axiom wears four masks to its own party and comes as four guests at once: electromagnetism, gravity, the strong force, and the weak force.

What shall we do now? the Four Forces sing. And what is Space? And what is Truth? And what is Goodness?

Oh hell, Matter replies. What's anything?

Over in the corner, Time takes a look up Her own skirt.

And Mcalister makes out a fragment, blurry at first, then clear as day; the mechanism behind the curtain of Being, beyond all its veils, garments, and classifications: the true purpose of matter and energy.

He tries to compress it in his mind. It won't compress.

He tries to rationalise it in his mind. It is not a rational object.

He lies back in the sand then, takes a deep breath, and begins to laugh hysterically.

"I know," the cat says. "I know."

THIRTY-NINE

Matilda finds John up in the belfry, looking out over the village.

"Philosophising?" she says.

"Hardly. It's just nice when it's quiet."

She listens to the silence. "Know what I really miss?"

"What?" John mutters.

"Kids."

"I thought you never had them."

"Sure, but they used to come into the library asking after books. I liked playing Mother Librarian."

Whistle gestures to Wilthail below. "We may as well be children for all the confusion of late."

"Maybe." Matilda drums her fingers. "I found Millie Connors hanging from a tree in the forest. She was seventeen. Been coming in to see me at the library since she was five. Her eyes were open."

"We'll work it out," Whistle says tiredly. "We'll work it all out and everything will be fine."

Matilda toys with one of the strange cubes, passing it from hand to hand. It glows gently green. She knows if she puts it up to her ear, Planck's constant will quietly ring out from inside, each number given its own special consideration by the distant woman's voice. "My mother is buried down there," she says, nodding to the grave-yard. "Every now and then I wonder if she might put a hand up through the soil."

"None of this is magic," John says. "The dead are staying dead, I'm sure."

FORTY

Eric Crane and his parents are preparing to eat dinner. Eric is sat at the table knitting his thumbs while his father reads a book and his mother is flitting from the kitchen to the lounge, bringing food in.

"Bubble and squeak," Mrs. Crane says. "If Uncle Alf were here he'd eat the whole thing to himself!" Eric and Mr. Crane exchange a glance. "If Uncle Alf were here he'd ask for seconds and thirds I bet, then still have room for pudding," she continues. "Do you remember that one Christmas when—"

"Yes," Mr. Crane says flatly. "Yes, we do."

Eric recalls it vaguely. Uncle Alf, his father's brother, staying at their house a few years before. A well-built man with scorched ginger hair and a serious face, always wearing a tweed jacket. Eric's father had gone to bed and his mother and Uncle Alf stayed up drinking sherry. He heard them talking until three, then put some earphones in and fell asleep. In the morning his mother was all new and shining like she'd been through a car wash.

Mrs. Crane brings cutlery in and sits herself down and the three of them eat in silence. The wind blows through the chimney, just a whisper now that Mr. Crane has blocked it up. The front door has wooden slats across it, nailed in. The back door is covered in newspaper, same with all of the windows of the house. Eric spied Mr. Crane loading a revolver a few nights before and slipping it into the back of his trousers like a cowboy. Maybe, Eric thinks, it's still there now.

"So," Mrs. Crane beams to Mr. Crane, "how was your day?"

"Well, mostly I checked the shutters on the windows and made sure we have enough food to last another few weeks."

"Delightful. And you, Eric?"

"I've been reading," Eric says.

Reading by candlelight, Eric thinks. Reading by candlelight and if there's a scream outside or a howl I just put my earphones in and listen to The Beatles, but the battery on my MP3 player is almost gone now.

"Gosh," Mrs. Crane says, "if Uncle Alf were here I bet we'd all be playing charades by now. He'd have us dancing about!"

Yes, Eric thinks, but Uncle Alf died last year in a yacht accident, so I don't think he'll be coming.

"He'd have us dancing on the chairs! Oh that man."

Eric and his father exchange another glance. Mrs. Crane's eyes narrow. "What is it? A joke?"

"No, not a joke. The food's delicious," Mr. Crane says.

"You're laughing at me."

"We're not laughing at you. Let's just have a pleasant meal."

"Well I'm not hungry, frankly." Mrs. Crane puts her fork down. "Frankly I'm not hungry at all these days. God, we'd waste away if I didn't cook."

"Yes," Mr. Crane says and smiles gently. "That's true."

"Not hungry, not hungry at all, and here you both are laughing at me all the time. God knows what you do all day. We should be outside, *out-side*, not cooped up in here. It's hot. It's far too hot."

"All right, yes. It's too hot. You're spot on."

"If Uncle Alf were here—"

"I don't think we should talk about Uncle Alf anymore," Mr. Crane says. "Let's talk about something else instead."

Mrs. Crane rolls her eyes. "Yes, what do the *men* want to talk about? Chainsaws and motorbikes, I should expect. A right drought of real men around here recently. We should be *out-side*."

"Well we can't go outside right now, you know that."

"*Well we can't go outside right now, you know that,*" she echoes.

"A few more days," Mr. Crane says. "Then the army will come in and sort all this out, I'm sure. Just a few more days now."

Wind whispers through the chimney again.

"There aren't any planes," Eric says.

"What's that?" Mrs. Crane mutters.

"There aren't any planes. There haven't been any all month. I've been watching out of the skylight."

"You just haven't been looking properly. Terrible eyes. Haven't I always said you have terrible eyes?"

"Could mean anything," Mr. Crane says. "Maybe it's affecting the whole country, but I'm sure Europe will be fine. They'll send help."

"Well I'm not leaving," Mrs. Crane says. "They're not taking our house. We worked hard for this house. We spent good money on this house."

"All right. We won't leave the house."

"We'll have to leave the house," Eric says softly.

Mrs. Crane brings her hand down on the table. "If you say that again I'll smack you into next week." Eric looks to his father, whose eyes are now fixed on the plate in front of him.

"*Leave the house,*" his mother says. "Try it then, you little brat. See how far that gets you. *Leave the house.* You know, you can just take your dinner up to your room. Or better yet, leave it there and you can have it in a few days when you've emptied your head of nonsense."

Eric puts his cutlery down and tries to catch his father's eye.

"Go on," Mrs. Crane says. "Off you go."

Three knocks from the door then.

Eric does not leave the table. The Cranes stare at their plates. The wind screams. The door knocks again, three more regular beats.

"We've a visitor," Mrs. Crane says.

"Go upstairs, Eric," Mr. Crane says. He is reaching for something at the back of his trousers. A knock again, followed by a crash. "Upstairs. Now."

Eric sprints through to the hall and there, between the stairs and where he stands is the front door, boarded up, but with a figure clearly standing on the other side. A boot comes through the wood. Eric runs back to his parents. Mr. Crane is loading the revolver. Mrs. Crane has picked up her fork and is starting again on her bubble and squeak.

"On second thoughts, stay here," Eric's father says.

Eric nods.

His father moves into the hallway. Eric stands at the living room door, unable to look away. The boot breaks one of the boards off the front door, then kicks away another and a hand comes in next; pale, male, and groping.

"All right," Eric's father shouts. "That's enough. I'm armed. Nothing of value in here. We're just waiting out whatever this all is. We're not going to bother anyone. Stop or I'll open fire."

The hand pulls back through the door. Mr. Crane tightens his fingers on the pistol. The sound of Mrs. Crane's fork against her plate echoes from the living room.

194

"Is that you, you old bastard?" comes a voice. Mr. Crane stands rigid. "It's Alf! Have you gone mad? Hey, I've got muffins. They were reduced!"

"Alf who?" Mr. Crane says.

"Alf *who*?" The figure bends down and through the gap in the slats comes Uncle Alf's red face, grinning. "Little Eric too. And Judy, is she here?"

"Alf!" Mrs. Crane whoops and runs to the door. "Let's get rid of these boards."

"Don't do that," Mr. Crane says.

"Come on, help. We need a hammer. Where's the hammer?"

"Alf is dead," Mr. Crane says soberly. "That is not Alf."

"He's obviously *not* dead, as you can see by the fact that he is currently standing on our porch and *not dead*."

"I second that motion," Alf smiles. "And I've got muffins."

"We don't want your muffins, thank you," Mr. Crane says.

"Look," Mrs. Crane shouts. "You're being ridiculous. Just give me the bloody hammer and I'll get the boards off myself. Yes, I know, don't let strangers into the house, but this isn't a stranger. It's Alf. Come to visit."

"Come to visit," Alf smiles.

"From Yorkshire?" Mr. Crane says.

"That's right!"

They stand in silence, Mr. Crane still pointing the revolver at the intruder and Mrs. Crane waiting for her husband to find the hammer and Eric peeking from the living room. Alf winks. "So, how about it?"

"What was the last thing you got me for Christmas?" Eric says.

"What's that?"

"We were just talking about you and now you're here. Doesn't make sense. What was the last thing you got me for Christmas?"

Mr. Crane tightens his hold on the gun again. Alf smiles, opens his mouth uncertainly, closes it.

"Yes," Mr. Crane says. "What did you get him?"

The wind screams. Alf smiles sweetly. "How about I come in and we talk this over?" he says.

"You see?" Eric says. "He doesn't know. This isn't—"

"Stop this rubbish at once," Mrs. Crane barks, catching Mr. Crane with the sharp end of a scowl. "You're both being just awful. Pull the boards back right this second."

"That's a fine idea," Alf says. "A fine idea."

Mr. Crane glances uncertainly at his wife, at his son, at Alf, then goes off to find a hammer.

FORTY-ONE

Aubrey Rhodes wakes with a start and quickly remembers his plastic condition. He is in Wilthail Library. Mannequin Derrick Thomas is already up, sitting at a table and reading a book, turning the pages with his clumsy plastic fingers. Rhodes waves. Thomas tries to make a thumbs-up gesture. They had come to find Matilda Sargent, the librarian, but she's long gone apparently. As is everyone else; confined to their houses given the recent strange weather. Matilda Sargent was rumoured as a Wiccan and she might have been the only Wilthailite willing to give the two mannequins a chance, Rhodes had reasoned.

The other villagers had not been so accommodating. Several weeks ago Rhodes and Thomas made for the high street, walking slowly, watching for pavements, taking enormous strides to make up for their unbending knees. There was movement in the corner shop and the mannequins approached. Mrs. Crane was throwing tins into a bag. She noticed them and paused. Aubrey Rhodes put out his hand. Mrs. Crane screamed and ran. They kept to quiet corners of the village after that.

Derrick Thomas has a marker pen stuck to his hand with an elastic band and he pulls a whiteboard over to Rhodes and writes shakily:

SO. HOW R U?

Rhodes touches his heart, the universal symbol they've arranged for I'm fine.

HAD AN IDEA. BEEN DOING A LOT OF THINKING.

Rhodes produces his own pen: GO ON.

Thomas: WE FIND OUR WIVES.

Rhodes: NO. YOU KNOW WHAT WILL HAPPEN.

Thomas: THEY CAN HELP US. JUST HAVE TO EXPLAIN WHO WE ARE.

Rhodes: THEN MAYBE WE SHOULD WRITE THEM AN EMAIL.

Thomas: HAHA.

Then Thomas' face is serious somehow, if plastic can seem serious. He writes: IF WE CAN'T FIX THIS THEN I KNOW WHAT TO DO.

Rhodes: WHAT?

Thomas: THERE'S AN INCINERATOR AT THE MORTUARY.

Rhodes thinks this over. WHAT IF WE ONLY COME BACK AGAIN?

Thomas: I DON'T THINK WE WILL AFTER THAT.

Rhodes: BUT WHAT IF—

Thomas bats his hand aside. WE WON'T. FIRE CLEANS.

FORTY-TWO

They have tried a few of the devices in Matilda's bag already. Among them is a sphere which floats about an inch off the ground silently and apparently without power, and a piece of paper both Matilda and John agree is a colour neither of them have ever seen before. Finally they lay the items back out on the altar and sit in the pews and drink.

Whistle nods to a gash on Matilda's shoulder, the tip just peeking out of her jumper. "How did that come about, if I may ask?"

"Stupidity."

"Ah."

Whistle lights a cigarette. The novelty of smoking in God's house has worn off already. He'll give up, he's promised himself, when this is all over. Or when Wilthail runs out of cigarettes.

Or when he's dead.

He tries to picture Rupert and Jamie Carnegie, trudging through the trees. "I think my daughter's dead," he says calmly. "She said she could hear voices in the forest. She wanted to go in. I told her she was stupid. We argued." He finishes his wine and pours another glass. "And now she's dead."

"She could still be alive," Matilda says gently.

"No one knows better than you how much of a lie that is."

The librarian nods. Her cheeks are flushed red. In the gloom, in the dusty murk of the church and with Jesus glaring down, she is the Matilda Sargent of Whistle's early twenties again.

"I don't think there's anything outwardly violent about the forest," she says. "Maybe we just don't understand it. A kid could burn herself on a cooking hob and never have any idea it was supposed to be used for cooking. All these things I've found, they must be for something. Someone knows how to use them. They can't just be weapons."

"What if they are?"

"I don't want to believe that."

Whistle eyes the cubes, still sat on the altar, flashing to themselves, chanting their little constants.

"I don't think belief changes anything one way or the other. Water stays wet however hard you wish it wasn't," Whistle mutters to himself.

"Doesn't it get a little dull, being so rigid?"

"I'd rather know the truth over a convenient lie, however miserable it might be."

"Your daughter's very different to you, you know."

"Thanks for pointing that out. It had never occurred to me."

"She came into the library, before all of this started. She wanted books on mental health, looking for something in particular." She squints, remembering. "Carl Rogers, On Becoming a Person. She talked to me about it for ages."

"She must know a lot about mental health now, I'll give her that, certainly."

"She said she wanted to know how brains work so she could fix hers."

"Sometimes brains are beyond repair."

"That's a strange thing to say about your own daughter."

He goes to shout but holds back. Matilda's dark, pointed eyes are on him now, waiting. Whistle says, "I've been nothing but a bank account to her since day one. I'm not going to sacrifice my life just because she wants to end hers. Her mother and I were always accommodating. All we ever got in return was spite and drama. At some point you've had enough. She's a woman, a grown woman."

"She's your daughter," Matilda says, loud enough for it to echo around the church.

"When did you get so high and mighty? You haven't even been married, how could you understand?"

She pushes her glasses up her nose. "I know what decency is. Everyone knows what decency is, even if some of us won't admit it."

"Reading about life is one thing, up in your literary castle. Living it is another. You can't just wrap the world up with a bow and call it all *decency* and *duty* and *right* and *wrong*. Everything's bigger than that."

"Everything *was* bigger than that," she says. "A month ago. Things are different now. She's your daughter."

Whistle is quiet for a long time. He finishes his glass and Matilda finishes hers and she refills the two of them and they finish those too.

Then quietly, from behind his beard Whistle says: "She is my daughter, yes."

FORTY-THREE

Jennifer Rhodes wakes to the blare of a car running idle outside. She opens the window. Suzie Lees is stood below in a sparkling dress, heels, and with a cigarette balanced between her fingers like a paintbrush. Robyn Appleby is locking the car, the thing now parked diagonally across the road.

"What in God's name," Jennifer says.

"Jennifer!" Suzie croons.

"One good thing about the apocalypse," mutters Robyn Appleby. "You can park wherever you fucking like."

"Are you mad?" Jennifer says. "You'll wake the whole damn town and everything else."

"It's midday. Nothing happens in the light. Can we come in?"

She throws the key to them and then they're clambering up the stairs, Suzie giggling, and finally standing in the bedroom. They look wrong here, two polished things in a world of dirty clothes and empty glasses.

"Why are you dressed like that?" Jennifer says.

"We've been dancing." Suzie does a drunken twirl. "The village hall was open so we got some Sinatra going and opened the bar up. And we danced." She tries to twirl again. "We *danced*."

Robyn and Jennifer exchange a glance and she's sure he's wearing the face of a man who has paid for the ticket, but is having second thoughts about the trip.

"There was lots of dancing," Robyn nods, his eyes red.

"I'm glad to hear that," Jennifer says.

"What happened here?" Suzie says.

"I've been living, Suzie. This is what living looks like."

"I never thought you'd be so messy."

"I never thought you'd be so rude."

"Excuse Suzie," Robyn says. "We've both had too much to drink. She thought it would be a good idea to come and see you. I thought otherwise."

"He's so boring sometimes. You're so boring sometimes, aren't you?" Suzie says.

"I don't suppose I could trouble you for a drink, Jennifer?" Robyn asks.

"There's gin downstairs. Help yourself."

"I'll have one too," Suzie calls after him.

Jennifer gets back into bed and centres her stare on the wall. I might be wearing it down, she thinks. That patch on the wall, with all that looking. I wonder how much more it can take. Maybe it's been looking back at me and that's why I'm wearing away too.

"Where's your husband, Suzie?" she says.

"Technically I'm now single, so I don't recognise that question as valid."

"Where's your husband, Suzie."

There's a clink and a crash from downstairs, Robyn in the kitchen. Suzie crosses to the window and smokes out of it and watches the afternoon twilight. "He's dead."

"How?"

"He left all angry, the night everything changed around here. I thought he'd just driven to a hotel or something. Well, the Mitchells tried to leave the village when the twilight started. They got as far as the glass wall and there was Kevin's car, all smashed up against it."

"Sorry."

"Strange day today, isn't it? All clear skies. I don't like those stars though."

"If you ever want to talk about it—"

"I'm fine."

Dying on an argument, Jennifer thinks. Imagine that. No chance afterwards to be right or wrong. "Is his body still there?" she says.

"Probably. Unless something's gotten to it."

"Maybe we should think about going to collect it. Do a proper burial."

"He's fine where he is."

Jennifer lowers her voice. "I don't think we should be leaving the dead unburied at a time like this. I'm sure Robyn would drive us out to where Kevin is, if we asked him nicely."

Robyn reappears with three glasses. "Made you one too, Jennifer. Don't know if you drink gin, but being your house and all…"

"Thanks."

He bends over to put the glass on her bedside cabinet and Jennifer notices his eyes then; the pupils more vertical than circular. And his skin, worked together in patches, like scales. He catches her glance and stares back for longer than she considers polite.

"Robyn," she says quietly.

"Jennifer," he says and joins Suzie at the window. She rests her head on his shoulder. The scene is ridiculous, Jennifer thinks. The two of them dolled up like they're going to the opera and standing in my little den of dirt.

"I was just saying to Suzie," Jennifer tries, "that we should think about burying Mr. Lees' body."

"Oh stop it," Suzie snarls. Then laughing, "I mean he'll be plenty rotten by now, won't he!"

"Not too terribly," Robyn says. "There'll still be something left to bury. I think that's a fine idea. He's out near the orchard, isn't he? We could be there in twenty minutes."

"No," Suzie says. "Let's just stay with our drinks, or drive about a little. We don't have to be serious all of a sudden."

What is that like, Jennifer thinks. To be left in a crashed car for weeks. A month now, if I'm counting properly. Imagine if you were still alive the whole time, but couldn't move a muscle. Imagine if you stayed like that for eternity, even after they put you in the ground. Just staring and thinking, staring and thinking, aware of everything and not being able to comment on any of it. You'd go mad in a few weeks. But after that, I'm not sure. It can't be too different to life in this room, in this bed.

"That's odd," Suzie says.

"What?" Jennifer says.

"There are two naked men coming down the street." Suzie squints. "They're mannequins," she says quietly. "Shop mannequins, you know the kind. They're walking wicked clumsy. I've never seen anything like it. Do you think it's a prank?"

Jennifer stares straight ahead.

If I was in hell, would I know? she thinks. Maybe that's half the torture, thinking you're still alive.

"They've stopped outside," Suzie whispers.

"I didn't lock the door," Robyn whispers back.

There is a rattling from downstairs, the door handle.

"Get something heavy," Suzie snaps. "You're a man, you have to fend them off."

Suzie peeks out of the window again, shuts it, and sits down on the floor in a ball. "Right, that's it, they're real and they're trying to get into the house and we're going to die."

"Do you own a gun, Mrs. Rhodes?" Robyn says. Jennifer throws him a disgusted glance. "No, all right. Worth a try."

The front door slams open.

"Oh sweet Jesus," Suzie whispers into her hands.

"There's a machete, Aubrey's. In the cupboard there," Jennifer says quickly.

Robyn hunts through mountains of books and clothes, then brandishes the thing in his hand. He hesitates at the doorway and watches Suzie, balled up still, and Jennifer in bed.

"Do your best then," Jennifer says, her eyes back on the patch of wall.

He peeks over the bannister. One of the monsters is at the bottom of the stairs now, trying to get purchase on the first step and failing. It glances up at Robyn and stops.

"Now listen, you bastard," Robyn says and raises the machete. "Metal versus plastic wins every time. You might want to think about that before you try coming up here." The thing puts its hands up, as though waving.

"What? Can't you talk?" Robyn says.

The thing shakes its head and tries the first step again, gets its foot down properly this time and raises itself up.

"I'm not joking. I'll cut you into next year if you take another step."

The mannequin looks back to its partner. The partner shrugs clumsily. The first puts its hands up again in a sort of peace gesture.

Robyn yells and darts at the thing with the machete. The first mannequin flings itself backwards and takes the second with it and they roll about for a moment on the floor.

"Up," Robyn shouts. They haul themselves to their feet. "Now I don't know where you've come from or what you are, but you best not be coming back here again or there'll be hell to pay. Understand?"

Both of them nod. They turn to leave.

"Hey," Robyn shouts and slashes at the first one's arm. The limb falls to the floor. "Something to remember us by if you think of trying that again."

The mannequin looks to the arm, then to its partner, then to the arm. They leave, waddling out into the afternoon, then back up the street.

Robyn locks the door, takes a few deep breaths, and climbs the stairs again.

"What a knight!" Suzie says and kisses him on the mouth. He seems to be standing taller now and his chest looks like it's inflated.

"What did they want with us?" Jennifer says to herself.

"Who cares, they're gone aren't they?"

"They could have tried any of the other houses. Why this one?"

Robyn finishes his gin. "I feel like a new man. Those bastards, who do they think they are? We'll take the car out, do a little reconnaissance, find your husband, Suzie. Give him a send-off. How about it?" Suzie stands uncertainly and watches his face. "We'll take plenty of booze for the trip. I found some old petrol in our garage earlier, so we'll be fine. Scott will tag along. And you'll come too, won't you Jennifer?"

Jennifer says nothing.

"Let's stay. Oh, let's stay," Suzie says.

"Shoes and socks on, I'll get the car warmed up. See you both outside in two."

When he's gone, Suzie looks back out the window and lights another cigarette. "Men," she says. "If they're not trying to get into your pants, they're trying to get you killed. I don't think I've ever found a good one and I've known plenty. They're made wrong. That's their problem. If you open up their heads there's a tiny speck of brain inside and the rest is all brawn. That's their problem, that is. They're made wrong."

The car engine starts up.

"Maybe," Jennifer says.

The sky seems darker now. Shapes dance high up, coils of light.

"What are you doing?" Suzie says, watching Jennifer, who is climbing into a skirt and tying her hair back.

"Coming with you, what does it look like?"

FORTY-FOUR

Rupert and Jamie Carnegie walk in silence for several hours. The forest is all gloom and a thick mist seeps from the ground and wets their boots and socks. Bogs lie waiting, and every now and then one of the Carnegies finds himself up to his knees in mud and water. Shapes linger way off in the trees, but the men don't talk of this.

There is the smell of death, Jamie thinks, like if someone left a morgue to thaw for a few months.

They come to a mess of vines. Jamie pulls at them and behind are windows and brickwork. The Rawlings' house, he realises.

They walk around the structure a few times. The garden fence is still standing. A spatula waits on the griddle of the barbeque. Rupert picks it up thoughtfully. "Strange man was Rawlings," he says.

Jamie pulls at a tangle of vines, but they won't give.

"Absolute nut if you ask me," Rupert continues. "Always talking about death. He was worse than the bloody Applebys."

"Old men talk a lot," Jamie says.

He catches glimpses through the vines now. The house is full of glasses, bottles, and plates: the aftermath of a party.

Rupert shrieks. Jamie turns about. The old man is on his backside, fallen and staring up at Mary Rawlings. She wears a cardigan, dressed exactly as Jamie remembers her on every other occasion, her hair immaculate.

"Scared me almost to bloody death, you did!" Rupert says.

Mary gives the old man a hand up, regards the two of them and says, "May I ask what you're doing here?"

"What *we're* doing here?"

"This is my house, as I'm sure you're aware."

"With respect, Mrs. Rawlings," Jamie says, "it doesn't look much like a house anymore."

"I'll concede that." She straightens her cardigan. "But where are my manners. Could I offer you gentlemen a cup of tea at all?"

Rupert catches his son's eye. "Tea?"

"Shortbread also."

As she approaches the house, the vines peel back like spider legs and she passes inside.

"Tea," Rupert says again.

Jamie lowers his voice. "What if her husband is in there?"

"Then I guess he'll be joining us. I'm parched."

They enter the house. Inside, the rooms are all murk and dark spaces, lit by vines which have grown illuminated spores. They jut from the walls, from the ceiling, from out of plug sockets and light fixtures. The two men join Mrs. Rawlings in the kitchen. She is working at the sideboard, filling the kettle and readying the cups. Jamie notices a vase. The dimensions are all wrong; the outside touches all the corners of the shape at once.

"Neither of you take sugar, I'm right in thinking?" Mary says.

The men grunt. They sit at the table, their feet aching and their eyes sore and their socks wet. Jamie glances at the vase again.

"So," Rupert says, "Mr. Rawlings not about today?"

Mary brings their cups over. "Milk, no sugar."

"Thanks. Was just saying about Augustus."

"I've got some little biscuits too. Gods, where are they?" She rummages about in the pantry and reappears with a box of shortbread, all misshapen and homemade. "Drink and eat up. All that walking will wear a fellow out, I'm sure."

Rupert sips his tea and lets out a sigh. Jamie does the same. They take the rest in gulps, not caring about the heat.

"What kind of tea do you call that? It's fantastic," Jamie murmurs.

"Special tea, from where I grew up."

"Sussex?"

"No. Not Sussex."

Rupert seems to glow now, Jamie notices. His eyes are wider, well-rested; five years have fallen off his face like dried mud.

"Perhaps save some of the biscuits for later," Mary says. "Take them with you, wherever you're going. Actually, where are you going?"

"The Whistle girl," Rupert says. "We think she's wandering about in here. Her father asked us to go looking. Shed any light on it?"

Mary shakes her head. "I've been keeping to myself."

"Your husband's not around?"

"He's out running errands," she says and sips at her tea.

Rupert glances at the glowing vines, at the impossible vase. "What kind of errands?"

"Just errands."

Her face relaxes then, wrinkles emerging. "How are things in the village?" she says quietly.

"Not good," Jamie says. "We think people are dead."

"They're dead in the forest too. If you travel deeper you may come across them. I hope you're quite ready for that."

Jamie spots a wooden cube with five corners on each face. And, when he looks properly, a chair that stands up in spite of only having one leg.

"More tea?" Mary refills all three cups from a teapot and adds milk.

"That's a very small pot," Jamie says, "for so much tea."

"You can hide anything away if you know how," she says, her eyes on him.

Jamie opens the teapot and looks in. It's full to the brim after six cups poured. He takes a teaspoon, pokes it into the pot, hunts for the bottom but feels nothing.

"This is bloody delicious," Rupert says, his mouth full. He grabs another shortbread.

The room is quieter than it should be, Jamie thinks. As though a freezer has been turned off.

"Unpleasantness ahead," Mary says.

Jamie looks up. "What?"

"There's unpleasantness ahead and you should prepare yourself for it."

Jamie looks to his father, who is still working on his shortbread quite happily, apparently unaware of the conversation.

"What are you talking about?"

"Attachments," Mary says without her mouth moving. "Perhaps it's time to tell those you care about that you care about them." She leans over the table and her face seems whiter now. The room — the impossible vase, the impossible chair, Rupert — dims to a vague outline. "Everything is more finite than usual these days."

"What the hell are you talking about?" Jamie whispers. Her old, dry hair lifts above her shoulders slightly.

Her wrinkles have disappeared. "All of this is to do with you, isn't it? Everything that's happening in Wilthail."

"In a roundabout way. Which families are still alive in the village?" Mary says.

"The Cranes, the Brightmans, a few others I think. Why?"

"That's it?"

"A bunch of bodies are scattered around the place. Not sure who they belong to."

She closes her eyes. "This is awful."

"John Whistle and some others are still holding out though. Why don't you go and join them?"

"I'm not supposed to interfere," she says quietly. "Not allowed, not really." She resembles a young woman suddenly, red-lipped, blushing cheeks. "Sometimes events are beyond our control, will you remember that?" Jamie opens his mouth, closes it again. "Will you remember that?"

I've gone insane, he thinks. As mad as my father; it's genetic. "Look—" he says.

"Mind if we take a few with us?" Rupert Carnegie says now, nodding to the biscuits.

Mary's wrinkles have returned. The underlying noise of the world is back in Jamie's ears.

"Please," Mary says, her mouth moving again. "Take them all, for the journey. They'll keep your strength up. I've already packed a little bag of sandwiches and lemonade for you both."

"Ah Mary, you're a bonnie lass," Rupert smiles. "Any whisky too, like? To keep us going?"

"My husband and I don't drink. We feel it dulls the senses."

Rupert wrinkles his nose at this.

"Mary," Jamie says.

"Well," the old woman says, "I've errands of my own to be off on. Sorry to turf you out so soon. Can I give you a hand with your things?"

"Mary," he says again.

She leads them to the door and through the vines, and then they stand in the garden, or what was a garden once, and she hands them a lunchbox.

"Head deeper," Mary says. "That's where everyone is, I should imagine. Head deeper until you find all the new structures."

"Structures? It's all fields that way," Rupert says.

"There have been some changes." She kisses them both on the cheek and passes Jamie a compass. "Follow this and you should be fine."

"Mary," Jamie says. "Can we talk a little more?"

"Safe travelling, gentlemen."

She enters the house again and the vines curl over the entrance and the two men are silent for a while.

FORTY-FIVE

Mcalister's feet are burning. He checks the soles and they're as pale and smooth as he's ever seen them, just like the rest of his skin. Into a city now and he and Beomus pass through markets selling objects of impossible dimensions, selling food Mcalister cannot place the smell of. Towers loom over their heads, miles high. Some of the folk are dressed medievally, in long shawls and cloaks and others wear only a short sari or nothing at all, and their faces are riddled with machinery and silver growths. Beomus leads them to a market stall selling cloaks. The seller is quiet and can't seem to take his eyes from Beomus' face. The seller hands them cloaks and a belt and the men dress themselves and make back into the main street.

"Who was that?" Mcalister says.

"Not a clue."

"He knew who you are though."

"Most people around here do."

A crowd develops before long, following at a distance, twenty townspeople tugging at Beomus' cloak, calling out his name. The boy pushes them away irritably and leads Mcalister down a side street, then another, and into a building of chrome and glass and some shimmering material Mcalister has never seen before.

"Hood up," Beomus says and Mcalister does so and the two of them appear as monks. Mcalister follows the sound of the boy's footsteps through the gloom and the passage opens into a room that extends ahead of them without end — or without visible end, the height of a modest skyscraper; bookshelves from the floor to the ceiling.

"Don't look anyone in the eye. If they speak to you, ignore them," Beomus says quietly and the room seems to catch even that small noise and throw it up to the ceiling.

Down through winding staircases then. Thousands of cloaked figures sit at reading tables, volumes piled beside them. Cherubs fetch books from high shelves while readers wait below. The library is in stages, Mcalister notices. The ground level where they stand is mundane, while the next one up is balanced on scaffolding and the shelves are made of glass. Just above, he can faintly make out, the books are in cabinets with only a few readers at the desks and the rest of the level empty.

Ahead of them a woman sits at a table reading into a microphone, hundreds, if not thousands, of small glass cubes laid out before her. "One point six one eight zero three three three nine eight eight seven—"

"What's she doing?" Mcalister whispers.

"The Arbiter of Fundamentals," Beomus mutters back. "She regulates logic."

"Does logic need *regulating*?"

The boy catches him with a sardonic stare. "Reckon circles just naturally form if left to their own devices? She broadcasts the constants out to the rest of the Etheria — keeps everything in agreement."

Almost at the reception desk now, Beomus whispers into the policeman's ear: "Tell the High Librarian you're a scrutineer and you need to see the arbiters' chronicles."

"What?"

"Just tell him."

"Why the hell do *I* have to?"

"Because if he sees my face we'll be promptly escorted out and exiled to the Addled Forest, all right? I'm not exactly in good favour with this lot at the moment."

"You told me these are your people."

"It's complicated."

Mcalister shifts his weight between feet. "Besides, I don't know your language."

"Plenty of Corporic diplomats come through here from time to time. Just stick to English."

"*Diplomats?*"

"Sure, from your future. It doesn't matter. You're a scrutineer. You're here to see the arbiters' chronicles."

The figure at the desk looks up from his papers; a young man well over seven feet high, dressed in a purple sari. "Gentlemen?"

Beomus pulls his hood down a little.

"Hi," Mcalister says. "I'm a scrutiniser."

Scrutineer, comes Beomus' voice in his mind.

"Scrutineer. I'm a scrutineer. I'm here for the arbitrage."

Oh Ganesha's dick, comes the voice again.

"I'm a scrutineer and I'm here about the arbiters' records."

The librarian bends to Mcalister's height and studies his eyes. "Is that so?" he warbles.

"Yes. My friend and I were hoping you might be able to assist."

"Have you a scrutineer's sigil on your person, might I ask?"

Mcalister opens his mouth, makes a little yelp sound, and closes it again.

You are completely and utterly useless, comes the voice in his mind and Mcalister feels something pushing through his body, starting from his chest and spreading out to his limbs. He tries to move his fingers, but they won't respond. He goes to open his mouth but it stays shut. Then, quite naturally, it opens by itself. "By the decree of Sardamon, First Scholar, I'm here to open an investigation into the records of Beomus the Arbiter of Mischief. No disrespect to you or your establishment intended whatsoever, but there have been reports of unauthorised persons gaining access to the records."

The librarian's face crumples. "I can assure you, sir, that no one has been up to the arbiters' floor in weeks. I man this post all hours of the day, I would know if there had been discrepancies."

Mcalister speaks again, beyond his control. "And I wouldn't intend for a second to dispute your testimony, but you must understand that we are duty-bound to investigate any claim, however small, when concerning such documents, especially given the recent crisis in the Corporia."

The librarian thinks this over. "Obviously if you're a scrutineer I will give you full access to whatever it is you require. If you'd kindly show me your sigil then we can proceed."

Mcalister tries to cry out but his body remains rigid.

Just stay calm, all right? Only another minute, comes Beomus' voice.

"I'm afraid I haven't the time to argue officious matters with you, sir," Mcalister's mouth says. "The arbiters themselves have commissioned me on their behalf, and if I'm to report back that the High Librarian sought to obstruct my investigation, it is unlikely said High Librarian is to remain in his post much longer."

The librarian begins to shuffle and straighten his papers. "If no proof of identification can be provided, sir, I'm afraid I will not be able to do as you ask, threats regardless."

Mcalister's mouth remains closed.

Now what? he thinks.

His mind is quiet. The sound of footsteps from behind.

"Please sir," the librarian says. "There is another patron waiting for assistance. If you would kindly step aside."

It's done, Mcalister thinks. *Turn me around, let's go. This is insane.*

His mouth opens of its own accord yet again and his body approaches the librarian. In a whisper: "All right, you've pushed me to it, and don't think I won't be writing your behaviour up in my report, you pencil-pusher." And out of his own mouth falls a noise like galaxies colliding, Mcalister thinks, if such a thing made a sound. His skin glimmers purple for a moment, then returns to its normal pallid pale.

The librarian nervously fumbles with his robe. "Please sirs, if you'll kindly follow me."

Mcalister feels his body returned to him and reaches out for the desk so as not to fall over. The three of them climb a staircase. "If you would, sirs." The librarian beckons to a glass lift. "Any further queries, please don't hesitate to let me know."

The two of them step inside and the doors seal.

"What the bloody hell was that?" Mcalister snarls.

"Clever, I'd say," Beomus mutters. "You sang a bar of Novelty's song. He taught it to me himself. Means we're directly associated with him. No one's going to mess with Novelty."

"Clever? I'll murder you, that's what I'll do. I'll poke your eyes out first, and then I'll murder you."

"Pu-pu-pu-please sir," Beomus says in a high voice. "I'm a scrutiniser with the governmentses. Honest."

The elevator doors slide aside. They stand in a perfect, transparent sphere; the cosmic strings dancing above, the city bustling below. There are only modest shelves here, each with volumes of one colour; red, orange, yellow, green, blue, indigo, violet, and then tens of colours Mcalister has never seen before. The rest of the library is visible below, corridors and passages and halls, each building made of some other material; of wood or brass or glass. Some of the buildings shimmer slightly and fade from view for a second, only to return suddenly.

"Those other rooms," Mcalister says. "What are they?"

"Other libraries in other cities. They all exist in a similar space, in another part of the Etheria. It's not easy to explain."

"But you could visit them, from here?"

"Yes." The boy cocks his head. "But most of them you wouldn't want to."

"Why?"

"They're not in particularly nice spots."

In one of the halls, figures walk hunched over, lugging a ball on a chain behind them. Mcalister points to it. "Like that?"

"Quite so, yes."

"Who are they?"

"All prisons have a library. Those balls, they're space-time singularities. It takes the effort of a planet to pull them along."

Beomus thumbs through a volume. Mcalister stares out over the city.

"What's it called, this place?" Mcalister says.

A few volumes in his arms now and crossing to a reading table, Beomus opens his mouth and a sound like shattering diamonds falls out.

Mcalister says slowly, "The Place Where the Knowledgables Gather and Make Their Knowledge Known."

Beomus looks up. "How in the hell do you know that?"

"It's what the sound means, isn't it?"

220

The boy keeps his eyes on the policeman uncertainly. "Yes," he says. "That's what the sound means. You're not supposed to know things like that."

"Guess I'm brighter than you think."

"It isn't about intelligence. If that's happening, then you've been here too long already."

Mcalister covers his eyes and turns away. "Hold up some fingers. Don't tell me how many," he says.

The boy does as he's told.

"Three," Mcalister says. "Try again." A pause. "Four. Now none."

"Why didn't you tell me sooner?" Beomus says.

"It started after I fell in the ocean. It wasn't much at first, just a little light at the edges. Now I can see the whole way around my own head. Is this what's it like for you? For all of you?"

The boy shrugs. "Sort of."

"What happens next?"

"I'm not sure." Beomus drums his fingers on the table. "All of this," he gestures to the library, to the city below, "it's a sort of skin, to make it easier for you to comprehend. There isn't really a city or a library or anything like that. Etherics aren't *people* in any sense you'd understand the word. Your mind has constructed these things to make it simpler. If you stay here too long you might start seeing things for what they really are. We can't wait for that."

"Why? I've coped up until now, haven't I?"

"This is child's play. If the rest follows, well, let's just hope it doesn't. I can't help you when that happens."

"I'll just have to handle it then."

"You won't. Your mind will turn to porridge. Look, you're the first of your kind to cross over, this quickly anyway. Your head isn't built to deal with this kind of thing. I won't be long now. A few minutes and we'll have what we came for."

Mcalister watches the cosmic strings twisting about overhead. "What *have* we come for, exactly?" he asks.

"This is a library of biographies. Everything that has happened and will ever happen to an arbiter is archived here."

"How will that help anything?"

"We need to know what I'm going to do next."

Mcalister considers this. "Won't it just be based on whatever you read in that book?"

"Yes," says the High Librarian, stepping from the elevator. "We would call that a paradox. If you'd kindly put the book down and vacate the premises, I'd be much obliged."

"Wait," Beomus growls and turns a page.

The book snaps shut and begins returning itself to the shelf.

"The authorities have been informed of your presence here and will arrive momentarily."

"Pencil pushing *idiot*," Beomus snarls and his eyes shine a furious purple.

"Rules exist for a reason," the librarian says. "Anything less than total adherence can result in all manner of damage to a society. Though, given your previous rank and title, this sort of behaviour is perhaps to be expected."

"We should go," Mcalister mumbles.

"Has anyone else been here recently?" Beomus says. "Any of the other arbiters?"

"Out," the librarian says. "Now. You should think yourself lucky I'm not detaining you."

"Just a moment, it's important." The librarian raises an eyebrow. Beomus emits a sound close to that of a planet's birth.

Mcalister understands the sentence with little effort: The Grudge is Almost Settled, and the Arbiter of Entropy May Well Soon Die.

"Now, *has anyone else been here recently*?" Beomus says.

"We have inspections from *actual* scrutineers occasionally, yes," the High Librarian replies.

"I said recently."

"Yes. One."

"Who?"

"The crone, if you must know."

Beomus grabs Mcalister's arm and rushes them over to the elevator.

"I understand," the librarian says, "you have something of an ongoing dispute in the Corporia."

Beomus reaches into his own ear, his whole hand disappearing for a moment, and plucks out a shining blue gem and offers it to the librarian. "Tell whoever arrives, whoever asks, that we're headed for my birth lands. Will you do that?"

The librarian looks down his nose at the gem, then at Beomus. "Your birth lands," he says quietly.

"My birth lands," Beomus nods. "That's real qualia, by the way. Test it if you don't believe me."

The librarian pockets the gem. "Your birth lands. That can be arranged, yes."

Beomus and the policeman step into the elevator. The librarian plays awkwardly with the cord of his robe. "I wanted to say that it's something of an honour to meet you, present complications excluded."

"Cheers a million." Beomus throws him a wink. The elevator doors slide shut.

FORTY-SIX

It's evening and John Whistle kicks open the church door and lays a huge box at Matilda's feet.

"You brought a surprise," she says.

He picks out the objects one by one: oscilloscope, voltmeter, Geiger counter, particle chamber, and a few Matilda isn't sure of. "For the toys you've found," he says.

"Where did you get all of this?" she says.

"My place. There's a laboratory in the garage, haven't used it in years. Seemed a shame to let it all go to waste now."

She watches him working at the altar, connecting devices to a makeshift generator, setting up a blacklight; his coat on askew, his hair a mess. She wonders how his skin smells, like an old man or a young man? Or is he one of those strange men who have no smell at all?

"What are we looking for?" she says.

"Any sign of how your toys work."

"And then?"

"I'm not sure."

"I'll leave you to it, might watch the evening from the belfry."

"Shout if you see anything, would you?"

"Will do. If you accidentally kill yourself while I'm gone, I'll be extremely annoyed."

"Noted."

He tries the voltmeter on the cubes. Nothing. Then the Geiger counter: no discernible trace of radiation. He puts one to his ear. "Two nine nine seven nine two four five eight…" The speed of light, as announced by the distant woman inside. Next he tries a few of the glass coils, then the copper-looking coil, and finally one made of a material he doesn't recognise, some kind of textured metal. Again, no voltage, no radiation. He checks Matilda has done as she's said and gone up to the belfry, chooses one of the larger cubes — Planck's constant, takes a few deep breaths, and launches it into the air. He closes his eyes. Silence, then a clatter. He picks the cube up, lying between pews, unharmed, tests it again with the equipment. No readings whatsoever.

At the bottom of the pile of Matilda's treasure is a stone; smooth, speckled midnight blue. He runs the normal tests: no more reactive than the others. He plays with the thing in his hands for a while, leaves it experimentally under the blacklight. Finally he checks Liptrot is sleeping and climbs the steps to the belfry where Matilda is leaning over the railing smoking.

"How's it going, Tesla?" she says and passes him a cigarette.

He shakes his head. "No dice."

The Applebys' study is lit up, a few of the Cranes' rooms too. "Of all the folk to survive," Matilda murmurs, "I can't say the Applebys were my preferred choice."

Whistle changes position so he can look out over the village properly. There are lights in the forest tonight: a first. "I saw you praying yesterday," he says.

"So what?"

"So nothing. I just didn't think you were particularly religious."

"I'm not, but given what's been happening around here, it wouldn't be unreasonable to entertain the idea of phenomena beyond our understanding."

"Most things are."

"You know what I mean."

"You think this is all supernatural?"

"It wouldn't be such a stupid suggestion, considering everything we've seen."

"What have we seen?" he says dryly.

"Blood rain, knitting needle rain, abominations, universal constants trapped in tiny glass cubes."

Whistle strokes his beard. "If we got hold of someone from the tenth century and let them loose in London, how long do you think it would be before they went mad?" Matilda shrugs. "Well, it's beside the point. I bet they'd soon start calling everything magic though. They'd see an airliner going overhead and call it magic. They'd see a car pulling itself down the road without a horse and call it magic. They'd see a computer and, hell, I think those are magical anyway and I'm from this century."

"There's a difference between computers and knitting needle rain," Matilda says.

"No there *isn't*. The only difference is that you know how the computer works, but not what's going on around here recently. Just because something's mysterious doesn't make it magic. Nothing, if you look at it hard enough, if you take it apart, if you smash it, freeze it, measure its temperature, ever turns out to be magic."

"And that?" she says quietly. "What's the story behind that?" She points over the railings. A church, identical to theirs, is some two hundred feet away, shimmering a little in the twilight. And another, to its right. And another.

Five of them in total, ending with their own, forming a circle.

"That," Whistle says, "I'm not sure about."

FORTY-SEVEN

Eric Crane crouches in the bushes outside the library. He has searched four abandoned houses and the charity shop now, looking for his laser. The last stop today is Jennifer Rhodes' place because she has been known to hoard all manner of objects ever since her husband died, or so Eric's father says anyway. He checks the road, then sprints across, shortcutting through the old mill. The road sign outside Jennifer Rhodes' house is covered in what looks like blood.

He catches something white and moving out of the corner of his eye. Two mannequins are stumbling up the road like fifties B-movie robots. Eric holds his breath. They pass and turn towards the church.

Rhodes' house is unlocked. The place smells of old food. Plates are stacked high in the sink. A severed plastic arm is lying in the hall without explanation. He checks the living room. No sign of the laser. Then the kitchen, the bathroom for good measure, and finally upstairs.

Her bedroom is the worst of all, cigarettes stubbed out on the windowsill, unfinished glasses of wine. He rummages through her drawers. Out of desperation he pulls back the bedclothes: a note underneath.

Aubrey.
Sorry.
I'm all hollowed out.
J x

Eric folds up the letter and puts it in his backpack. Then he checks the spare bedroom; still no laser.

Back home and he climbs the trellis up the outside of the house and back into his bedroom. His machine is still sitting silently on the rug, gleaming, almost finished, the gravity petals open and refracting the twilight. There is the smell of cooking and he follows it downstairs. Uncle Alf is sat at the dining table with Mr. Crane.

"My boy," Uncle Alf beams. "Sit down." Eric sits. "Haven't seen much of you today."

"Been busy," Eric says.

Mrs. Crane enters bearing all the makings of a roast dinner and lays steaming pots and plates on the table. She's wearing an old dress of hers, Eric notices, a short red number which leaves little to the imagination. "Dinner is served," she announces.

Uncle Alf claps. "Bloody fantastic!"

They eat.

"Miserable day today," Alf says with a mouth full of potatoes. "Did you see it? Blowing a gale, it was."

"Like every day now," Mrs. Crane mumbles.

"And the sky all lit up with those strange ribbons. They ought to do something about that."

"Alf," Mr. Crane says and puts his cutlery down. "There's a small matter we wanted to raise with you." Alf smiles, bits of potato pushing their way through his teeth. "You say you came all the way down from Yorkshire?"

"Drove," Alf nods.

"Did you happen to notice the huge glass barrier on the outskirts of Wilthail?"

"This mint sauce, bloody delicious. Is it homemade?"

"No," Mrs. Crane says. "But thank you."

"The glass barrier," Mr. Crane says. "Did you see it at all?"

"Nope. Didn't see anything."

"Well, is the outside world still in order? Have they got knitting needle rain too?"

Alf squints. "Knitting needle rain," he says slowly. "Don't know if I've come across that one. Mind if I grab some more potatoes?"

"Please," Mrs. Crane says.

"And," Mr. Crane says, "there's also the small matter of your death."

Mrs. Crane slams her knife down on her plate. "That's e-bloody-nough. Just the other day we were talking about how much we missed Alf and here he is and all you can do is pick at him."

They eat in silence. Eric plays with his peas and thinks again about the laser.

"I don't want to cause a fuss," Alf says sheepishly. "If staying here is going to be a problem, then I don't mind sleeping in a hotel."

Which hotel would that be? Eric thinks.

"No," Mrs. Crane says. "You're here now. You've come a long way. You must still be tired from the journey."

"I am quite tired actually."

"So you can darn well relax here for a little while and get your strength back."

They finish the meal in silence. Then, with the plates cleared, the evening proceeds in much the same fashion as the last month, with Mr. Crane drinking himself into a stupor. Only this time Alf and Mrs. Crane drink too, and before long the three of them are laughing like old friends. They play The Rolling Stones through a portable speaker with the last of the battery and Alf and Mrs. Crane dance while Mr. Crane falls asleep on the sofa.

Eric peeks through the cracks in the boards across the window and thinks about Zoe Whistle for a while.

"Do you remember that night in Brighton?" Alf says, spinning Mrs. Crane around.

"Of course."

"And the bar and…"

"Oh, I remember."

Mr. Crane opens his eyes for a moment, slouches further into the sofa, then falls back to sleep.

Is everyone insane? Eric thinks. Or is it me? Which one would be worse?

Alf glances over at Mr. Crane. "The old boy's asleep," he says quietly.

"How about we go upstairs and I show you all my old albums?" Mrs. Crane says.

"But we've nothing to play them on."

"Oh, that doesn't matter."

They dance a little more, their noses almost touching, and Mrs. Crane says to Eric, "Will you look after your father — make sure he doesn't throw up or anything?" Eric nods. "See you in the morning, darling."

They disappear upstairs.

And if you were the one who'd gone mad, how could you possibly tell?

He shifts his father up to a sitting position so he won't choke if he vomits. Something bulky is in his father's pocket, a wallet. Eric opens it up. Credit cards, train tickets, and a picture of Uncle Alf. His cheeks are red and his hair is red and his face actually looks like Alf as Eric remembers, not this new visiting Alf.

The newcomer, Eric thinks, is closer to Kevin Lees. Just with red hair in the right places.

FORTY-EIGHT

Robyn Appleby pulls up a fair distance from the Porsche.

"That's the one?" Scott says quietly, nodding to the car ahead.

"That's the one," Suzie says.

The four of them get out, Robyn, Scott, Jennifer, and Suzie. The air is cold and damp, and with the dark coming on now, it makes Jennifer think of a war zone. Robyn strides ahead and looks in through the car window.

"There's no one here," he says. Suzie approaches. "You might want to hang back a bit though."

She barges past him and looks in herself. There's blood all over the driver's seat and the windscreen is smashed. Some human-looking matter is lying on the passenger seat with veins attached.

"No blood trail," Robyn says, looking under the car. "Can't have gone far though. We'll split up. Suzie, you're with me."

Scott makes an exasperated noise and glances at Jennifer.

"We'll take the forest," Jennifer says. Scott hesitates. "It's all right, I'm a trained Girl Scout."

They fork off, Jennifer and Scott trudging over the marsh and into the forest, Suzie and Robyn hand in hand, striding out into the fields.

"If you see anything, maybe just tell me first," Jennifer says. "No surprises."

"No surprises," Scott says.

Leaves and twigs crack under their boots and the sound seems louder than it should be. The air is strange too, heavy, clinging to their clothes.

"Do you have a torch?" Scott says.

"Sure."

"Might be time to get it out?"

"No, we don't need a torch."

Who are these men one meets from time to time? she thinks. Light-willed, always afraid, scheming, lying. Is it their upbringing or their genetics, or both?

Aubrey was not like that.

Maybe we're all too coddled. We've grown used to running water and express delivery and legal recourse and social media.

"What's that?" Scott whispers.

Jennifer squints. "Just a branch."

They head closer. She's not wrong, it is a branch, and from it something is dangling back and forth in the wind.

"I really think we should use the torch now," Scott says.

Jennifer produces it from her pocket. She angles the beam up and a girl is hanging from the branch, her hands and legs dangling free, the noose still tight around her neck. "Don't run," Jennifer says and looks Scott straight in the eye. "If we split up, we might not find each other again."

Scott nods slowly.

The girl is Millie Connors, a sixth form student Jennifer counselled for a time, mostly about an unwanted pregnancy. Her eyes are half open.

233

"She's been here a while," Jennifer murmurs.

"I don't think so. Still some blood in the cheeks. We best be getting on."

"We can't just leave her here."

"It'll be a busy day if we're going to bury all of them," Scott says and nods to the forest. Jennifer makes out seven other figures nearby, all of them sixth form students she recognises to one degree or another.

This is hell, she thinks. I'm already dead and this is hell. "Everyone here, all their parents' houses were in the forest. It must do something to them," she says.

"Like what?"

"I don't know, but teenagers don't just all kill themselves for no reason."

"Maybe it was a pact."

"They wouldn't do something like this."

"How do you know what people would and wouldn't do?" Scott says irritably. "I'm going back. Lees wouldn't have come this far in anyway."

"He might, if something was chasing him."

"No, I've had quite enough, thank you."

"Just wait," she says. "Give it a second and calm down, all right?"

She notices a boy sat in the trees some ten feet away. He's dealing cards out to himself on the floor. She approaches. "Hello."

"Hi," the boy says without looking up.

"What do you have there? Trading cards?" She tries to place his face. Is he one of the Turner children maybe? "What are you doing out here all by yourself?"

He meets her eyes. "What are *you* doing out here all by yourself?"

"Is Mummy or Daddy around?"

"We should go," Scott mutters. "Best we don't get involved."

The little boy picks up all of the cards, shuffles, then deals them out again. They don't look unlike Tarot, Jennifer thinks. "What are those?" she says and bends down. They all bear faces, some smiling, some crying.

"You're the widow," the boy says and turns over a card and Jennifer's face is there, hand-drawn. She starts back. "You're the mouse," the boy says to Scott and turns over another card, Scott's face clearly depicted.

"Fuck this," Scott says and sets off running for the car.

"I'm the widow," Jennifer says. The boy nods slowly. He lays the rest of the cards out: Zoe Whistle, John Whistle, Matilda Sargent, the Crane family, the Thomas family, Suzie Lees, then Robyn Appleby.

"What's he?" she says and points to Robyn Appleby's card.

"The serpent."

Wind rattles the trees and all the dead leaves fly off in a mad bid for freedom. "Where is Kevin Lees?" Jennifer says.

The boy takes the fragments of a ripped card from his pocket and Jennifer can just about make out Kevin's face. "The cuckold," the boy says.

"I really should be going," Jennifer says and begins to back away.

The boy nods and collects up all of the cards, shuffles, and deals them back out to himself.

FORTY-NINE

Rupert kept in the lead and lazily kicked bushes and branches out of his way. Jamie was thinking of Burger King very hard. They'd eaten through Mary's shortbread the evening before and their skin felt like it was glowing and the world took on a pleasant sheen.

They came across a racing bicycle, the front wheel warped at ninety degrees. They had walked on, well over ten miles it felt like, and caught sight of something through the trees only to find it was the same bicycle again. Rupert put his head in his hands and the two of them said nothing. Then they laid out on the floor exhausted, and used branches and shrubs for pillows and slept a black, dead, dreamless sleep.

Jamie wakes to a yellow face above him, slits for eyes, the mouth a slit too, smiling. He scrabbles back into a tree.

"Today," says the figure from behind his mask, holding a microphone, "we're playing for high stakes indeed: a father-son duo, intent on beating the odds."

"Christ," Rupert says, who is awake now too and standing.

Thirty or so other masked things sit to their right, in lines of chairs like a theatre, and some of the smaller figures are eating popcorn from great buckets.

"What the hell is this?" Jamie says.

The main figure leans in to whisper, "So, do you think the old man's still got it? Just between you and me, of course."

Jamie says nothing and looks about. The trees have fashioned themselves into crude fences, a mess of branches and vines in the perimeter of an enormous square around them. "What the hell is this?" Jamie says again.

The audience laugh, some of them practically screaming. A red APPLAUSE sign shines in the air, supported by nothing at all, and the audience clap manically. The sign fades and the audience quieten down again.

The host leads Jamie to a podium which has appeared in the centre of the stage and motions Rupert to do the same.

"Jamie," Rupert whispers breathlessly. The old man's eyes are still heavy, half asleep; his hair full of dirt and twigs.

"Gentlemen," the host says, putting on an American accent now. "Are you both ready to begin?"

Rupert shakes his head violently.

"No," Jamie says.

"Well then," the host says. "There it is."

The APPLAUSE sign shines again and the audience clap and cheer. Jamie tries to step off of the podium, but his feet are stuck firmly to the floor.

The host takes centre stage. "Now, for those of you watching at home who might be new, the rules are very, *very* simple. Whoever has the most points by the end of the game wins the privilege of staying alive."

The audience cheer again.

"I don't want to play," Rupert shouts. "I don't want to play, you hear?"

"No problem at all!" says the host. "Then you forfeit the game, is that correct?"

"No," Jamie says. "He doesn't. He wants to keep playing."

"I bloody don't," Rupert yells.

"If you forfeit, you've lost," Jamie says. "They'll just kill you anyway."

"The younger Carnegie is rather astute," says the host. "That'll come in handy."

Rupert pats his inside pocket out of habit, looking for his whisky bottle, but the pocket is empty. "All right, all right…" he mutters.

A high-pitched jingle plays, all wrong notes over wrong notes, then a spotlight is on Jamie and Rupert and the audience hush to silence. The host takes out a card and reads from it. "Question one, to Jamie Carnegie. When you were six years old, your father spent the family's earnings that week in the Working Men's Club, and you had to attend your first day of school without a uniform. True or false?"

Rupert nods excitedly at his son, then doubles over and screams. "No cheating, boys," the host says. "I'm afraid conferring is strictly prohibited. Jamie?"

"True," Jamie says in a flat voice.

The host examines his card. "True!" Another horrific jingle plays. "Five points to Jamie Carnegie. Now, Rupert. For five points, when asked about his father, Jamie usually tells friends the old man is dead. True or false?"

Rupert glances at his son, who has his eyes pinned to the ground. "False."

The host peeks at his card. A new jingle plays, a minor key with screams overlaid on top. "I'm afraid the answer is *true*, Mr. Carnegie. Kids, eh? Little scamps!"

The audience cheer again.

"Another for young Jamie. Short of money one month, Rupert smashed open your piggy bank when you were seven years old and denied the entire incident when later asked about it."

"True," Jamie says.

The sad jingle plays again. "*False!*" says the host. "You were in fact eight, nine, and ten when the aforementioned happened. Bad luck!"

"What if we both forfeit?" Jamie says to his father.

Ten thousand needles on his skin then. He screams and falls onto the lectern.

"*No conferring,*" the host says. "I think we made the rules quite clear. Rupert, for ten points now. Jamie lost his virginity to a man named Samuel Biddle, Wilthail's former postman."

Rupert tries to glean the answer from his son's face. Jamie keeps his eyes to the floor.

"False," Rupert says finally.

"In fact it was *true!*"

The audience cheer and whoop.

"Ah, he was a handsome chap, Samuel Biddle. Ten points for the next one, Jamie. Rupert Carnegie killed a woman, leading to the end of his marriage to your mother."

The audience all lean forward slightly in their chairs. Jamie grips the edges of the lectern. "False," he says quietly.

"You would be absolutely correct," the host says delightedly. "If you'd said *true.*" Another cheer from the audience. The APPLAUSE sign dies suddenly and the spotlights fade except for Rupert's, and the old man looks about, feckless.

"Yes," says the host, "it was a quiet Thursday and you had been working at the mill in Croftbury. You thought you'd treat yourself to a few drinks at the pub there before driving back home for dinner with your wife and son."

"Enough," Rupert says.

"Before long you were shooting down country lanes at well over sixty miles an hour."

"Stop," Rupert says. "I forfeit. I forfeit, you hear? I don't want to play anymore."

"That very same day, that very same evening in fact, Irma Sargent was cycling back from the library, where she worked part-time. She was wearing a florescent jacket and the lamps on her bicycle were working perfectly. At home, she would be greeted by her husband and infant daughter Matilda, who had been with a childminder all day and was looking forward to seeing her mother."

"I want to stop playing," Rupert shouts and tries to pull his legs from the podium.

"At six fifty-three PM, medium humidity, sky overcast, you turned the corner on Hensting Road and slammed into Mrs. Sargent at just over fifty-five miles an hour. She landed hard enough to crack her helmet and sustained intense cranial trauma, as well as breaking her back. This was quite beside the point though, as when the ambulance arrived—"

"Stop," Rupert screams.

"—she was already dead from cranial bleeding. Isn't that so, Rupert?"

"I forfeit," Rupert whispers. "You bastards, I forfeit."

"That's your final word on the matter?" the host says. Rupert nods. "Well then, today's undisputed winner is Jamie Carnegie!"

The audience begin to cheer.

"I forfeit," Jamie says. "I forfeit too."

The audience fall back to silence.

"You're absolutely sure?" the host says.

"Yes."

"Well, in these rare cases we like to show contestants what they *could have* won."

"We don't care," Jamie says. "Really."

A spotlight illuminates the back of the stage now.

"Hi," Zoe Whistle says, sat cross-legged in a lion's cage.

The host reads from a card: "Today's prize is Zoe Whistle, a twenty-six-year-old manic depressive with a history of attempted suicide. Zoe enjoys tea, colouring books, Scandinavian death metal, and deviant sexual acts." He turns to Rupert and Jamie. "You're both absolutely *positively* sure you'd like to forfeit?"

"Are you okay?" Jamie shouts.

Zoe shrugs. "I'm doing all right."

"This is a trick," Rupert says.

"No tricks," the host says.

"Don't do anything stupid," Zoe yells.

Jamie looks to his father. He has never noticed what big, worldly eyes the old man has, the irises blue and wild, the pupils like manholes. "Irma Sargent on her bike. Is it all true?" Jamie says.

Rupert nods.

A corridor opens up ahead of Jamie, a new space: adulthood or something close, where everything is a grey area and no decision will please everyone, if anyone at all, and each story has some other side to it you hadn't considered before.

"Don't do anything *stupid*," Zoe yells again.

"Last chance to reconsider, gentlemen. I'm afraid I can only take final answers now," the host says.

"I'll keep playing," Jamie says.

"I forfeit," Rupert says.

"Well there it is," nods the host.

"What?" Jamie whispers.

"Don't be stupid, Mr. Carnegie," Zoe shouts.

Rupert looks to Zoe, then to the host, then to his son. "Aye. I forfeit."

Zoe presses herself up against the bars of the cage and begins to scream. Jamie tries to pull his legs free from the podium again, but his father only puts up his hands in

241

a *never mind* gesture. His face is light and creaseless. He smiles to his son. "Get her out of here," he says. "Damn proud of you I am."

He turns back to face the host, who is taking off his mask now; Augustus Rawlings appearing from underneath, one corner of the mouth twisted into a snarl. He reaches out a hand for Rupert.

"Dad," Jamie says.

The bars of Zoe's cage part. Jamie's feet are unstuck from the podium.

Rupert eyes Rawlings' black, withered fingers. "Always knew there was something off with you."

"Likewise, Mr. Carnegie," Augustus purrs.

"Dad," Jamie says again.

"Damn proud of you I am," Rupert says and puts his hand in Augustus'.

The scene is evaporated in one great clap of amethyst purple. Jamie and Zoe stand alone in the forest.

FIFTY

Matilda admires the belfry to her right through binoculars. She watches another Matilda, also holding binoculars but turned away, looking to her own right. She tries the other side. The next Matilda is looking left. Matilda raises her hand. The other Matilda does the same, in exactly the same motion, at the same speed.

"It may as well be a mirror," John says. "I told you."

"What if it is?"

John cracks off a little plaster and hurls it at the belfry to the right. It rings out on impact. "Pretty solid mirror if it is one, eh?"

"If they aren't mirrors," Matilda says slowly, "then—"

"Parallels," John says. "Most likely. Parallel, identical versions of our church on identical causal trajectories."

"What if we all flip a coin?"

"Whatever you do, however many coins you flip, events will be exactly the same for them. It's all the same causal chain."

"What about Heisenberg's thing?"

"I've already thought of that. It still won't work. Same chain, same events, on a macro-scale anyway."

They sit for a while and watch the other Matildas and Whistles in their belfries.

"What if we go visit one of them?" Matilda says.

"Then they'll have already left by the time we arrive."

She groans. They drink a few glasses of wine, waiting for the existential horror to subside. Then, silently, they collect up their things and watch the others through the night collecting up their own possessions and disappearing into their own stairwells. The smell of Matilda's shampoo wafts back at Whistle as they descend and he's a teenager again for a moment.

Downstairs, he goes to check on Liptrot while Matilda blows out the candles. The priest is asleep, groaning and snoring, his wrists still red from trying to rip himself free from the binds. Whistle touches him with Matilda's sleeping coil just to make sure and empties the lavatory pan and fills up the water jug.

Yea, Whistle thinks, though I walk through the valley of the shadow of death.

Back at the bedrooms now, he calls out goodnight but Matilda's room is dark and there's no reply. He blows out his own candle and makes into the bedroom and undresses in the dark and kneads his sore joints and gets into bed. There is the smell of shampoo again. A mouth finds his.

Afterwards they lie quietly. This is how humans are supposed to be, John thinks. All the time.

He lights the candle by his bedside and the two of them share a cigarette.

"They're all doing this, aren't they? The other versions," Matilda says from the crook of his arm.

"Probably," Whistle says. "But I'm sure we did it better."

"No doubt."

He puts a hand through her hair.

"You look sad," she says.

He eyes her body under the covers. "I can assure you I'm not."

"I mean generally. You always do."

Whistle thinks this over. "My parents were academics," he says.

"I know, I met them."

"And when I was a kid they used to have lots of people over for dinner. Most of them were famous mathematicians and scientists, but others were total idiots and I could see my parents were just taking pity on them. After they'd gone home, my parents would give me a quick summary of their life story, and it was usually something sad like drugs or divorce or some weird personality flaw they'd never ironed out. So I always wondered how people made such stupid decisions. Didn't they realise what they were doing at the time? I promised myself I'd never end up like those sad cases at the dinner table. Naturally I did anyway.

"But if you think about it long enough, you'll always come around to the same conclusion, I reckon. There's no grand plan and no one's in charge. It's all just fumbling about in the dark, and half the time you're not even sure why you're fumbling. You're so desperate for something to pin your peace of mind to that you'll do all sorts of stupid things in its name. You don't mean to break up a marriage, but if breaking it up might let you sleep like a normal person again, suddenly you start considering it. You don't mean to become a drunk, but if drink is the only way you can keep a handle on some tiny compartment of your life then it's straight for the bottle."

The wind screams through the rafters. The candle has a little seizure, then settles again.

"And before you know it, you're just another balding idiot with nothing to show for himself but bankruptcy and a few keepsakes. All those sad bastards at my parents' dinner table were good people at some time. Something just got big on them and they folded. It could happen to anyone."

Matilda says quietly, "It's why I never hated Rupert Carnegie."

"Then you're braver than me."

"It wasn't bravery."

"I think it is. If you're going to forgive someone for something terrible, you have to be courageous, because you might forgive them and still feel angry about it, and then you'll never get it out of you. It's a gamble. It's a kind of courage."

"Thanks," she says.

"Don't mention it."

After a while she begins breathing deeply and regularly and John goes to close his own eyes, but notices something glinting on the desk: a small opal, cycling through the visible spectrum.

"Oi, wake up a second," he says. "What's that over there?"

"From my satchel. It's the same as the others," Matilda says sleepily.

"No," John says. "It's not."

FIFTY-ONE

The boy leads Mcalister to a warehouse on the outskirts of a deserted town. Everything inside is glittering and enormous, made of chrome and glass and some kind of fluid that vibrates, but holds a solid shape in the air. There is debris all about the floor, broken parts, tubing, balled parchment.

"I came here once when I was a boy," Beomus shouts, foraging behind a gigantic chrome cube.

"You're still a boy," the policeman says.

"When I was young then, pedant."

Mcalister cranes his neck up at the structures, some of them shapes that don't sit well with the eye when enough attention is paid. A walkway spirals up into the air, then meets with itself back on the ground without losing any height.

"This is a laboratory?" Mcalister says.

"Correct. Don't touch anything."

Beomus begins sorting through junk on the floor. "There was a man, the Arbiter of Worldworks. He was commissioned by Novelty himself to work here, given all the equipment he needed. This is back when we were all scientists of course, near on a universe ago."

"Where is he now, the arbiter?"

Beomus holds a glass cube up to the light, the thing glowing faintly purple. "Who knows? He insisted on asking certain pressing questions about the nature of reality. I don't go in for all that stuff myself, but he had a touch of obsession about him." The boy points to a hectic column of mesh and glass. "That, for example, is an entirely objective thermometer."

"Aren't they all?"

"No. They're relative to a scale, if you think about it."

"Who cares?"

"The Arbiter of Worldworks did."

Mcalister ambles aimlessly about the warehouse.

"To your left," the boy shouts. Mcalister looks to a structure, easily the largest device, the size of a small building, speckled with gleaming nodules and bubbles; antennae-like rods sticking from its bulk. "Have you ever wondered if you weren't just dreaming?"

"Sometimes, I guess. Doesn't everyone?"

"The arbiter grew obsessed that he might be. He disappeared for years and let no one inside the laboratory. Finally he announced that he had built a machine to *prove* the world was objective and not an illusion."

"You all have far too much time on your hands," Mcalister mutters. He runs a finger over the machine's body. One of the little nodules explodes.

"*Don't touch*, I said," Beomus yells. "Anyway, there was something of an argument about this at the time, between the philosophers. Say the arbiter's machine worked and he proved somehow that this layer of reality was a dream, or a really elaborate deception. What then?"

"You'd wake up, presumably."

"Sure, and then you're back to square one again, because how would you ever prove the next world up was anything more than just another trick?"

Mcalister says, "I suppose you'd eventually have to decide to do something else with your time. Like taking a walk. Or having a life."

"Or you build something so powerful that it's bound to collapse all of the realities above you, if there are realities above you."

"*Collapse?*"

"Destroy."

"That seems unnecessarily aggressive."

"He was that kind of arbiter."

The boy begins on another pile of discarded rubbish. "Novelty took issue with this, obviously, and banned his research. The arbiter disappeared into the Addled Forest after that. He left all of this junk behind."

Mcalister kicks at the debris. "And you're an *arbiter* too, right?"

"Sure. Of mischief."

"That sounds exciting."

The boy shrugs. "Duller than it sounds. You throw a little chaos into quantum mechanics and suddenly they're giving you official titles."

"Chaos into quantum mechanics? Then doesn't that make you Schrödinger's ca—"

"Don't," the boy growls. "Just don't."

Mcalister resists the urge to pat the youth on the head.

"Anyway," Beomus says. "The arbiter left in a hurry. I reckon there are a few useful things of his still here."

"Looks like junk to me." Mcalister sits himself on a workbench and watches the boy foraging. "Do you love, up here?"

The boy turns around suspiciously. "What?"

"I mean, how does it work? Do you have children?"

"This really isn't the right time."

"I feel like there isn't going to be a right time."

The boy puts a glittering sphere up to the light and peers through. "Yes, we love."

"In the same way we do?"

"No."

"How?"

"Why are you so curious about all of that? Hell, I take you to a storehouse of near on *magic*, and you want to know, what? If we screw?"

"Not just that, but yes."

Beomus gestures to the warehouse. "This is all a skin, to make it easier for you to understand. I told you that. Your little primate brain wouldn't be able to handle the reality in itself, okay?"

"Right."

"We aren't bags of meat. We don't have genitals. But yes, sometimes we do something similar to what you're referring, and yes, sometimes we have children. But it's a different kind of love. It's deeper."

"How?"

"Can we just finish what we've come here to do?"

"Why are you being so strange about all of this?"

The boy groans. "Because it's pointless. Even if I described it, you're not going to understand. How much about the intricacies of marriage could you explain to a Dalmatian?"

"I'm not married and I have a cat, not a dog."

Beomus rolls his eyes. "You're all getting worried about artificial intelligence right now, aren't you?" The policeman nods. "Well, judging by your books and movies, you think it's going to be mechanical and emotionless. It isn't. The higher you get on the intelligence spectrum, the more complicated the emotions a mind can experience. The reason why your dog, or your *cat*, wouldn't understand your marriage is because they aren't built to love, not really, not in the same way. We live longer than you. Our minds are different. We love in other ways. It's more consuming and love isn't even the correct word for it anyway, all right?"

"All right," Mcalister nods.

"And trying to explain it to you is pointless. Not because you're an idiot, but because you don't have the mental apparatus. So can we drop the subject?"

"Mmm…"

"What?"

Mcalister kicks idly at some metal filings. "Not to drag this out, but you said you've had other…*incarnations*?"

"That's right."

"So, people *come back*?"

Beomus cocks his head. "Ah, this is a big one and you lot are centuries away from cracking it."

"You can make an exception, can't you. Considering the circumstances."

The boy looks off into the distance. "Everything is a little bit conscious."

Mcalister waits for more. Nothing follows. "And *what does that mean*?"

"Yeah, just give me a second." He tries on the beginning of a sentence in his mouth, abandons it, tries another. "Everything is a little bit conscious, even atoms, all right? It's a fundamental property of the—"

"This sounds like New Age bullshit."

"Just shut up a second." Mcalister mimes zipping his lips closed. "Sentience is a fundamental property of matter, just like spin and charge. It's a pattern, a recursive one; doesn't matter if it's being run on a brain, a computer, or a planet — same as you could open a Word document on a PC or a phone, right? It's the information that's important. As long as that pattern is transmitted in its entirety from one point to the next, we can still say it's the same thing. If I took a snapshot of all of your molecules right now and destroyed them, then made an exact copy in Australia, it would still feel like you, wouldn't it?"

Mcalister considers this a moment. "Well…yes, but it wouldn't be me."

251

"Why not?"

"Because—" the policeman bites his lip. "I'm not sure. It just wouldn't."

"You all get over that obsession in a few centuries with the nano-fabricator, don't worry about it. Anyway, the point is that all matter, if arranged properly, is capable of supporting consciousness. It just needs to be able to carry high-level organisational structures. I know this is a lot to take in."

"Just a bit, yes."

"When an arbiter chooses to end their life, as they all do eventually, their mindstate is recycled, then reconstituted as a new arbiter. It's the patterns that are important, not the stuff supporting the pattern. The more complex the supporting base, the more complex the patterns it can support."

"And we're *reconstituted* too then?" Mcalister says. "People, I mean. When we die."

The boy eyes him seriously. "Yes. Mindstates are recycled in the Corporia."

"Then why don't I remember—"

"You really wouldn't want to. Think yourself lucky. That's a curse only arbiters enjoy."

"How many times do we come back?"

"Baby steps. Don't push it. However, to answer your question, yes, that's how Djall, Zorya, and I have been turning up in new bodies. Perfect transmission of a mindstate from one point to another. Etheric stuff."

"And that's how you brought us *here,* from Wilthail?"

"And that's how I brought us here, yes."

"Then what happened to our original bodies?"

"Oh, vaporised. Immediately actually." Mcalister stares, horrified. The boy tries to smile encouragingly. "It's the code that's important, not the computer. You still feel like you, right?"

Mcalister shrugs. "I guess. And this is all technology, not magic?"

The boy throws him a frown. "What did I say about not trying to put it in a box? You can't compress this stuff, not with your current apparatus. Baby steps, all right?"

"Yeah, yeah."

They go trudging back into the debris. Mcalister turns the new ideas over in his mind, looking for a mental shelf to leave them on. "You all seem extremely human," he says carefully.

"Not really. The Etheria is just trying to accommodate your miniature brain. We're closer to forces than people. That's the nearest I can get you to the truth."

"And you all speak in…you know, fantasy-language, with long words."

Beomus taps the policeman's head. "Again, the Etheria's trying to be nice to you. Evidently some part of your mind thinks we should talk like Tolkien characters. It's your lack of imagination to blame, not ours."

"Lack of imagination," Mcalister echoes quietly.

He stares at the walls, at the machines, at the boy.

To see what is really there, he thinks. All the time. Behind the veil. To know Things in Themselves, Truly. That's a noble goal.

The boy plucks a drawstring pouch from the ground, looks inside, sniffs. "Before the Arbiter of Worldworks built his machine, he tried other methods of waking a mind up to the realities above it. Some were violent. Others," he proffers the bag, "were less invasive."

"What's that? Drugs?"

"Drugs induce hallucination. This powder does quite the opposite."

"How can you be sure?"

"Ah," the boy smiles. "Now you're thinking like an arbiter. You can't be sure, of course. Hence why the Arbiter of Worldworks was such a lunatic."

The boy buries his nose in the bag for a moment and closes his eyes. When he opens them again, they're raging purple, and his face is dancing with pale fire.

FIFTY-TWO

Derrick Thomas and Aubrey Rhodes live in the Wisteria Bed and Breakfast for several days, learning Morse code from a book they found in the library. They sit for seven or so hours at a time with bells from the reception desk on their laps and ring them at each other, then consult the book.

"The raik in Spain," Derrick rings in dots and dashes.

"*Rain*," Aubrey replies.

"Rain," Derrick rings. "Yeah."

Robyn Appleby's car has driven past a few times, but otherwise the village is silent. As the sky dies to dark again towards the evening, there are sometimes howls and screeches and footsteps passing by the door.

They have not felt tired in these bodies, or hungry, or thirsty. There's no sense of fatigue from their walks. Aubrey has looked for a battery or power source several times, but the effort is pointless, always tracing his smooth plastic skin and finding no lip or aberrations of any kind. They dress themselves in clothes left behind by guests, in corduroy and dressing gowns and they feel a little more like real men then. Derrick has adapted to missing an arm.

"I think I remember dying," Derrick rings out with his bell one afternoon.

"Same," Aubrey replies.

It is the silence that's so horrible, Aubrey thinks. Just the creaking of plastic for weeks on end and trusting that there's another person in that strange body.

There is a screech from outside, then a cry like a dog being butchered.

"How. You. How happen. Death," Derrick rings, ignoring the noise.

"Brain tumour. Went on for ages," Aubrey rings back. "Not sure how I went."

Aubrey considers this delicately, then opens the green notebook and searches for a page and hands it across. A few days ago they broke into Officer Mcalister's place. They weren't sure what they were looking for, but it was the last house they hadn't checked. They took a few of his books and looked through his family photos, then Aubrey came on a small green notebook with almost illegible scribble inside.

Aubrey points to a particular section on the page now: "*Third suspicious death in 4 years. Derrick Thomas was diabetic, type 1. Last prescription actioned by Robyn Appleby. Financial issues with funeral business. Possible motive for murder. Needs further investigation.*"

Derrick is motionless for a while, then rings out, "Never had any problem with Robyn."

Aubrey turns the page, points again. "*Recovered insulin vial from Thomas' premises. Label indicates U-100. Sent away for testing. Residue in vial is at least five times that.*"

Derrick gets up and methodically throws each item off of the mantelpiece. When that's done, he tries to hurl the television, but the thing only slips in his plastic grip. Instead he smashes the screen with the poker from the fire. Finally he picks up his bell and rings very slowly: "T-H-E F-U-C-K-E-R."

"Yes," Aubrey rings.

"T-H-E F-U-C-K-E-R."

"What do you want to do?"

"Kill."

"How?" Aubrey holds up his plastic hands to serve as a stark reminder of their current condition.

Derrick is still.

There is a clattering from outside, light at first, then like sheet metal being twisted. The knitting needle rain has begun again.

"The incinerator," Derrick rings. "The incinerator. The incinerator."

"How do we get him there?"

"Not for him. Us."

Derrick balls his fists. Animals must feel like this, he thinks. All hatred and no outlet, no room for love or stoicism anymore, just the desire to witness something die, watch its eyes close for the last time.

"Okay," Aubrey rings. "When?"

"Tomorrow. When it's light. We go in together."

Aubrey nods. "You think that will work?"

"Only choice we have. Can't live like this."

They read newspapers all evening and watch the coils of light dancing in the sky, and by eleven the next morning they're ready with their backpacks. They make out into the street, Derrick leading as always, their little reception bells tied to their necks. They turn down Precosa Street.

"Where are you going?" Aubrey rings on his bell.

Derrick keeps walking and before long they have rounded the street. Thomas' former house is ahead, boards over the windows. He peeks in through a crack: just dark and dust.

"Want to go inside?" Aubrey rings.

Derrick shakes his head. They continue walking.

FIFTY-THREE

Eric joins the dinner table, Alf and Eric's father already waiting there. Alf grins and hands the boy a napkin. Mr. Crane is only staring at his empty plate, face blank. Mrs. Crane brings in vegetables first, then a tray of steaming meat and sets it down on the table and deals each of them a huge serving. Eric pokes the meat with his fork.

"What's this?" he says.

"Alf caught it today," Mrs. Crane says.

"Like, hunted it?"

"That's right," Alf says. "Know a thing or two about hunting, I do."

"What is it?"

"Eric," Mrs. Crane snaps.

There is a little fur on some of the meat and Eric tries to cut around it. It looks a bit like chicken. He puts it to his nose. It doesn't smell like chicken.

"I'm rather *thirsty*," Alf says and toys with his glass. Mr. Crane looks up from his meat. "I said I'm rather *thirsty*," Alf says again. Mr. Crane collects his brother's glass mechanically and returns with a little beer in it. "Perhaps I should take young Eric hunting someday soon," Alf says.

"Would you like that, Eric?" Mrs. Crane says.

Eric shrugs.

"Put some hairs on his chest," Alf says. "Bit of a scrawny chap at the moment, aren't you?"

"Doesn't eat his greens, that's his problem," Mrs. Crane says.

Eric nods.

"You've done very well, Alf," Mrs. Crane says. "The meat is delicious."

"Don't get used to it. The army should be here any day soon and we'll be back to caviar and champagne in no time, you see if I'm wrong!" Alf says.

"I do hope you'll still be staying with us, even if things return to normal."

"Just say the word and I'll stay as long as you like," Alf replies in a rather deep voice.

Mr. Crane puts his fork down. "Thanks. That was nice."

"But you're not even finished," Mrs. Crane mutters.

"I'm not hungry."

He pushes in his chair and the three of them listen to him traipsing upstairs to the study and shutting the door.

"Miserable. So so miserable…" Mrs. Crane says.

"Always was the angsty one," Alf says.

Eric averts his eyes from the table, examines the living room. The sofa is an unmade bed where Mr. Crane has been sleeping the last few nights. His alarm clock and a book lay on top of the sheets. Eric intentionally does not consider the reasoning behind this change of sleeping arrangements. The politics of adulthood rarely yields pleasantness when inspected closely, he has learned.

Alf shoots a glance at Eric. "I went for a walk today, into the forest. What's that boy's name who used to bully you? Tom Downing? Well, he was hanging from a tree.

All dead, he was. How about that! His whole family too. Who got the last laugh, eh?"

Eric stares at the man, at his glaring red cheeks, at his red hair and sideburns. I hope something terrible gets at you, Eric thinks. I hope it eats you up.

The room dims slightly. "I am quite happy here," Alf says without his mouth moving. "You and I could be the best of friends."

Eric looks to his mother. She's still eating contentedly.

"I don't want to be friends," Eric says.

"Well I do, and I'm going to be staying here a long while, so you might as well just get used to it, I'm afraid."

"What have you done to Mr. Lees?"

"Kevin Lees was finished with his body. I'm fascinated with bodies, you see. Recently I'm all about your mother's."

Eric's heart hammers. A knot is pulling tighter and tighter in his stomach.

I hope something terrible gets at you, he thinks again.

"No," Alf says. "Not today, thank you."

"More vegetables, Eric?" asks Mrs. Crane. The room has returned to its usual shade of gloom. Eric shakes his head.

"Puts hairs on your chest," she says and gives Alf a wink.

Alf keeps his eyes on the boy.

Eric rearranges the meat on his plate to keep his hands busy and there, underneath a slab of the stuff, is a small metal disc on a chain. He hooks the disc with his fork and it reads: *Polly*, followed by a home number and vet number.

"What's that there?" Alf says and grabs the disc and puts it in his top pocket. "A little wishbone? I'll save it for later."

"That wasn't a wishbone," Eric says.

"If I say it was a wishbone, then it was a wishbone," Alf smiles.

The blood rain begins and the smell of iron seeps into the room. "I'd like to be excused from the table," Eric says.

"Permission denied," Alf says.

Eric pushes his plate away.

"You've barely touched your food," Mrs. Crane says.

"I'll eat it later."

"Boy," Alf barks, but Eric rushes out and climbs the stairs in double steps. He spies his father through a crack in the door of the study, sitting at his desk and drinking something brown from a glass.

"Hi," Eric says.

"I think I've gone mad," Mr. Crane says wearily. Something in Eric does not want to witness his own father like this. He is vaguely aware of the fact that the man isn't really immortal or all-knowing, but the thought of being presented with actual evidence to support this is too much to bear.

"It's all right," Eric says. His father tries to smile.

They stare out of the window for a while. The blood rain has stopped now and the streets are red, and gelatinous lumps of clotted blood sit in gutters and on car bonnets. House windows are smashed and front doors are left open and driveways are empty. The streets are full of debris, of tyres, of food, of shoes, of open suitcases with their insides scattered.

Eric sits on his father's lap and puts his head on the man's shoulder.

"Reckon you still want to hang out with me if I've gone mad?" his father says.

Eric nods.

There is an animal cry from the next street and Mrs. Herrity and her daughter appear below, running hand in hand, pursued by dark blurs. The women pause at the intersection for a moment, look left then right, and finally decide to head left. Mr. Crane puts a hand over his son's eyes. Mrs. Herrity lets out a strangled scream and her daughter's follows shortly after. The street is silent again.

FIFTY-FOUR

Jennifer Rhodes waits for the sound of Robyn's car driving off, then comes out from her hiding place behind the tree and walks back through the forest. It is perfectly quiet now. She finds the little boy again easily enough. He is still sat on the ground, dealing out cards to himself. She hikes up her dress and sits cross-legged opposite him and watches in silence for a time. The cards bear new painted faces among the old ones now: Derrick Thomas and Aubrey Rhodes.

"What are you?" Jennifer says.

"What are you?" the boy replies.

"I'm not sure how to answer that."

"Well then." He deals out the whole pack, takes Rupert Carnegie's card, rips it into pieces, and puts the pieces in his pocket.

"What's going on?" Jennifer says.

"Entropy," the boy says.

She spies the hanging figures through the trees. "Did you kill them all?" she says. The boy shakes his head. "Then what did?"

"Entropy," the boy says.

She watches him rearranging the cards into new positions, grouping the villagers with one another and separating them again.

"Are you from Wilthail?" Jennifer says.

"No."

"Where did you come from?"

The boy stays quiet. Jennifer lies down on the ground. The dirt smells like death. She lets it stick to her face. The boy puts his cards away and lies down next to her. She lights a cigarette. The boy takes it from her, smokes a while, passes it back.

"Now you can ask me what you came here to," the boy says.

Jennifer turns the question over in her mind for a moment. "Why is there death in the world?"

"Life's even stranger, but you don't ask after that."

"I guess death is the only one I want to understand right now."

"There is understanding," the boy says, "and then there is knowing." He brings something from nothing, a noose in his hand. "You can know it, if you like."

She takes the rope. The boy produces his cards again and begins dealing them on the floor. He gives Jennifer her own card. She rips it up without much hesitation, hands him back the pieces, and tousles the child's hair a little. "Thank you," she says.

"It's all right."

She looks for a quiet patch among the hanging bodies and finds one, not far from Millie Connors. The girl's face is peaceful.

All trials ended, Jennifer thinks. All assignments handed in and no homework.

With her skirt rolled up, she climbs the tree and fastens the noose and ties a triple knot to make sure. She watches her thoughts idly and waits for something profound, but nothing comes, not a quote, not a line of old poetry. Then she puts the noose over her neck and sits on the branch for a while. She can still make out the boy below, dealing his cards.

None of it meant anything, she thinks. Or maybe it did and I was just too stupid to figure it all out. God, I tried but there are so many moving parts. Maybe I'm just a dumb animal staring at a chalkboard covered in some brilliant equation and it's all going right over my head.

She tightens the noose and moves to the end of the branch and her bare feet dangle free.

I hope it all meant something and I was just too stupid to get it, she thinks. I hope it's that, because if it's the other thing then I'd rather have not been born at all.

Aubrey. You meant something. Everything, I'd say.

She looks for the boy again. He still sits cross-legged, but has been replaced by a man now, grey-haired, wearing purple robes: Augustus Rawlings. He nods to her.

She nods back, then pushes off from the branch.

FIFTY-FIVE

Matilda watches John in the half-dark. He gesticulates with the flashing opal in his hand. "If you were going to put someone in such a strange situation, why make the whole thing a hall of mirrors?"

Matilda shrugs, still in bed. "Maybe they're just reflections and that's it."

"There'd be no point to a game like that."

"It doesn't have to mean anything, you know." She frowns. "God, I'm starting to sound just like you."

He holds the opal up. "This was designed. It has a function. All the artifacts do. The other churches appeared when the first stone ended up under the blacklight. Why?"

"Look, this is all very serious. Why don't you come over here a minute?"

When they're done he waits a polite ten minutes or so, then gets out of bed and studies the opal again.

"I'm a little tired," Matilda says. "I might drift off."

"You're no fun when you've got what you want," he murmurs.

"I hope that wasn't a complaint. If it was, we can always go back to sleeping in separate beds."

"Complaint rescinded."

"That's good."

He thumbs the opal idly for a while, watches its frenetic cycle through the rainbow.

Matilda dreams a little: all black, punctuated now and then with faces, mostly her mother's, the old woman frail and quiet, though still alive.

Then Whistle's voice: "Hey."

"Jesus Christ, John."

"Put some clothes on. We'll sleep later."

"What is it?"

He leads her up to the church, the two of them barely clothed, aged, sagging a little, fat around the middles. The original stone is still under the blacklight on the altar, keeping the other belfries visible.

"Even if you wanted to tease someone, you'd still give them a chance. Where's the fun in an impossible puzzle? Watch this," John says and puts the flashing opal alongside the stone. Drenched in UV now, it settles on a single colour: purple.

They say nothing for a moment. Matilda squints. "What does that mean?"

"Tell me the first purple thing that comes to you." John fetches a sketchpad and marker pen.

"I don't know — an elephant?"

"Elephants aren't purple," he mutters and draws a half-decent one with its trunk raised all majestically. "Come on."

He starts up the steps to the belfry. Matilda follows. At the top they make out the other Johns and Matildas, all stood in their own belfries under the midnight dark. Whistle raises the sketchpad in the air. The others do the same.

Matilda glasses the other churches with the binoculars.

"Well?" Whistle says. "*Well*?"

"A giraffe," she says quietly. "And a monkey. And I'm not sure what the hell that is." She puts the binoculars down. "What's going on?"

"We've cleaved all the permutations. All it took was a variation, just a tiny one, enough to deviate what would've been an identical course of events. The other opals chose their own colours. That's what they were for. We're on separate tracks now."

"So we can talk to them?" she says slowly.

He hands her the sketchpad and pen. "We'll light the torch if we want to speak," he says. "The other versions will have worked that out too, let's hope."

John holds the torch up and Matilda scribbles, then raises the sketchpad as high as she can: *Guten Abend.*

A pause, then another torch, distant. Matilda squints through the binoculars. *John's pretty clever, huh,* the sketchpad reads.

All right with his hands too, Matilda responds.

"Stop that," John snaps.

She examines the other couples through the binoculars. "Are they still us?"

"Depends on what you mean. Yes, for the most part, but leave it a few days and the divide will get larger."

"What do you mean?"

"They're going to start having new experiences, experiences we won't in our church. Small things I expect, but significant. One of them might stub their toe or something and voila, you've got a completely divergent set of causal chains. It's like two identical twins — the same genetics, the same parents. From the beginning they may as well be the same person, but just a little variation in the way they're treated, in the experiences they have, and suddenly they're wildly different people."

"How different?" Matilda says. She squints through the binoculars again and notices she's the only Matilda doing so.

"Different enough. Who knows?"

"One of the sets is turned away."

"What?"

"They're turned away. I don't think they want us to read their lips."

"Maybe they're just standing at an angle. There hasn't been enough time to diverge yet. We can get nervous when they start behaving in ways we don't recognise."

They watch the scene in silence for a while. The night is windless.

"We should meet, all of us," Whistle says finally.

"Do you think that's a good idea?"

"I haven't a clue, but we've come this far."

FIFTY-SIX

Jamie lies with his head on the ground. Time passes at an indiscernible rate. The mist conjures abstract shapes in its folds and dissolves them again.

There is a voice, a woman's, and she says, "Drink."

Water trickles into his mouth and he swallows. A little more and he bats it away. He opens his eyes. Zoe Whistle stands over him. "There's a stream a little way off," she says.

Jamie grunts.

"You want to see?"

"No."

"If you don't get up, I might just pour the rest of this cold water on you instead." He rolls back over in the mud. "I'm sorry about your father, but we don't have all that much time," Zoe says.

Jamie grunts again.

She gives him a kick. "Fucking snap out of it. We *don't have time.*"

He lies still and focuses on a leaf in front of him, the thing all dry and dead. Zoe produces a load of daisies plaited into a chain and puts his hand through and ties it off. "There," she says. "You're all pretty now. Have you ever seen a pretty person in the mud? That's not where they live."

"This isn't my permanent residence, it's just a holiday," he says. He listens to the sound of his own breathing for a long time. Then he says, "Where were you before the... gameshow?"

"Around and about."

"What?"

"Something was calling to me. It was a very low voice. I first heard it when I was dreaming, then all the time."

It had been a murmur at first, like a distant ocean. It grew closer and closer until it sounded right outside the window. She mentioned it to John Whistle, but he only stared at her vacantly. Her medication was low already and she didn't want him worrying. The growl called her name like a lover would. And again. She grew to yearn for it, a sort of sexual pull.

She waited until her father had left the house for soup and made out into the evening. Shadows stalked her in the streets, but she wasn't so afraid.

They will leave you alone, the voice assured her.

She entered the forest and there was a lit trail of glimmering trees to guide her. She walked for an hour or so until she was thirsty like she couldn't ever remember being thirsty before. A figure stood ahead of her, Fikri, who had marked her arms with his knife. He called her name, but she ignored him and walked on. There was Donya next, fat and old, and she called Zoe's name as Fikri had, but still she walked on.

Figures were chained to the trees, creatures twice her size with rippled chests, with too many arms, with blood on their mouths and their noses, and they bayed and cried and watched her with hungry eyes. She was not sure if they were real, but she passed them by, drawn on by her thirst and the voice.

Finally she came to a clearing. Centrally there was a table with two chairs. A figure sat in one of the chairs. He gestured to a glass on the table, full of water.

"Please," he said.

She drained the contents in three gulps. The glass refilled itself. She drank again and put it back.

"Mr. Rawlings," she said. "I think we met at Derrick Thomas' funeral."

Augustus smiled and beckoned her to sit and she sat. "A fine evening for stargazing tonight," he said. "Only, I think you don't recognise these constellations." Zoe shook her head. "I knew all of them once, their names and stories. Ah, how we forget as we age!"

Softly Zoe said, "How old are you?"

His face turned the colour of roadkill and his bottom lip fell off to reveal rotten teeth. "Old," he said.

She went to stand. The chair flew into her legs and pushed her back to a sitting position.

"Let's talk a while," Rawlings said sweetly.

"What were those things in the trees?"

"Creatures that couldn't age properly. It takes *courage* to live so long. It takes *stamina*. Some minds aren't suited for it. They warp. They come here."

"I don't understand."

"You're used to institutions now, I should think. I trust you to recognise one more."

"There were usually beds in the ones I've been to before."

"These patients don't sleep, as is conducive to their recovery!" He slapped his leg. "Ah! I was a doctor some time ago, took the oath. And I was a grave digger too. Such misfortune that I wasn't incarnated as a germ, then I might have seen the whole game from both sides!"

"I think I might go home," Zoe said.

"You're closer to home here than you would be out there," Rawlings said and leant into the table. One eye was missing now, just a bleeding socket. The other bore into her. "I cannot decide if you have forgotten, or you're only pretending. You can be such a tease."

"I really would like to go home now."

"I have been chasing the boy all of this time," he said. "I did not imagine I would find you here also."

Figures emerged from the trees with spines that jutted from their backs, hunched, their eyes glazed and red and bulging. They all stared at Zoe Whistle.

"I have sought to undo everything of yours," Rawlings said. "It's been a fine game so far."

"I really don't know what you're talking about," she said and stood to her feet.

The creatures hissed and Rawlings jumped from his chair and grabbed her face. He stared into her eyes and his pupils burned purple. Inside the pupils, she saw, was a kaleidoscope of infinite stars, all dying. She tried not to scream.

He threw her aside. "You're Corporic, yet you reek of Novelty. What kind of a trick is that?" His skin began to fall away in clumps, revealing the muscles and tissue beneath.

"I don't know what the fuck you're talking about," Zoe shouted. The creatures sauntered back into the trees, unimpressed. "I'd just like to go home, please."

FIFTY-SEVEN

Beomus and Mcalister trudge silently through a desert of green sand. Finally they come to a great canyon, stretching ahead for miles, the whole thing apparently made of glass and glowing faintly purple. Beomus leads them to a small shack along the edge and knocks on the door. The door is drawn back slowly and an old woman waits behind it. Her eyes are pupilless and her hair is full of twigs and plant matter. She looks the boy up and down, then the policeman. "You're an idiot," she says finally.

"I know," Beomus says.

"You're a damn idiot."

"Yes, I know."

She shows them in. The shack is simple inside, only the most basic requirements for living. The old woman sets a kettle above a green flame and motions that the two men sit down.

"He's a damn idiot," she says.

"I know," Mcalister nods.

"And you're a damn idiot too."

"Am I?"

"Yes, to get mixed up in all of this."

"I don't think I had a choice."

"Terrible excuse." She pours three cups of tea when the water is ready and distributes them.

"This is the crone," Beomus says. "She's been good to me so far."

"As one might show mercy to a moth, were it trapped in your house," the old woman mutters. The purple canyon glows to itself beyond the window. "How many incarnations now?"

"Enough," Beomus replies.

She squeezes his cheeks and looks into his eyes. "You're not so old yet." She catches Mcalister's gaze. "You've no idea what you're embroiled in, do you?"

Mcalister shakes his head. "Not really, to tell the truth."

"Your friend, your *feline*, is a romantic; the classic sort, who would take another man's wife from him just for the pleasure of it."

"That's hardly fair," Beomus murmurs.

"Isn't it? If there's more to the matter, now would be the time to tell me so. I've been watching."

"Have you?"

"Of course." She takes a bound volume from the desk and flicks through the pages idly. "Beginning in 25,654 BC. You were maimed by a mountain lion, a complete waste of an incarnation. 4,560 AD, thrown out of an airlock for trying to incite mutiny aboard a starship. I've been keeping notes on the others too."

"Zorya," Beomus says.

"Yes, she's in here, passing by, sometimes born only weeks after your death. Centuries before on other occasions."

"But you've found each other in Wilthail," Mcalister says. "Mary Rawlings, right?"

"Through no effort on his part," the crone says. "Djall sacrificed the rest of his own incarnations to bring them all together, to your village. A stupid strategy. Took the last of their incarnations too."

"We went to the library," Beomus says.

"I know."

"I read my own histories."

"I know. Idiot."

The boy shrugs and sips his tea. "Best course of action I could think of. The histories said you're living in exile?"

"Djall was less than best pleased about me helping you those years ago, banished me here, via his minions. It's no matter. Your biography, did you read ahead?"

"No."

"You're lying."

"What does it matter?"

"It matters," she says, a hair's breadth from shouting, "because if you read ahead then the future is fixed. As you damn well know."

"Wouldn't it have been anyway?"

"*No.* It doesn't work like that. Ah, but you've that I-know-better look in your eye. You think you're going to change it, no doubt."

"I didn't read ahead. The librarian ruined everything."

"You're a damn idiot."

She sets her gaze on the policeman. "And what have you done to him?"

"Nothing," the boy says.

She squashes Mcalister's cheeks and peers into his eyes. "He's turning."

"Yes," Beomus says quietly.

"*Turning?*" the policeman says.

"Like I told you," Beomus groans. "You've been here too long. You're changing."

"Into what?"

Beomus and the crone exchange a glance. "We're not sure," the crone says. "But you've been speaking in our tongue from the moment you stepped in here."

"We're going home, aren't we?" Mcalister says. "I'll be fine when I get back to Wilthail."

Beomus and the crone exchange another glance. "No," Beomus says gently. "You won't."

The crone rolls her eyes. "The lad brought you here so I can put you to sleep for a while. He thinks that will halt the process."

"You said we were close to Wilthail or the forest, or Novelty, or whatever it is. We can just go home," Mcalister protests.

"We're close, yes. That isn't the problem," Beomus says in a schoolteacher's voice. "Wilthail and the forest is right on the other side of the Glass Canyon." He points to the great glowing mass beyond the window. "But you won't survive the trip through it."

"It's where we send our children," the crone says, "when they're ready. It changes them."

"How?" Mcalister says.

"It shows them the World in Itself, Truly. One doesn't return from that still caring about racing cars and cleavage."

"I don't care about those things anyway," Mcalister mutters.

"In fairness I still like both," Beomus says.

"I'll walk through it with you, I don't care. Whatever we have to do," the policeman says.

"Haven't you been listening?" the boy says. "There's no coming back. Probably it will just turn your mind to mush and that will be that."

"Stay," the crone says. "I'll put you to sleep, a dreamless one. When all of this is over, I'll wake you. The world-schism will be open again and you can go back home that way instead, as you are now."

The policeman eyes the old woman suspiciously. "*When all of this is over.* What do you mean by that?"

"When Djall is dead," Beomus says. "I have to end him in the Corporia. He can't be hurt elsewhere. It's the only way to settle this."

"It's not the only way," the crone says.

"It's the only way I'll accept. Then Zorya and I can return to the Etheria and we won't bother Wilthail again." To the crone: "But you've written the histories. You must know how this ends."

She shakes her head. "I drink a brew to forget whenever I finish a volume. Besides, even if I knew I wouldn't tell you."

"Then see ahead, just a little. Tell us what to do."

"Not in ten billion years, not again. You're better for staying ignorant anyway. It'll give you hope."

"I don't want hope. I want certainty."

"Too bad." She gestures at Mcalister. "Now you know how it must be to live like one of them." They watch the policeman in silence as he finishes his tea. Then the crone asks, "Jennifer Rhodes. You knew her?"

"Of course," Mcalister says.

"I'm afraid something has happened."

"What?"

"She's passed away. It wasn't distressing. She chose to."

"Then she lives here now?"

"Not quite," Beomus says slowly.

"What about the ocean, all my dead twins?"

"That's just a stopover point before mindstates are recycled."

"To go where?"

"The same place you all go when you die."

"Back into the Gestalt," Mcalister says flatly, thinking of the universe living in Beomus' eye.

"Back into the Gestalt, back into the world," Beomus agrees. "We can't track her, she's not an arbiter. And she won't remember much of her life as Jennifer Rhodes. She could be centuries away now."

"Why did she die?" Mcalister asks.

"Djall has been terrorising the village, trying to goad the idiot boy back," the crone says. "There's nobody

278

around to stop him. With the Addled Forest trapped halfway in the Corporia, he has all the mad arbiters at his disposal that he needs. They'll be possessing dead bodies and all sorts of merry hell by now. Rawlings is on his last incarnation. Desperation breeds a certain malevolence. He's turned the village into a—" she searches for the correct word.

"Hell," Beomus says.

The crone nods. "Nothing short of a hell. All the mad arbiters stalk the streets at night. They've been eating children, tempting folk into the forest, doing unspeakables."

"Only cloak and dagger stuff so far. He's scared if he acts up too much, Novelty will make an appearance and kick his ass," Beomus says.

"Delightful," Mcalister nods. He looks out over the Glass Canyon. "Who else is dead?"

"Kevin Lees. An accident," the crone says. "A barrier came over Wilthail when it was split from the normal timestream, thanks to your little prince of milk here."

"Would you all stop fucking calling me that?" Beomus snaps.

"Lees drove straight into the thing. A number of families have ended their lives out of despair also. That's all I know."

"And they're all just gone now…recycled?" Mcalister says.

The crone nods. "Most of them. Better that way, perhaps."

"When does it stop?"

The crone catches him with her pupilless stare. "What's that?"

"When does the process stop? From life to life, not remembering any of it. What's the point?"

"I showed you the Gestalt," Beomus says. "Don't you remember?"

Mcalister rubs his forehead. "It's hard to hold on to. The thing was so big and weird."

The crone refills the policeman's teacup and bends down to his ear and drops to an almost-whisper: "It just keeps going. Up and up."

"Then how many souls, how many *mindstates*, are there? In the whole of the...Corporia?"

Beomus winks. "Just one."

Mcalister takes a deep breath. "Then how many are up here?"

"Just one," the boy says again. "There's only ever one. It starts as an atom in the Corporia, and ends in the Etheria as Novelty himself. Ten to the power of ninety-one incarnations. That's how many it takes. One mindstate coming back, over and over."

"I think that's enough for our Corporic friend today," the crone murmurs.

"No," Mcalister says, trying not to raise his voice. "What about your kind? If there's only one of you, then you remember all of it? Every life — you remember being each other?"

"Sure," the crone says. She glances at Beomus. "*He* wasn't my fondest incarnation."

"Then don't you also remember what everyone you've been is going to do?"

"That's right," the old woman nods. "But our memories aren't perfect. We recall some of the highlights, certainly."

"You must remember the rest of it, then," Mcalister says carefully. "Being everyone in the *Corporia*."

"That's right. Being *you*, tubby," Beomus grins. "And the ham you ate in your sandwich last month. And the fish in your pond before that. Only one mindstate doubling back on itself. Up and up. It's a long game."

"You said you were another species."

"A white lie. You lot, just later. Does that sound better?"

"One mindstate…" Mcalister says.

"One mindstate," the boy echoes. "Isn't evolution fun?"

"One mindstate coming back until what?"

"We're not sure. Novelty's got that covered, hopefully. The old man knows what he's doing."

The two Etherics stare at the policeman, his face blank now. "You've broken him," the crone whispers.

"Give him a second," Beomus says. "Anyway, speaking of Novelty, the plan was to find him."

The crone raises an eyebrow. "You think *now* is the time?"

"Who the hell is Novelty anyway?" Mcalister says.

"I told you, an arbiter," Beomus explains. "He's been hiding in Wilthail this whole time as a Corporic, expunged his own memory for safety. Probably thinks he really *is* a Corporic now."

"Seems a bit of a coincidence that you, Novelty, and the Rawlings couple end up in Wilthail at the same time, doesn't it?"

"No," Beomus says, his eyes on the crone. "Likely someone engineered it that way."

The old woman shrugs. "I can neither confirm nor deny."

A silence. Then Mcalister asks in a dark voice, "And what if Novelty was Jennifer Rhodes or Kevin Lees?"

"Then everything is lost," Beomus says.

"Then everything is lost," the crone agrees. "He'll be recycled right back to the beginning of the Gestalt. It's a loop."

"Back to an atom?" Mcalister asks carefully.

"Back to an atom, yes."

"How many atoms?"

Beomus grins again. "Oh, all of them. One by one." The policeman lets out a small involuntary whine. "If it makes you feel better, you've already done that bit. Lucky you don't remember, eh?"

"Every atom, every molecule," Mcalister says quietly.

"And rock," Beomus agrees.

"And fly," the crone adds cheerfully. "And bird, and tiger."

"One mindstate. From birth until death," Mcalister says.

"From birth until death, to the end of creation and back again," Beomus says. "Then up and up, to the next level. Physics, chemistry, biology, teleology, chronology, the Etheria, Entropy, and finally Novelty. Capiche?" He gestures playfully to himself, head to toe. "Look where you'll be in a few trillion incarnations, tubby. Isn't it grand?"

"Your girlfriend," Mcalister says slowly.

"What?"

"You've…been your girlfriend?"

"Mary Rawlings?" Beomus says, as though to a child. Mcalister nods. "That's a rather personal question, but she's older than me, actually."

"Then—"

"It's complicated."

"She's screwing herself," Mcalister says.

"Really, it's complicated. I don't expect you to understand all of the nuances."

"She's literally screwing herself. That is disgusting."

The crone smiles. "In any case lad, you should go."

Beomus stands and kisses the crone on both cheeks. "Stay," he says to the policeman. "Stay here and sleep. There's nothing in Wilthail for you now. The crone will see to it you get home safely, when this is all done."

"When you're dead. That's what you mean isn't it?"

"When the grudge is settled, however it pans out." Beomus nods to the canyon. "That's the only way through, and you almost certainly won't survive it. We've told you what will happen."

"Stay, Mcalister," says the crone. "For everyone's sake. I'll make you a little sleeping tea and you'll be in the land of nod before you know it. Your prince of milk will be fine without you for a while, I'm sure."

Beomus puts a hand on the policeman's shoulder and speaks to him mentally. *They might all die, your friends. Some of them are dead already. I don't want you watching. And I don't want you going the same way. Stay here with the crone. This is where we part ways. The great tragedy isn't death. It's losing each other across history. You understand that now, don't you? I'd like to see you again. So stay here until it's over.* He rubs the policeman's ear a little as one might a pet's. *I don't want anything happening to you.*

FIFTY-EIGHT

It had taken three hours to arrange. First, each set of couples assigned themselves numbers one to six, and wrote them on their respective sketchpads. One of the couples, Matilda 4 and John 4, flipped a coin until it was decided by process of elimination that all of the sets would meet at Matilda 4 and John 4's church.

John and Matilda made downstairs. The opal was still glowing purple under the blacklight, its five sisters lit some other colour in the neighbouring churches. They packed a few things into a holdall, then woke Father Liptrot.

"Mmm," the priest moaned, red-eyed.

"Father, we're going now. We might not be back for a little while," John said. He untied the rope about Liptrot's arm, then the other. "You can do what you like, but please don't follow us, understand?" The priest nodded. "There's water upstairs and a little food. It should keep you going for a few days if we don't come back for some reason. After that, there's still some stuff in the village shop."

"Let's go," Matilda said.

It was four o'clock by Whistle's watch, several hours before the dark shapes usually appeared from the forest and came knocking on the church door.

Outside, the graveyard is all mist and marsh and something has broken a few of the gravestones in two. They close the door behind them. The five other churches appear like ghosts through the murk and vanish again as the fog warps.

Matilda takes John's hand. He feels himself in a book, the kind with ghouls that suddenly appear from behind trees and beheaded brides who shriek and wail and brandish knives. He threads his fingers through the librarian's.

They come on a leg, a woman's judging by the shape, severed above the knee. John stops to examine it but Matilda pulls him on.

There is the noise of a church door closing to their left, then the same noise to their right.

"Sometimes," Matilda says quietly, "when I was a kid, I used to stay up as late as I could. I thought that when I went to sleep I would die, and then I'd be replaced in the morning by someone who felt exactly like me and had all my memories, but wasn't really me at all."

"But it would be you," John says. "Sort of."

They walk in silence for a little while, then John points through the murk: two figures up ahead.

"Hi," the other John mumbles.

John nods. "Not sure what to think about all this."

"Let's not and say we did."

They walk further, the four of them, into the gloom and towards the church that was agreed as the meeting point. More couples join them in silence until they're ten strong. John watches his doppelgängers from behind, the movement of their shoulders. My posture's all wrong, he thinks. And no one ever thought to tell me.

The meeting church is close now, the doors already open. The ten of them trudge around the wall to the gate.

"A queer gang," says a small bespectacled old man, sitting on the wall. The group pauses. "Many similar faces."

"It's a long story," John says.

"I've a moment. Care to tell it?"

"No thank you. We're here to meet our friends."

The old man looks over his shoulder at the waiting Matilda and John inside the church. Then he vaults off the wall and stands blocking the gate. He peers up through thick glasses at one of the Johns. "Standard deviation, nothing major as yet. I had rather hoped you'd stay isolated a little longer, a few more days perhaps. To really diverge, you understand."

"What is going on?" John growls.

"A get-together," the little man says, "by the look of things." He touches the church gate with a silver hook and it fuses itself to the wall.

"Get the hell back from there," John shouts.

"Your women are clever. They've found my devices."

"You can have them all back."

"That would make me something of an Indian giver." He peers up at a Matilda. "Abnormal deviation with this one, elevated oxytocin. The chemical beginnings of more than mere infatuation?" He touches her with the silver hook. She screams and doubles over. "Two seeds," continues the little man, "both from the same flower. Now, exposed to the same amount of sunlight we would expect them to grow to the same height, yes?"

The Johns crowd over Matilda. Blood gushes from her stomach and her face is deathly white. A John rolls up her jumper. The flesh is torn wide open and there is a cavity where her stomach and intestines should be.

"But of course there is more to it than that," the little man says. "The ground might be slightly higher for one seed. There may be a little more nitrogen in its soil. And at that moment, a miracle: they become entirely separate agents."

Matilda gurgles a little and stops breathing. John rests her gently back on the ground, then lunges. The little man brandishes the silver hook.

"You bastard," one of the Johns screams.

"Subtle variations in a complex system lead to large-scale effects later," the little man says. He nods to the waiting John and Matilda by the church door. "This set rigged the coin toss, of course — the only pair to lie. As a result, they will probably remain alive considerably longer than the rest of you."

Another John lunges. The little man only puts out his hook and the John crumples, his flesh coming away from his face like a child pulling dried glue from a finger.

The crowd backs away. One of the Matildas is crying now, the Johns shouting.

The little man continues. "The deviation was small, a wavelength of light. Yet admire the variation! Egotism, deception, and conspiracy. The three hallmarks of your species."

"Retreat," one of the Johns shouts and they all turn about. Five more of the little men are waiting behind, identical, holding their silver hooks.

"When the experiment is over, the mice are retired," says the original little man.

One of the Johns grabs a Matilda and kisses her on the mouth.

Inside the meeting church, John goes to close the main door. Matilda blocks his path. "Let's not watch," he says.

|||

THE PRINCE OF
MILK

FIFTY-NINE

Robyn watches the snake's eyes. The vivarium looks warm inside. It would be good to bask in the heat of the lamp. It would be good to have something live and terrified dangled in from the sky once a day, to swallow it whole and feel it kicking about inside you like a baby. It would be good to kill for pleasure. He fetches a mouse and holds it up to the glass of the vivarium. The snake comes alert.

"You're teasing him," Suzie Lees says.

"The meat will taste better for it."

"Look, he's all frustrated."

A shame we didn't find your husband's body, Robyn thinks. I would have opened my mouth wide and swallowed him whole.

"His skin's all pale," Suzie says. "Look. He's ill."

She's right. The snake's skin is turning a pinkish hue. There is even a little hair growing at the bottom of its tail.

"When a vet becomes available, I will take him to one. Until such a time, mice will suffice as his medicine."

He throws the mouse into the vivarium. It tumbles about like a barrel. The snake does a few laps of the vivarium, no urgency. The mouse plays dead. Like my brother, Robyn thinks. If he were a mouse he would do the very same thing: roll over, lie still.

"Maybe we should let him go," Suzie says.

"What?"

"The snake. Maybe we should let him go, in the forest. He can't be happy here, cooped up."

"Maybe you'd be happier in the forest," Robyn says. "We could let you go with him."

"Stop it."

"You could fend for yourself, eat mice, slither about on your belly."

"Just stop it."

"God knows he's more productive than you. All you do is drink."

She lights a cigarette. "You're being mean."

"Go and amuse yourself," he barks.

"I want to go home."

"Then go."

"I want you to drive me."

"I'm busy. Can't you see I'm busy?"

She storms down the hall. "*Scott*," he hears her calling, then a knock on Scott's door. "Scott?"

The mouse is still cowering, shivering a little. Robyn knocks on the glass and points to the rodent. "Hey. Lunch. That's lunch." The snake lies down and appears to be trying to sleep. Robyn picks the mouse up by the tail and looks into its little eyes.

No fight in it. Just like my brother.

He puts the thing in his mouth. The feet claw at his tongue and the tail writhes about in his throat, and in one determined motion, he swallows. He feels it descending his gullet, still thrashing, then going motionless in his stomach. There is a sense of being whole, suddenly.

"What the hell are you doing?" Scott says, stood at the doorway now with Suzie.

"Waste not, want not," Robyn says.

"We have plenty of food downstairs."

"Oh, it's horrid, *horrid*," Suzie cries. "Scott's going to take me home."

"All right."

"There's something wrong with you."

"Good," Robyn says. "Go back then. Go back to your empty palace with your dead husband's things, the one who never gave a damn about you anyway. Go back to your empty palace with your lace underwear and stockings and you can put them on for no one and strut about like a stupid peacock. Go back to your empty palace with nothing in it and see how long you last without anyone to leech off."

The snake watches Robyn with sad eyes.

"I know what you did to Derrick Thomas," Suzie says quietly.

"The world is a fundamentally harsh place."

"You gave him too much insulin. Scott told me."

"What of it?"

"You're a murderer."

"Our father would have turned in his grave to see the family business disintegrate. Advances in modern medicine have allowed people to live well beyond their allotted years. During hard times one must get creative, especially in our profession."

"Well I'm glad all of this happened," she says and points to the twilight sky. "Before you could do anything else."

"That's cute," he smiles. "You think Thomas was the first?"

"Take me home please," she says to Scott.

"Yes, brother. Take her home," Robyn says. "You who are of course in no way complicit in any of this. You who didn't know about any of it and certainly didn't help me make the arrangements."

The snake pecks at the glass. Scott puts his head down and appears a great, fat, shamed egg.

"You were next, of course," Robyn says, locking eyes with Suzie. "No one would much have missed you, and by then you'd have inherited your husband's wealth. We would've done the full works; a horse-drawn hearse, a choir, the lot. The only thing still left undecided was the method. You don't have any allergies I'm aware of. You don't go out much at night, so a chance stabbing by a passing lunatic was out of the question. How would you have done it, brother?"

"Let's go," Scott says and the two of them shuffle out the door.

Robyn looks back to the snake, the thing still watching him. Its eyes have turned almost entirely blue.

SIXTY

Only one hour of daylight left now; the shadows are huge and short-lived. Matilda and John take shovels from the cellar and dig ten graves in an empty patch of the graveyard and haul the bodies in one by one. When it's all done, they stand over the mounds and try to think of something to say.

"What if the little man comes back?" Matilda murmurs.

"Then he comes back."

The other churches and belfries are gone, dissolved away when Whistle took the stone out from under the blacklight. Now there's only mist.

Later, John sits up in the belfry and watches the sun disappearing. Nothing stirs.

It must be sixty feet down, he notes. If one were to throw themselves off head first, the job would be done in seconds.

And there, the Crane's living room lit, figures moving about inside.

What was it like being a boy? Whistle thinks. Everything smelled new, smelled good. The days were longer. The sun shone hotter. Nothing bit you. Now the sun barely shines at all, and if nothing bites, you call it a good day.

Donya. Our daughter's gone. I'm sorry.

Matilda appears from the hatch with two cups of tea and hands him one. He grunts thankfully.

"Any sign of Liptrot?" she says.

"Nothing. He's probably out in the forest forming a new congregation."

They watch the village in silence, a museum of old, dead relics: the flower shop, the book shop, the pharmacy, their windows all smashed, their doors open or ripped off the frames.

"I buried the devices," Matilda says. "And everything else."

"All right."

A light wind starts up.

"Was it all just teasing?" she says.

"Maybe."

"I want to feel sad, but I barely even knew them."

"If it hadn't been for the coin toss, it'd be us instead."

"I've been thinking about that too."

"It was the right thing to do. They would have done the same."

"But they didn't," she says a little louder.

"No. Deviations, I suppose."

A pause.

"What now?" Matilda says.

Whistle nods to the trees.

"That's suicide," she says.

"Maybe, but there isn't much else to do."

"If Rupert and Jamie find her, then they'll come back. Just wait here, with me."

"It's time," Whistle says. He glances over the belfry railings at the ten mounds below, all in a line. "Time we went into the forest."

SIXTY-ONE

Suzie dreams of a wedding, her own. She arrives at the church in a carriage to the beaming smiles of Wilthail. A gang of photographers greets her as she steps onto the road. The groom is already standing at the altar, his back turned. As she enters the church she realises it is almost completely empty, save for the Crane family and John Whistle and Matilda Sargent. The organist begins playing.

There is a clatter from downstairs and Suzie starts up in bed. She is in the spare room, where Scott left her, promising she'd be safe there and that he would drive her home the next day when it was light.

She moves to the bathroom to brush her teeth. Another noise from downstairs. The brothers' bedroom doors are both open. Barefoot, she pads softly down the stairs. There is a rhythmic thumping from the living room. She rounds the corner. A great, green snake the size of a fridge is writhing about on the floor. In its mouth is the backend of a mouse, also enormous, flailing about, trying to grab at the furniture to pull itself free. She screams. The snake turns about, bringing the mouse with it. The mouse's eyes are human, pale blue, desperate: Scott's.

Suzie backs away, falls over, stands again. The snake crawls towards her and tightens its bite on the mouse.

"Back," she screams.

The snake nears, its eyes narrowing. The mouse wriggles some more and blood trickles from its sides where the snake has sunk its teeth in.

She runs to the kitchen and tries the back door. Locked. The snake rounds the corner. She smashes the door glass with her elbow, screams, blood everywhere. The snake eyes her blood hungrily and guides the mouse further into its mouth.

She notices Robyn's pet snake in the vivarium. It has been bitten clean in half.

"Help!" she screams through the smashed glass.

"Help," the mouse echoes, halfway inside the snake.

She rummages through the kitchen drawers but all of the sharp knives have been reallocated by Robyn, she remembers, to his travel bag for excursions outside. The largest thing she can find is a wooden spoon and she brandishes it like a sword.

The snake pauses for a moment, laughs, the noise of it muffled by the mouse in its mouth, cackling so hard it closes its eyes in ecstasy. The mouse reaches out a desperate paw to Suzie. She tramples over the two of them and runs for the front door. Also locked. The snake turns about and takes the mouse further into its mouth until only Scott's furry head protrudes.

Into the living room and she grabs book after book from the shelf and launches them at the snake. It only sidles closer.

"Bastard," she screams. The snake chuckles again. Scott's head disappears into the thing's mouth entirely and the snake swallows, delighted. Suzie hurls the computer monitor, misses. She tries to block the monster's path by moving the sofa, but isn't strong enough to lift it properly. The snake watches idly. Its belly is fat.

"Please," Suzie whispers. The snake smiles again. "Please."

On the desk, she notices, is Aubrey Rhodes' machete. She grabs it with both hands.

The snake slinks a little closer. It pulls up to her height and a tongue appears and vibrates like a mad flame. The eyes are unmistakably Robyn's.

"Please," she whispers again and raises the machete.

The snake explodes at her, the jaw dislocated and wide open, and she hacks with the machete, with her eyes closed, and hacks again and again and cries out. Two piercing teeth sink into her arm, down to the bone, then relent and sink in again. She hacks with the other hand now.

She opens her eyes to blood, pints of it everywhere, and the snake has retreated and is lying on its side, groaning. Suzie's arm is completely numb and she can see the bone where the flesh has been pulled away.

The snake's eyes flutter, then fix on her. She raises the machete again and it cowers, tries to pull back through the living room door. The rug is scarlet with blood and all Suzie can smell is iron. The snake opens its lipless mouth and rasps like a broken accordion. She bends to its height. Its mouth opens again. Something close to human speech falls out. She strokes its nose, strokes its cheek, then pushes the machete past its tongue and all the way down its throat and twists.

SIXTY-TWO

Eric wakes early and goes downstairs for breakfast. Alf and Mrs. Crane are sitting at the kitchen table.

"The boy lives," Alf smiles.

"Hi."

"Eric, sit down a second, please," his mother says. He sits. Alf watches him from behind a cigarette. The skin of his uncle's face is pocked and cracked like wartime porcelain.

"Your father's gone," Mrs. Crane says coldly.

"Did you know about this, lad?" Alf says.

Eric shakes his head. "Gone where?"

"No idea, but he took a rucksack and food with him, so we guess he's not coming back," Mrs. Crane says.

"He seemed okay," Eric says quietly.

"Sometimes life can be complicated," Alf says to himself and chomps on a slab of meat. "Adults, you know? Your father did what he thought was best and went looking for pastures new. Who knows where he got to? Somewhere nice, we hope. Don't we?" He rubs Mrs. Crane's hand. She pulls it back quickly.

"We should look for him," Eric says.

"I admire your courage lad, but it wouldn't be wise to leave the house."

"Why? You go out all the time."

"Yes, but I'm learned in the ways of combat. It's far too dangerous for you and your mother."

"Then you go look for him."

Alf puts another piece of mystery meat to his lips. "Hm, no, I don't think so."

"Why?"

Alf slams his hand down on the table. "Because your father has already made his decision."

Eric goes to storm out, but a knock comes from the door.

"It's the morning," Mrs. Crane whispers. "They don't come out in daylight."

Alf heads into the hall without hesitation. There is the noise of the boards being pulled away and the whine of the door's hinges. A soft murmuring, then he reappears. "It's for you," he says to Eric.

Reluctantly, the boy pads into the hall. The Old Curmudgeon is standing a little hunched in the doorway. "Hi," Eric says.

Whistle smiles. There are too many lines in his brow. "How have you been?" the old man says. Matilda Sargent is waiting at the top of the driveway, smoking.

"Okay," Eric says uncertainly.

"Strange times, huh?"

"Yup."

"I have something for you," Whistle says. "I should've returned it sooner, but you know how things are."

He takes something bulky and square and black from a carrier bag: the laser. Eric checks it over. Perfect condition.

"My daughter told me you were looking for this. I found it on the road the day Derrick Thomas…well, I found it on the road."

The boy weighs it in his hands. "Thanks."

"It's fine." Whistle leans in a little closer and lowers his voice to a whisper. "Everything okay here?"

Eric shrugs.

"The man who answered the door, who is he?"

"He says he's Uncle Alf."

"But he looks like Kevin Lees," Whistle says.

"Yeah."

"Listen, Matilda and I are going on a little adventure." Matilda waves from the road. "We won't be back for a while. If you and your mother need somewhere to stay, it's safe in the church. No one can get in. If you go while it's still light, you can make it there safe and sound."

"Thanks."

Eric examines the laser again. An ugly, black miracle. "Is Zoe okay?" he says.

"I hope so. We're going to try and find her."

Matilda checks her watch. "John," she shouts.

"We have to get going." He gestures to the laser. "I trust that helps with whatever you're doing."

"It helps," Eric says.

Whistle pats the boy's head. "When I was young I used to build things too."

Eric closes the door.

Back in the kitchen, Alf and his mother are standing. "Well I won't let you," Alf shouts.

Mrs. Crane tries to dart past him, but he pushes her back.

"What's happening?" Eric says.

"Your mother wants to go outside and get herself killed."

"He's all alone out there," she says. "All alone..."

"Best thing for him. He was miserable here."

"Don't you think it's strange that Uncle Alf looks so much like Kevin Lees?" Eric says.

All three of them are quiet except for Alf's heavy breathing. "Go upstairs," he says to Eric in a low voice. "And I will be up to deal with you when I'm done with your mother."

"No," Eric says.

Alf raises his hand to strike the boy, then falls to his knees and cries out. In Mrs. Crane's hand is a rolling pin. Alf cowers for a moment, then stands. Eric and Mrs. Crane move to the doorway. Alf's eyes glow slightly purple and the cracks in his face grow a little wider. Mrs. Crane raises the rolling pin again, but Alf doesn't flinch. She pushes Eric into the living room and shuts the door, and Eric watches from behind frosted glass. His mother, a blur now, stands her ground for a few seconds. Alf charges. The two of them disappear out the front door.

Eric concentrates on his breath for a long time, waiting for his mother to reappear. After half an hour or so he shuts the front door and goes upstairs. Nothing moves beyond the window; no sign of either of them, nor his father.

He takes stock of his machine. The battery still holds a charge. The gravity petals are unfurled and shining in the daylight. He fits the laser to the frame and sticks it down with tape and aligns the beam emitter with the focusing dish. Then he connects the laser itself up to the battery and activates it. The beam glows a brilliant red through the dish and refracts it a hundredfold: a light show whipping about in the mirrors of the gravity petals. There are no parts left to acquire.

SIXTY-THREE

Matilda and John walk silently through the drab afternoon. They don't talk about the body parts in the gutter. Matilda's cold hand finds his.

John recalls one night walking home from a gig with Matilda some forty years ago, their fingers threaded like this, the sun coming up.

Only now the sun is going down, he thinks. And if it comes back up tomorrow, I think we'll both be quite surprised.

"If there's a heaven," Matilda says, "do you think all of the—" she pauses, "all of the other Johns and Matildas, would they go there?"

"I hope not, because by the time we turn up they're all going to be quite pissed at us."

A figure made of rags steps out from behind the Lees' house. It bandies about with dangling arms. A head appears from behind matted blonde straggles.

"Suzie," John says cautiously. "You don't look well at all."

"I'm okay." She glances at their linked fingers. "It's all been horrid, hasn't it?"

Matilda nods. "Sure has."

"Where have you been living?" John says.

"With the Applebys. But they're gone now."

John notices blood on her hands and up her arms a little. "I see."

"I think I want to go to the sea. I want to get in the water and wash my hands," she says.

"When all this is over, I'm sure you can do that," Matilda says.

"*When all this is over,*" Suzie echoes sceptically.

"It will be over," John says. "We promise. We're going to settle it, in the forest."

Suzie nods. "I haven't heard of anyone coming out again, but good luck anyway."

"Suzie," John says. "Don't do anything silly, all right? We'll get everything back to the way it was. I know things haven't been great recently, but that's no reason to give up."

"Do you have any cigarettes?"

Matilda hands her one and she lights up. "Where are you going now?" Matilda says.

"I want a drink."

"There's still booze we left behind in the church."

"That sounds good. A quiet night in."

John looks to Matilda. "I suppose we should get going."

"I don't like it when it's dark," Suzie says.

"We'll see you soon, all right?"

Suzie smiles but the muscles look atrophied, as though she hasn't done it in years. "Yeah," she says.

She watches them pass down Marls Street still hand in hand. There is a slight twinge of jealousy in her that two oddballs could find each other despite recent events.

In her mind she wears a great, flowing white wedding dress and the streets are lined with onlookers. Her hair is washed and she is clean and her face is heavy with makeup. She is beautiful, she knows. The sun is fat, though not too hot. The newspapers will feature photos of her on the front page the next morning; the village will talk of it for days. She daintily brushes her hair behind her ear and tightens the flowers in her grip and smiles for the photographers.

Mrs. Crane runs past and the two of them lock eyes for a moment. Then the woman is gone, disappeared down a back street. Tailing her comes a man, red-haired, red-faced, and stops in the middle of the street.

"Oh," Suzie says. Cameras flash in her mind. "*Oh*," she says again. She looks the man over. He is scruffily dressed, but she ignores this. "Your hair," she says.

"My hair," he replies.

"They said you were dead. I found the car."

"It's complicated."

"You look good," she says darkly. "And your eyes. God, they're purple."

He approaches. "It's complicated," he says again. He takes her hand.

"Are you back now?" she says.

"I'm back now."

"For good?"

"For good," he says.

"That isn't Kevin Lees," Mrs. Crane screams from up ahead. "And it isn't Alf either."

I wonder if I care, Suzie thinks. No, I don't.

"Shall we go home?" she says.

"Let's," the man agrees and Mrs. Crane watches them disappear into the Lees' house in silence. She leans against the flower shop for support.

A blinding light from her son's bedroom suddenly, emerald green, cerulean blue, and a noise as though the world is splitting apart, as though time is splitting apart. She squints and covers her ears. The light fills the entire street and she calls out her son's name. Then the noise and the light show is over as soon as it began, and she knows, or thinks she knows, that if she returns to the house, Eric will not be there, however hard she searches.

SIXTY-FOUR

With the crematorium in sight, the two mannequins slow a little. Derrick Thomas finds the backup generator easily enough, still full of fuel, and gets it running. Aubrey Rhodes looks the incinerator over and, satisfied, starts the thing up. They watch the flames twist about inside, licking at the roof of the machine. Thomas takes the bell from his neck and rings in dots and dashes, "So?"

"So," Rhodes rings back. "This is it then."

"Yup."

Rhodes cranks the thing up to full power.

Thomas puts his hand into the incineration chamber. "Can't feel anything," he rings.

"Good. Will be painless then."

Painless, Thomas thinks. Not unlike going to sleep.

"Wouldn't mind a drink," Rhodes rings.

"Same. A last meal too."

Rhodes nods. The two mannequins hug awkwardly, unable to bend their arms enough to really complete the act.

"Wish you all the very best," Thomas rings.

"Likewise."

"Will be painless."

"Painless. Sure." A pause. Then Rhodes rings, "Me first."

"You sure?"

Rhodes nods. "Don't watch."

"Fine."

Another pause, longer, the two of them motionless.

Not unlike going to sleep.

Rhodes hugs his partner again. Then he steps up to the opening of the machine. Air warps on its lip. He tries to imagine the feel of the heat, but the memory of heat itself is gone, just like the taste of fresh bread, the sensation of grass between his toes, the curve of his wife's back.

None of it meant anything, he thinks. Or maybe it did and I was just too stupid to figure it all out. God, I tried but there are so many moving parts. Maybe I'm just a dumb animal staring at a chalkboard covered in some brilliant equation and it's all going right over my head.

He waddles closer to the incinerator.

I hope it all meant something and I was just too stupid to get it, he thinks. I hope it's that, because if it's the other thing then I'd rather not have been born at all.

He thinks of his wife.

You meant something. Everything, I'd say.

He begins crawling into the contraption, nothing but flames ahead. It's an odd sensation, fire all around and not a lick of heat. This isn't so terrible, he thinks, and tries to slink in further.

He's stuck, his damn foot caught on something or other. He pulls, pulls again. Nothing. A glance behind. Thomas is trying to drag him back.

The hell? Rhodes goes to shout, mouthless. Thomas pulls harder.

Reluctantly, he slides himself back out, about to start making vulgar gestures. A new mannequin is in the doorway, standing uncertainly. It's shorter than the two of them, but still made of the same seamless plastic Rhodes and Thomas recognise from their own bodies. The two men look to each other, then back to the newcomer.

Finally Thomas waves a jolly hand. The newcomer waves back. Rhodes takes the Speak & Spell from his rucksack. "*Au....Au...Aubrey Rhodes,*" he types out and points to himself.

He passes it across. The new mannequin fiddles a moment with the buttons.

"*Rhodes,*" comes the reply. "*Jen...Jen...Jennifer Rhodes.*"

SIXTY-FIVE

John and Matilda watch the hall from a distance. It only took a few hours of walking through the forest to find it. The structure is old, the stonework all cracked. They approach slowly. Gargoyles line the outside, some with heads, others without; some eating the flesh of other gargoyles. One turns to watch them.

A cast iron door opens. A woman steps out, plump and bronzed, with plaited black hair. She beams and kisses John on the cheek.

"Who, exactly, is this?" Matilda says frostily.

"His wife," the woman says. "Donya Whistle. I kept the name even after the divorce. Naturally."

John examines her face. "Donya," he says.

She strokes his cheek. "You do look so tired. Would you like to come in and sit down?"

He peers over her shoulder, through the door. There's only dark inside. "You can't be real, surely," he says.

"Does it matter?"

"I think so, yes. You're not supposed to be here."

"Is anyone, really?"

She beckons them inside and disappears into the dark.

They hesitate for a moment, then follow after. Their footsteps echo in cackles. The door closes behind them. Total darkness.

A note rings out, a cello. Another clashing chord follows on top of it, an oboe, joined by a clarinet, a trumpet, and a violin. A stage appears in the murk of a dim spotlight, packed with musicians, an entire orchestra, some playing familiar instruments, others with bizarre many-sided shapes in their hands that emit steam from improvised holes. A conductor stands at the centre of the orchestra keeping time with a severed human arm which bleeds over the stage.

"Yea!" the conductor shouts over the racket, "though I walk through the valley of the shadow of death I shall fear no evil."

Matilda and John approach through the chairs. The auditorium is half-full and the audience turns to watch them; figures, some decapitated, some not, some beautiful, others hideous, young and old, their faces gleaming with purple fire. Donya sits among them with Mrs. Thomas and her children, with some sixth form kids, with the Simpson lot, and a whole set of Wilthail families John has never said hello to, but vaguely recognises.

"The players," John whispers. Matilda squints. She doesn't recognise the musicians for the most part, save for ten Matildas and Johns, each one disfigured or cut on, playing their respective instruments. Their eyes are fixed on their music, except for one Matilda who has no eyes at all and only shakes her head about in time and plays random notes on her violin.

"Thy rod and thy staff they comfort me," the conductor croons. The severed arm continues to spew blood. The dead fingers clench and unclench. "You prepare a table before me in the presence of my enemies. You anoint my head with oil. My cup overflows."

The orchestra holds a single horrific chord, then the music dies and the players turn to John and Matilda. Augustus Rawlings whirls around now, still holding the severed arm. He salutes with it and blood leaks onto his suit. "Good evening."

"Hello," John says. "If you're busy we can come back later."

Augustus gestures to some chairs at the front. "Please, sit down. I insist."

They sit. Rawlings starts the orchestra up again, a waltzing number. He throws the arm aside and leaves the orchestra playing and vaults into the audience.

John peers behind. Mary Rawlings is watching the orchestra with vacant eyes. The little man with the silver hook is sat just to her right, staring ahead, grinning.

And closer yet sit ten or so life-size wooden carvings that John quickly recognises as enlarged versions of his own. A few of them appear to be breathing.

"Is this a concert?" Matilda says.

"An impromptu one, for you both. Our special guests." Augustus smiles again and his face tears at the sides slightly.

"I've come for Zoe," Whistle says.

"She's performing at the moment. Her posture is terrible, but we must work with what we've got."

Sure enough, at the back of the violin row is Zoe Whistle, her eyes sad and set on her sheet music. John shouts her name. She doesn't stir.

"Now, the stage set, the players ready," Rawlings says. "If the doors of perception were cleansed, reality would appear to man as it is. Infinite! A fine platitude, but what did William Blake know, really? Ask a depressive and a lover what the world is made for and you'll get two conflicting answers. What *is* the world for? I'll tell you, if you like. To wither. Isn't that a thing?" He eyes Matilda and

John. "Why else be burdened with *wanting* and *wanting* and *wanting* all the time? And guile. And grief. And guilt."

"I think there's more to the world than that," John says soberly.

Rawlings bends down and sniffs at the old man. "Well, you would." He peers into his eyes. "Do you even remember? Any of it at all?"

"You're insane."

The orchestra begins again, quietly, building up to an almost deafening clash, then louder still. "Insane," Rawlings says. "One would strain to tell the difference between insanity and a mere annoyance, depending on the context. If a fellow had been wronged enough, perhaps he would take on the appearance of a man insane, but he is only insane with rage."

John and Matilda cover their ears. "Stop it," John shouts. The orchestra grows louder, and Rawlings' voice rides over the top of it somehow. He screams, "The world is a garden. The world is a gutter. Which is it?"

Whistle's wooden creatures bind the couple's hands. Augustus opens his coat. Inside is a world of glittering steel: scalpels, knives, a dagger. He settles on a scalpel. "The answer, of course, is a gutter." He puts the scalpel to Whistle's eye. The orchestra finds a melody, all sharps and flats. "In the beginning there was only cold, lifeless matter."

"Stop this," John shouts.

"And in the end there was something sublime, an ideal. The whole of creation tending towards perfection. Doesn't it make you want to throw up?" To the whole auditorium: "In all of my incarnations, I've never known a bed of depravity quite like this village. Your little dalliances, slinking off at night to rub loins outside of marriage. Your little murders, contrived to prop up a business." And to Whistle: "Your little acts of neglect, disowning your own daughters. I came here because a fool tried to steal my wife and I vowed to end him. But I chanced on an old friend then, one of far greater sophistication, Novelty himself. His stink is unmistakable. The fug, it has gummed up my nose for years. I stalked each and every house. I interrogated the villagers in a gentle way. But He was clever, hid Himself well. What a thing." He puts his face close to John's. "It *is* you, no?"

"Just what is going on around here?" John yells.

Augustus smirks. "Unlikelihoods. Demoting the impossible to only the highly improbable. The Applebys, I saw to it they got what they deserved. Young Eric Crane, a child's fantasy now a reality. Rhodes and Thomas, tourists once again in the Kingdom of the Living." He throws the scalpel aside and takes a sledgehammer from his pocket instead, pulling it from nothing at all. The couple writhe in their binds. Rawlings beckons the little man with the silver hook over.

"This is the Arbiter of Worldworks," Augustus says proudly.

"We've met," Whistle says.

"He's a rather gifted gentleman, technologically speaking." To the arbiter himself: "Is it him?"

The little man takes a glass rod from his pocket and runs it over Whistle, mumbling to himself.

"What's that?" Whistle says.

"A scientific instrument," the little man says.

"And?"

Rawlings snatches the device. "It detects the number of incarnations of a mindstate."

"Ten to the power of ninety-one!" the little man says and points to the device.

"Ten to the power of ninety-one, sure enough," Rawlings agrees, examining the thing. He gestures to the audience, stares at Whistle. "You've been all of them, old man. What a career." He raises the sledgehammer. "Fitting indeed then that I should be the one to relieve you of your position."

"We could talk about this," Matilda says diplomatically. Augustus grins and goes to swing the hammer.

A blinding purple flash. Two figures appear before Rawlings: a fat policeman and his cat.

"Long time no see," the policeman says.

Augustus yells, brings the hammer forward. The policeman puts up a hand. The hammer pauses in its flight.

"What you are," Mcalister says, his face all dancing with violet fire, "is a total, total prick."

Sergei sprints through the audience and up onto Mary Rawlings' lap. The old woman coddles the animal, kisses its ears. Augustus Rawlings growls and takes a step back. Mcalister levitates him several feet into the air, the old man's eyes bulging, robes dangling.

"I've seen the Gestalt," Mcalister snarls in Etheric. His pupils have disappeared into a haze of purple plasma. "God, the enormity, I've seen it. And the whole of time, before, during, and after — stars birthing, living, and dying. Entire timestreams blooming and waning. I've seen the True Shape of Being, all Her twists and convolutions. I've seen our lives here, from the perspective of the all-sky. It was an infinitely small mark on an infinitely wide map. Yet your mark was smaller even than that."

The Arbiter of Worldworks launches himself at the policeman. Without turning, Mcalister explodes the little man with a wave of his free hand. "I've seen the heart of the Glass Canyon, no less," the policeman yells.

Another purple blaze and a hunched old woman has appeared. She starts work on Matilda and John's bindings.

"Emelza?" Mary Rawlings cries.

"I intervene," the crone replies, "on special occasions."

The orchestra put their instruments down and look about, drunk. "Get out," the crone shouts to them. "You've all had a rather long day. He's powerless over you now. Go, get out."

Zoe runs to her father, kisses him on the forehead.

"All right?" John Whistle whispers, eyes wet. "Thought I'd lost you."

"Have to try harder than that. What happened? Actually, what's happening?"

"We all need to get to safety," the crone shouts. "Unpleasantness is imminent, no doubt."

The Wilthailites move back through the auditorium. Whistle's wooden figurines stand to their feet but do nothing, unsure. Mary Rawlings scoops Sergei onto her shoulder and joins the others. Whistle fumbles with the auditorium door handle. "Shit, it's locked."

"The grudge," the crone says. "No one's leaving until it's resolved, it appears."

They turn back, all of them, to the stage. Augustus is in Mcalister's Etheric grip still, the old man frail and dangling, and the policeman growing suddenly in size, doubled already. "Like an ant taken riding in a hot air balloon," Mcalister shouts, "the whole landscape of cause and effect was rolled out beneath me, every decision and regret."

Augustus tries to scream but only wheezes a little.

"End him," Sergei calls out. "You have to end him now, Mcalister. The way we agreed."

Augustus and the policeman are wrapped in a purple curtain of fire, both levitating.

"The whole of creation, top to bottom," Mcalister screams. "Laid out like a rug." He tightens his Etheric grip on the old man's neck. "And it means nothing, just as we suspected all along, little better than ants, hot air balloon or none. It doesn't mean a damn thing."

The crone catches Sergei's eye. "What have you done?"

"Just wait," the cat murmurs.

"He's out of control already. This is your daft doing. Stop it immediately."

"Mcalister," Sergei calls out. "You have to end him now. Otherwise it'll be too late."

"It doesn't mean a *damn thing*," the policeman spits. "Creation, endurance, destruction, all of it. For what?"

"What the hell is going on?" Whistle says.

Sergei and the crone exchange a glance.

"He's power-drunk," Mary Rawlings says flatly.

"What?"

"He's had too much already. Your kind aren't built for using Etheric."

"And what does that actually mean…" Whistle says.

"It means that maybe the Glass Canyon was a bad idea," Sergei mutters to himself. "He insisted we walk through it. He bloody *insisted*."

Mcalister roars and launches Augustus at the ceiling, lets him fall, levitates him again.

Whistle says, "Sorry, not to sound like an idiot here, but what does *that* actually—"

"It *means*," Mary Rawlings says, "that if we don't stop him, he's going to consume himself with Etheric and vaporise the lot of us. And possibly quite a large portion of Southern England too."

"Oh, it's fucking Armageddon is it?" Whistle groans. "Why is it always Armageddon when the gods are involved?"

"It's Southern England, not Armageddon," Sergei snaps. "And for the last time, godly status is relative."

The crone bends down to the cat. "It's time. We're out of options. You did this. Resolve it."

Mcalister's voice comes over them, from all directions, in English, in Etheric, in their minds and ears:

"The whole game was just some frivolous dance, no rules and no salvation."

"It's time," the crone repeats. She takes a pouch from her robe.

"*No*," Sergei says. "I gave that to you for safe keeping, not to use like this. Put it away."

"There's no choice. This was your doing, if you recall. We could've just left him to sleep in my cabin, but no — you knew better, as always. You're an idiot."

"We'll fight him," the cat says. "He's only a Corporic after all."

"*Was* a Corporic," the crone corrects.

"We'll fight him and put him to sleep. He'll be back on his feet in a week. If we all attack together—"

"Have you taken a look at yourself?" the crone says tiredly. "Your ears are adorable, but black and furry nevertheless. You're in no condition to fight, not as an animal."

"You and Zorya then." He nods to Mary Rawlings.

"He's already a monster, too powerful. This is the only right course."

"No," the cat says quietly. He stares at the old woman. "Please, please don't."

The crone shakes her head. "Mr. Whistle," she says formally. "You'll need to inhale from this bag now."

Whistle eyes her suspiciously. "And what would that be? Cocaine is my daughter's vice."

"Much stronger than that. An old technology belonging to the Arbiter of Worldworks. Smelling salts, to wake you up."

"I would say I'm quite awake already, thank you."

"No. You're not."

All eyes on Whistle. Matilda kisses him on the cheek and steps back.

"What the hell is going on?" he growls.

"You're one of them," Matilda says softly. "You're one of them and you've forgotten. That's right isn't it?"

The crone nods.

Whistle chuckles. "I think I'd bloody well know if that was the case."

"No," Sergei says. "You wouldn't. You chose to forget, to hide a while. Now you're going to remember. And then you're going to stop Mcalister for us."

"Why the hell would I choose to forget something like that?"

"There isn't time. You need to—"

"*No*," Whistle shouts. "I don't need to *do* anything, much less sniff your bag of whatever it is on the basis of some ridiculous story." He takes his daughter's hand. "My name is John Whistle. I'm sixty-seven years old. Interests include archery, homemade cider, and not fraternising with whatever the hell you lot are. I'd know if there was more in my head than that. There isn't. So just sod off. You've got the wrong man."

"Tell him," Sergei grumbles.

"*You* tell him," the crone shoots back.

The cat glances over at Mcalister, even larger now, Augustus little more than a toy soldier in his grip. "Your name is Novelty," the cat says reluctantly. "The Etheria was in a more or less perfect balance until some time ago when a certain mutual friend of ours, Augustus Rawlings as you know him, began killing when killing wasn't needed. Many of us tried to reason with him, but he was a sadist through and through. Our kind can't end each other, not in the Etheria. Except for the Arbiter of Entropy himself, of course."

"Still," the crone says, "we knew if Djall...*Rawlings* was left to his own devices, he'd end us all eventually, one way or another. It was decided that he would be lured down here into the Corporia, your world, to end" his reign, however we might go about it. To end him for good, if need be."

"I was lured down here too, to settle all of this," Sergei says. "Wasn't I?"

"It was the only way," the crone says quietly.

"You utter bastards."

"I…perhaps made sure Djall would find your little love letter those eons ago. When he learned of what you were planning with his wife, it was fairly likely he'd chase you into the Corporia. We assumed the two of you would eventually come to an arrangement, rather than live out your days as Corporics. Djall would give up his position and you'd both amicably return to the Etheria. We hadn't counted on your…perseverance. It was my idea originally. I'll take the full weight of the blame. It wasn't supposed to unfold like this."

"You told me not to go," the cat spits. "You practically begged me."

"And it only spurred you on, didn't it?"

"Screw you." He turns to Mary. "You knew about this too then, did you?"

The old woman says nothing, only keeps her eyes to the floor and nods.

The crone says again, "It wasn't supposed to unfold like this."

Whistle takes a few steps back. "And what does any of that have to do with me?"

The crone says, "Novelty was Entropy's polar opposite, tasked with building new forms in the world, shaping matter. The last incarnation of them all. He was the first to journey down here, to hide himself away before the plan was executed. He chose to forget his own identity so as to throw Djall off the scent, waiting until one of us brought his memory back."

The three Etherics stare at Whistle. The old man smiles disbelievingly. "And that's me, is it?"

The crone nods. "That's you, yes."

Whistle feels something enormous pushing at his mind, a battering ram ten times the size of the largest thought he's ever had.

"Dad," Zoe says. "It's all right."

What's all right? he thinks. God, am I a lie? "Am I a lie?" he says.

An explosion of purple fire. Mcalister is almost as tall as the auditorium, his head only inches from the ceiling. Rawlings is a mouse by comparison.

A terrible heat is on them all then. The room erupts into screaming. Mary Rawlings flees to the side of the hall with the cat in her arms, and ducks down behind a nest of chairs. The ceiling begins to collapse. From every direction comes Mcalister's roar.

Matilda takes the bag of smelling salts from the crone. She whispers into John's ear, "Wish we could've done this all for longer, but you're not mine to keep." She holds the bag under the old man's nose. "You're not anyone's to keep anyway. I won't take it personally. Go on."

Mcalister yells again, an animal cry. The walls shake. The ground tremors. The hall is all dust and fire and tumult and blinding light.

"I'm sorry," John says to his daughter. "God, I'm sorry for all of it."

Zoe smiles like he's just told a brilliant joke. "No one asks to exist," she says.

He nods at this, kisses her on the cheek.

"Go on," Matilda says. "Time to face the music."

He goes inwards, looking for his essence, a ledge to hold on to; something beneath all the wanting and opinions and angst and fantasies and plans and grievances and mental detritus of a lifetime; something enduring that will not be subdued, something he can grasp at and say, *I was here.* Donya. Cairo. His parents. Childhood.

His body. Holidays. Tax returns. Zoe. Morning coffee. A desperate attempt to mean something before the lights go out. The smell of grass. A bout of mononucleosis once. The swinging chair in the garden. Guilt.

No, he thinks. There's nothing tangible in there. Not really.

But it felt that way.

It always felt that way.

He closes his eyes, takes a long draw from the bag of smelling salts, and collapses.

The ceiling struts cry out. Mcalister's body begins to bulge unstably, wreaths of purple fire evaporating from his skin. His entire outline flickers like a candle. Mary Rawlings holds the cat close, kisses his ears, covers his eyes.

"It's too late," Sergei whispers.

"It was a good run," Mary whispers back.

The hall is an inferno. The walls turn a scorched black. Chairs ignite. Mcalister cries out again, a bass warble. The whole building rocks left to right, left to right; dust everywhere, so thick it blinds. Matter begins to come apart, gluon by gluon. Atoms twist and shriek.

Zoe Whistle covers her ears, screams.

Yes, she thinks. No one asks to exist.

Silence.

She opens an eye. The dust is hanging in mid-air. Mcalister is standing perfectly still, frozen. The crowd are staring wide-eyed. Zoe follows their gaze.

John Whistle is getting back up, face wrinkleless, his body swaddled in purple plasma. He stands in a silent, petrified snapshot of dust and winks to his daughter. "Hello," he says.

"Hi," she says.

"Shall we continue then?"

She nods.

The dust resumes falling. The room is deafening again. Mcalister's cry rings out. Whistle puts up a luminous hand. Mcalister gasps and falls silent. He lets Augustus free from his grip, and clutches his own head. Shrinking rapidly, he stumbles, stumbles again, turns about to the crowd with wide, frightened eyes, and collapses in a haze of fiery dust.

Sergei vaults off after his fallen master.

Augustus Rawlings stands, brushes himself off, takes stock of the hall, and sets eyes on John Whistle.

"That'll be quite enough," Whistle says and raises his hand again. Augustus Rawlings cries out. The pendants about his neck evaporate. His face is robbed of its purple gleam. "I revoke all privileges," Whistle says formally, "and relegate you to a permanent role as the Arbiter of Pleasant But Ultimately Meaningless Coincidences."

Augustus wheezes, "That's not even a real—"

"I know, just made it up. Good, isn't it?"

Augustus goes to attack. Whistle propels the old man back with an idle flick of his hand. "You'd rather I end you? No? Then keep your mouth shut. You've everything to answer for and nothing to complain about. Keep your damn mouth shut."

Augustus slumps against the auditorium wall and covers his eyes.

The curtain of dust evaporates finally. Behind it, Officer Mcalister is his regular pudgy proportion once again, lying on the ground. Sergei licks his master's face frantically. He paws open one of the policeman's eyes, peers in. "Bring him back," the cat shouts.

"It's not possible," Whistle says softly. "You know that."

"*Bring him back*. He's almost dead."

Whistle crosses the auditorium, bends down to stroke the animal. "It's not possible."

Sergei looks to Mary Rawlings. The old woman shakes her head. "Novelty's right," she says.

The cat climbs up onto Mcalister's chest and listens to his master's fading heartbeat. "You can't just let him die."

Whistle says, "Bringing a Corporic back from wherever it is he's bound next is way beyond my abilities. Let him go to sleep with dignity now."

The cat licks at Mcalister's nose, curls up on his chest.

The crowd watches in silence. The crone's voice comes quietly from the back: "Not to interrupt, but if there's no entropy…"

Whistle considers this. He examines the crowd, from the Thomas family, to the Simpsons, to the rest of Wilthail, to the Etherics, all of them staring back like startled cattle. Finally he sets eyes on his daughter. "How about it?" he says.

"What?" the girl says.

"You love death so much, want to make it an occupation? I'll set them up. You knock them down."

She stares vacantly.

"There are constants required," John says, "else everything falls apart. I keep one side in balance, always have." He nods to Augustus Rawlings. "Dickless over there used to keep the other side in check until he got greedy and malicious. The position is vacant again. We'll be needing another Arbiter of Entropy before we can resume business as usual."

Zoe frowns, waiting for the punchline. "And do what Mr. Rawlings did? Become a sadist?"

"No, you needn't. You won't. The job can be done with purpose, not malice. Disorder is a necessary coffee break on the highway to infinity. You can make an art of it. You've got the gift already, I reckon."

"But Mcalister—"

"He became one of us too quickly. We'll ease you into it. It's possible if done right. Probably." Zoe stays quiet. "So, how about it then?"

"Are you still…" she starts.

"Dad?" John interrupts. "Sure am. And more."

"And you're a decent boss?"

"He's a decent boss," the crone calls out.

Zoe shrugs. "I've needed a real job for ages anyway."

"It's settled then. You and me," John says.

"You and me." She toys with her hair. "Is that why I've been so miserable all this time? Does it do something to a person, being the child of one of your kind?"

"Nope, life's just unfair in places. Sorry."

The Wilthailites and Etherics stare blankly.

Jamie Carnegie appears from behind the crowd. "There have been…deaths."

John nods. "I'm sorry, for all of them. That wasn't part of the plan. They'll be bound elsewhere and elsewhen now, I'm afraid." Then quieter, his eyes on the cat: "As our policeman friend."

"We should probably all get a move on," the crone says.

"Agreed," John says. "The grudge is settled. Wilthail will rejoin normal space shortly. You should all be out of the forest when that happens. Get going. I'll sort the rest out."

The auditorium door opens of its own accord. The crowd turns to leave.

"Beomus," John says. "It's time to go."

"Be my guest," the cat replies. "I'm staying."

"Don't be a fool," Mary Rawlings chides. "We'll hold a proper funeral for him later, but we have to leave before it's too late."

"I'm staying," the cat says again.

"Don't even think about it," John growls.

"What's going on?" Zoe says.

"He's going to do something extremely stupid," Mary Rawlings shouts at the cat. "And just when the grudge is over, too."

The cat rears onto his hind legs, hackles raised. "You got what you wanted. The ruse worked, no? Go home then, all of you."

"Whatever you're planning..." Mary Rawlings says.

"Mine to plan." He licks at Mcalister's face again. "I give my mindstate for his."

"No," Mary says. "Not like this. It's all over. Come home with us."

"I give my mindstate for his," the cat says again. "That's possible isn't it?" To John Whistle: "If you help."

The old man nods reluctantly. "Theoretically, yes."

"Well he won't," Mary Rawlings snaps. "He bloody won't."

The walls have a translucent quality to them now, fading.

"We haven't much time," John says. "The spaces are cleaving. Whatever happens next has to happen now." He turns to the crowd. "Go home, wherever home is." He winks to his daughter. "Meet you back at the house, all right?"

All exit the auditorium until just John, Sergei, Mary, Mcalister, and silent Augustus remain.

"How does this work?" Mary says in Etheric.

"Get going already," Whistle says.

"Just out with it."

"My essence for his," Sergei says from down on the policeman's chest.

Mary bends down, strokes his tail. "And what happens to you?"

"He'll be gone," John says gently. "I had to disassemble Mcalister's mindstate to stop him. I'll reconstitute it using Beomus."

"Then he'll be dead."

"There may be a little left over after the process," John says. "If it's enough, it might reassert itself. I'm not sure."

"How?"

"No way of telling. Probably in some new incarnation. Maybe in a few years, maybe in a billion."

"You see?" the cat says. "It's not death, not really." He rubs his cold nose against Mary's. "You have to go now."

"I'll stay," Mary says.

"Don't be stupid."

"I'll wait for you. Here, in the village."

"Then you might not be able to get home."

"Doesn't matter. I'll wait."

"I'll probably never come back, you understand? Novelty's trying to be kind, but that's the fact of it."

The old woman nods. "I'll wait for you," she says again.

John puts a hand on her shoulder. "In any case," he says, "you need to leave. The procedure has to be performed alone."

"And what about…" Mary glances at Augustus.

"Don't worry, I'll bring him back to the Etheria when we're done here, blunt his claws. For now, just get yourself to safety."

The walls of the auditorium are almost completely transparent, the forest fading too.

"Is this it then?" Mary says.

The cat tries to smile. "I think so."

"Back to waiting again?"

"Don't. It's been an age already."

"I don't care."

"Just go. Really."

"Beomus."

"I'll miss you. Wherever it is I'm going, I'll miss you."

328

The walls fade to almost nothing. A great creaking approaches in the distance.

"Zorya," John yells. "*Go.*"

Mary kisses the cat on the head, rubs his ears. "Come back to me," she says. "Bloody well come back to me one day."

The cat licks her nose. "I'll give it my bestest."

IV
EULOGY

SIXTY-SIX

Eric Crane wakes with a start. The air is thin and pure here. Darkness in all directions.

"Hello?" he yells. His voice echoes right out into infinity.

Ah, but what happened?

Yes, the machine. He had pressed the lever forward and the world accelerated. The sun ascended and descended like a wild piston. The days turned to flashes of dark and light, then constant half-light. Wilthail seemed to resume its normal business soon enough, with cars flying up and down the street beyond his window.

The houses changed from brick to glass, or something close to glass, and then to great towers that shot up like needles. Machines flew into the village, flew out of the village, cargo dangling from their bellies. Fashion altered swiftly; men and women wore garments not unlike dresses and grew their hair long and wayward, or went entirely bald. Eric peered up through the skylight. Alongside the usual constellations were a thousand, ten thousand, a million stars zipping about: satellites or some such.

He altered the machine's speed, slowing here and there to take stock of the new eras. Miller Farm was replaced with a huge metallic structure shaped like a giant tear. More of them joined alongside. Soon the entire horizon was populated with abstract shapes: art or technology, Eric Crane was not sure. Wilthail was part of a bustling metropolis then, some men and women recognisably human, but most closer to something out of a comic book: seven or eight feet tall, with multiple limbs, or short and furry, or covered in machinery, or politely followed by gigantic black swarms that did their bidding. The air was thinner. It was harder to catch his breath.

And then the launches came, fleet after fleet of elegant pencils making up into the clouds without the aid of combustion. A new structure dominated the sky, a great ring that stretched from horizon to horizon, and vehicles shot up to it and descended from it. He checked the temporal coordinates. Recognisable faces in the street were persisting past the two hundred year mark, still living in Wilthail. Great bustling black swarms tore buildings down and replaced them, modified the roads, tended to the strange new plants, and soon the village appeared more organic than constructed. Banners lined the streets for a time, written in an exotic form of English Eric only half-recognised, boasting of a successful trip to Alpha Centauri, wherever that was.

New banners were raised, asserting the dominance of the First Terran Empire. More followed, urging disenfranchised Terrans to resist oppression, citing galactic tyranny and interstellar corruption.

Звездите не са за продан! - THE STARS ARE NOT FOR SALE!

The air grew thinner still. He set the machine to maximum speed. One hundred, two hundred, three hundred thousand years. Any trace of recognisable humanity vanished. The horizon teemed with movement; great artificial monoliths hovering with ease.

One million years and counting.

The landscape evaporated suddenly, restructured into geometric tiles. The sky was illuminated with shining glyphs; the sun was covered in geometric spots, an artificial quality to them. The moon boasted oceans.

And the constellations, Eric realised, were moving. Slowly, impossibly slowly, the stars altered in their positions; the heavens themselves reshaped by the hands of intelligence and technology.

No vehicles hovered in the sky. Humanity was either dead or elsewhere.

The landscape coalesced into a single, swirling entity; swishing about, swarming.

That was it then.

Matter was awake.

Eric tried to catch his breath, could not. Unconsciousness followed.

"Hello?" he calls out again.

"Hi," says a deep voice beside him. An enormous cow peers at Eric with burning purple eyes. It smells quite strongly of alcohol. "It's okay," the cow says. "We've been waiting for you."

"Where's my machine?" the boy whispers.

"Safe and sound, young man. Quite the trip. You tried to travel past oxygen. Didn't you think to bring any?" Eric shakes his head sadly. "Rookie error. That's all right."

The sky lights up all of a sudden, billions of stars, and dancing eddies of light between the stars. The horizon dips down below the land and wraps right under their feet. "When is this?" Eric says slowly.

"The end of the line. No time left to travel into, I'm afraid."

"The Big Crunch?"

"Closer to the Big Shindig, I'd say." The cow winks. "Would you mind?" It motions to a bottle strapped to its neck. Eric opens the bottle uncertainly, the inside full of a golden liquid that smells like alcoholic honey. The cow yawns its mouth wide. Eric pours until the bottle is finished, and the cow lets out a satisfied groan. It nudges the boy with its great, fat head. "Go on then, young man. On your feet. Places to be."

Eric stands. "I don't want to end up in a museum," he says.

"We don't have those anyway." The boy stays rooted to the spot and watches the sky. "Ah," mutters the cow. "But you miss your parents already?" The boy shrugs. "Well, you can't go back. Paradoxes must be avoided, understand?" Eric nods. "Augustus Rawlings played something of a trick on physics. Don't take this the wrong way, but your machine wasn't supposed to work, you see."

"I wish it hadn't," Eric says quietly.

They watch the sky in silence. The cow belches. "Tell you what," it says.

From out of the stars appears a village, Wilthail, no bodies in the woods, no blood on the fences. Suzie Lees is buying stamps at the post office. Matilda Sargent is watching the afternoon from behind a library window. Officer Mcalister is making his rounds, plump and mincing as usual.

And there, from their house, comes Mr. and Mrs. Crane, older now, their faces a little crinkled, Mr. Crane towing a Springer Spaniel by a lead.

"See?" the cow says. "Business as usual. Everything's fine."

"This is the past," Eric says.

The cow nods. "From our perspective, yes. Time is a bit more fluid here, you understand?"

Eric shrugs, still watching his parents.

The scene begins to dissolve. "They lived fine lives after you left," the cow says. "Sad in places, yes, but fine lives. Come and find me whenever you want to see it

336

again. I'll show you anything you want, or if I can't, I'm sure the crone will. She's clever like that. Shall we get going?"

"All right."

The cow lets out another belch, echoing out into space. "You can get on my back if you want. I don't do that for just anyone, you know." The boy climbs on. "Sitting comfortably?"

"Sure."

"Then off we go."

The cosmic strings shimmer. The sky is its usual shade of twilight. Cherubs observe from on high.

"Do you have lunch here?" Eric says.

"From time to time. Hungry?"

"Yeah."

"Lunch it is then. Ah, a small matter first though, if you don't mind. Mr. and Miss Whistle would like to see you, a job interview of sorts. A vacancy in mischief is currently open, I'm told."

Several billion years and an evolutionary jump away, Jamie Carnegie keeps a steady pace on May Hill. Below, Wilthail is as he remembers. Down in the meadows the lavender is fresh, and a tractor is ambling into the afternoon.

He pauses at the grave, sweating. He touches the stone, runs his fingers along the grooves of his father's name.

Further down the hill now, the Whistles' graves. He stops a while at Zoe's, picks a few daisies, binds them into a chain.

Back into a run, down towards the town, all the flowers are coming out for summer. Children play on the green. The fountains gurgle to themselves.

And Mary Rawlings is in her garden, tending to her hedges with shears.

"Ah," she says without turning around, "but it's the young lad, is it?"

"That's right."

She nods to the hedge. "I've never been able to get these damn things right. What do you think, left or centre?"

"I think it's fine."

She throws the shears down. "You've come to talk about serious things, haven't you?"

"No, just passing. Honestly."

"Give me a moment then." She disappears inside, comes back out with a tin. "Fruitcake," she says, passing it across. Jamie smiles politely. He knows, like the jam she gave him last month, that there will be no bottom to the tin, nor end to the cake. This has ceased being amazing to him.

"You're looking well," she says.

He wants to say the same, but can't with a clean conscience. She was an old woman before. Now she is a dry stick. "Are you all right?" he says instead.

"Fine," she smiles.

"You're always welcome to come for dinner, you know. Jenny's a fine cook."

"Maybe I'll take you up on that one day." She brushes a little soil off her trousers. "And how is the lovely Miss Dunne doing?"

"No problems there."

The shouts of children finishing school in the distance. "You best be going," Mary says. "Don't want to be swamped with kids on the way home, do you?"

"You're brave," Jamie says quickly. "I just think you're really brave." The old woman smiles and picks her shears back up. "I'll be going then," Jamie says.

"Good lad. Come and see me again soon."

"Sure."

A nod between them. Mary starts on the hedge again.

Jamie takes a glance at her garden. A rake. A wheelbarrow. A bed of geraniums. The chair Augustus always sat in while admiring the evening.

And there, a cat bowl — full of milk and changed daily by Mary Rawlings.

Untouched. Never touched.

Not yet.

GLOSSARY
AND FURTHER
READING

Backward Causation/Time Travel –

At one point Beomus/Sergei meets his future self in a Russian labour camp. This is usually called a paradox, but it doesn't have to be. There seem to be two modes of time travel in science fiction at the moment: Type 1, the Back to the Future kind and Type 2, The Time Traveller's Wife kind. With Type 1, it's totally acceptable to go back and change your own past. This is usually the mode favoured by Hollywood, as it makes for interesting viewing. Type 2 seems a lot more likely though. In The Time Traveller's Wife by Audrey Niffenegger (which is an excellent book, by the way), the hero, Henry, regularly travels back through time and influences his own past. However, he's unable to change it. This seems far more reasonable, if temporal travel comes about. Plenty of physicists appear fond of reminding us that linear time might just be a convenient simulated experience for human brains to make sense of the world. When no one's looking, the universe might be quite happy with events all happening simultaneously — *whatever that even means.* Philosophers generally call this distinction The A and B Theory of Time.

On a technical note, it's mentioned that Eric Crane uses some kind of 'gravity bubble' to travel into the future. This is largely informed by Einstein's Theory of Special Relativity. Gravity is usually understood today to be a distortion of space — a kind of geometric effect. That idea in itself is pretty mind-blowing. Black holes are thought to be so powerful that they not only suck light in but warp time, meaning the closer you get to one, the slower time passes for you relative to the rest of the universe. This is the idea behind Eric's time machine, and is one theoretical candidate currently being pondered by a few physicists at the moment for a method of temporal travel.

Causality Locking –

In one section, Matilda and John are incapable of communicating with other versions of themselves, since all the sets are now on the same timeline, making the same decisions. Astute lovers of science might bring up Heisenberg's Uncertainty Principle at this point, a weird quirk of quantum mechanics. Since the position and velocity of a particle can't be known simultaneously, this implies any parallel universes would immediately start to deviate from each other based on random differences on a subatomic level. Perhaps, yes. It's still very early in humanity's scientific career to say for sure.

What we do know, however, is that macro-objects like planes, cars, buildings, and — most importantly — humans, do indeed obey predictable physical laws. As far as we're aware, quantum indeterminacy (to use the posh term) doesn't manifest in the world of the everyday. There are some theories out there, (most notably espoused recently by Roger Penrose) that consciousness is predicated on quantum mechanics. If this is the case, it might have serious implications for all the Johns and Matildas. Still, as above, it's a little early in our history to say for sure.

Colander –

A colander is a device with holes in it used for draining water, usually found in the kitchen. Perhaps you're already aware of what a colander is. I wasn't until I began writing this book.

Determination of the Future –

The crone implies that if Beomus reads his own future, it will be fixed. This is largely informed by the old Determinism vs. Free Will debate. For example, imagine one day a fortune teller informs you the date of your death will be this coming Tuesday. You find this a bit alarming and decide to take matters into your own hands. On the day of your predicted death you lock yourself in a safe, to stay protected from any murderers or nuclear blasts, and to spite the fortune teller of course. Unfortunately you overlooked the small matter of oxygen and quietly asphyxiate, proving the prediction correct. Had the fortune teller not told you the date of your death, you would not have locked yourself in the safe in the first place and probably lived quite comfortably into old age. The prediction itself was an integral part of your death.

This kind of determinism is something to keep in mind if accurate prediction of the future ever comes about thanks to exotic physics somehow. (Faster-than-light particles might also allow for this kind of causality violation.) The idea is brilliantly played with in a short story (and later a movie with Uma Thurman and Ben Affleck) by Philip K. Dick called Paycheck. Sam Harris has also written a fantastic book called Free Will, which largely falls in the determinist camp. It's not a difficult read and the arguments are extremely powerful and succinct.

Entropy and Novelty –

You may recognise these characters from my previous book, The Bridge to Lucy Dunne. Entropy is an especially famous celebrity in the world of physics, the name given to the force that's responsible for the gradual decline of order in the universe. Novelty, the opposite force (not officially recognised in physics, as such) was brought to my attention by the fantastic — and now unfortunately dead — Terence Mckenna, who often made a case for the universe being a kind of 'novelty conserving engine'. As the universe winds down and speeds towards heat death a few billion years from now, Mckenna argued that novelty is working alongside, fighting against that trend. When one level of novelty is perfected, such as atoms forming into molecules, the molecules then form into some new level of novelty above themselves, and the process continues. At some point in the chain we reach human beings, which appear to be the most complex structure the universe has made to date. It's a fairly sobering thought that these two forces are currently battling each other, cosmically, with the outcome yet undecided.

Higher Dimensions of Space –

There are quite a few mentions of higher dimensions of space in the story. These seem to be mathematically feasible to a certain extent, but we're still not sure whether they have much to do with real space. Some models in theoretical physics, such as string theory, seem to require higher dimensions for the sake of mathematical consistency. Edwin A. Abbott wrote a brilliant book called Flatland which explains the concept of transitioning between dimensions very well indeed. I'd also recommend Diaspora by Greg Egan, which is not only a fun exploration of the above, but easily one of the most underrated gems of fiction you'll ever read.

Iceland –

If you've read my previous book, you may've noticed a bit of a fascination with Iceland. Likewise, it briefly makes an appearance in one of Beomus' incarnations. This stems from a book I read some years ago called Independent People by Halldór Laxness, which should be recommended reading for all humans. Apologies to Icelanders for any misrepresentation of your culture. It's pretty arrogant to write about a place you're only familiar with from books and documentaries. Still, people do that with Mars all the time and those guys haven't complained once.

Nothing Means Anything –

My 'work' on YouTube seems to be increasingly associated with the idea that if you're an atheist, it's impossible for the world to mean anything. Quite a few of the characters in this novel seem fairly down about it. It's a fun idea for comedy, but not believing in a god doesn't in any way preclude you from finding meaning in just *being alive,* I would argue anyway. And actually, if you really think about it, what kind of meaning would you be holding on to if you were actually religious? The universe would certainly have a purpose, but only in as much as a god has given it one. Nothing against the religious, by the way. No doubt we all struggle with this one sometimes, whether religious or not.

I should say, for those of you who will inevitably fall — or have already fallen — into this nihilistic pit, that there is a nice antidote out there. It's called Man's Search for Meaning by Viktor Frankl and it's a brilliant case for just how much we rely on finding purpose, and how it's entirely possible to construct your own. If, like me, you occasionally despair at having been plopped on this planet with little to no explanation, and the fact that no one seems to have a damn clue what we're doing here, I highly recommend giving it a read. We might just be here to party.

Panpsychism –

Sergei/Beomus gives a speech at one point suggesting the universe is inherently made of consciousness, or that consciousness is a fundamental force in the universe alongside all of the others, at least. One of the strongest proponents of this theory today is a very polite and reasonable philosopher called David Chalmers. Chalmers' argument is roughly as follows. Consciousness has — so far — been impossible to explain in terms of already existing phenomena. We can map certain sensations to certain areas of the brain, but the actual subjective feeling of the sensations (*qualia* is the posh philosophical term ((and also the stuff Beomus bribes the High Librarian with))) hasn't yet been explained. This is usually called the Hard Problem of Consciousness among philosophers.

Well, Chalmers argues, we've been in this position before. Electromagnetism didn't fit into any physical categories. Today we accept it as a fundamental force in the universe. What would happen if we did the same for consciousness? It's a bold idea and if it does turn out to have any explanatory power, it'll presumably do to neuroscience what the combustion engine did to the horse and cart. Let's wait and see.

Parallel Universes –

It's heavily implied that the multiple Johns and Matildas originate from universes adjacent to each other. This is currently pure science fiction, but the many-worlds interpretation of quantum mechanics does seem to suggest such a thing *might* be possible. When subatomic particles are observed (in terms of measuring them, not just *looking*), they cease being 'clouds of probability' and appear to condense into actual, tangible particles. The many-worlds interpretation implies that this condensation may occur quite differently in parallel universes, simultaneously, at the moment of observation. The scientific jury is out on that one at the moment. As with all the other wacky explanations out there, we'll just have to wait and see. If all of that sounds silly to you, perhaps try pilot-wave theory instead.

Relativity of Power –

Sergei/Beomus bangs on quite a bit about how something appearing to be a 'god' is only a result of how powerless you are compared to it. This is not too far away from Arthur C. Clarke's now famous quote, "Any sufficiently advanced technology is indistinguishable from magic." If this kind of thing interests you, you'll certainly enjoy the novel version of 2001: A Space Odyssey, which plays with the idea. Likewise, Roger Zelazny also wrote a fantastic book dealing with the 'technological gods' idea called Lord of Light.

Talking Cats –

The Master and Margarita is a great read. Sabrina the Teenage Witch was all right too. I'll leave it at that.

Theories of Identity –

Several of the characters mull over what it means to be the same person as when you were a child. The issue of teleportation is also touched on. This isn't a new idea. It seems to have first been documented by Plutarch the Greek essayist in the 1st century. The original example was with a ship, but we can just as easily use a human brain. Imagine, in a few decades, replacement brain parts come onto the market. So, say if your hypothalamus is acting up for some reason, you can get it surgically removed and replaced with a mechanical, more reliable version. Well, are you still you? Probably. Only a bit of your brain has been replaced. Fine then. Next your corpus callosum starts behaving strangely so you opt to get that replaced. And you carry on, taking parts out, putting mechanical versions in instead.

At what point do you stop being you? It's hard to say. Somewhere between the first replacement part and the last. Some people would even argue you're still you, as long as the original pattern of your personality is preserved. Ray Kurzweil, a rather famous technologist and 'Chief Futurist' at Google, has often talked about resurrecting his father from the dead. He claims he could feed all of his father's letters, voice recordings, and general written material into an AI algorithm of some kind, and the AI would take on his father's personality. Kurzweil believes this would be so accurate that one could consider it a true replica. Others disagree. In any case, as AI creeps into our daily lives over the next few decades, this issue is likely to become more and more topical.

Unknowable Realities –

Sergei/Beomus informs Mcalister at one point that there is no Great Library, and no Etheria, not really. It's just a convenient visual lie to stop Mcalister losing his mind.

This crops up from time to time in theology and science fiction. An example I like is Carl Sagan's Contact, in which (mild spoiler follows) the protagonist's father — really an alien — explains that he has taken that shape to make the experience of first contact more palatable. It's heavily implied that the experience of communicating with aliens as they really appear would be so incomprehensible that humans couldn't process the interaction. When we get higher up the spectrum, towards technological gods, the problem gets even more absurd. You may be aware of Kant's Critique of Pure Reason, which is a famous attempt to find out just what the limits of reason really are, and if there are aspects of the world we'll just never be aware of.

Turns out, according to Kant, there are sides to reality we'll never be able to experience. Limited to our senses, boxed in by reason, Kant makes a case for there being another world beyond our perception (the 'noumenon' as he calls it) that we'll just never have access to. If this kind of thing sounds up your street, I strongly recommend getting hold of one of the companion guides to Critique of Pure Reason, or watching one of the hundreds of lectures about it available on YouTube. More than that, Heidegger and a number of other philosophers argued that we need to work out what "Being" is in the first place. Why is anything here at all? That, to me (and I hope to you too), would be the real jewel in science's crown. All of human knowledge — physics, chemistry, biology, mathematics, philosophy, anthropology, geometry, the whole game — might be groping in the dark for the same elephant: Absolute Truth.

It's fun to think that one day our great, great grandchildren may get that much closer to understanding what the hell creation is doing here in the first place, and glimpsing the underlying structure and nature of matter itself. Hopefully they won't live with the same existential horrors we all quietly face today in our own lives.

There is a kind of bravery to our condition, I reckon: brought into being without an explanation, in a potentially infinite and apparently dead universe, and expected to just get on with it as though nothing strange is going on. Well it fucking is. And it's all right to have a meltdown about the whole affair from time to time, faced with the pressures of modern existence, trying to be a good human and a good worker and a good son/daughter/parent, trying to be a good citizen, trying to be wise without condescension but uninhibited without recklessness, trying to just muddle through without making any silly decisions, trying to align with the correct political opinions, trying to stay thin, trying to be attractive, trying to be smart, trying to find the ideal partner, trying to stay financially secure, trying to just find some modest corner of meaning and belonging and sanity to go and sit in, and all the while living on the edge of dying forever.

We're all in the same strange boat, grappling with the same strange condition. But it isn't quite so scary if we all do it together. So let's do it together.

Exurb1a runs a YouTube channel of the same name, centred around philosophy, theoretical physics, and dick jokes. He has also written a book of short stories you might like called The Bridge to Lucy Dunne. Then again it might be shit. The book is available on Amazon, and will shortly be out as an audiobook also. For queries/insults, please write to: exurb1achannel@gmail.com

Made in the USA
Middletown, DE
09 December 2023

45177116R00210